Lost American Fiction

Edited by Matthew J. Bruccoli

The title for this series, Lost American Fiction, is unsatisfactory. A more accurate series title would be "Forgotten Works of American Fiction That Deserve a New Public"—which states the rationale for reprinting these titles. No claim is made that we are resuscitating lost masterpieces, although at least two of the titles may well qualify. We are reprinting works that merit re-reading because they are now social or literary documents— or just because they are good writing. It isn't quite that simple, for Southern Illinois University Press is a scholarly publisher; and we have serious ambitions for the series. We expect that "Lost American Fiction" will revive some books and authors from undeserved obscurity and that the series will therefore plug some of the holes in American literary history. Of course, we hope to find an occasional lost masterpiece.

Ten titles have been published in the series, with three more in production. The response has been encouraging. We are gratified that many readers share our conviction that one of the proper functions of a university press is to rescue good writing from oblivion.

M. J. B.

FLESH IS HEIR

An Historical Romance

By
Lincoln Kirstein

WITH AN AFTERWORD BY THE AUTHOR

SOUTHERN ILLINOIS UNIVERSITY PRESS
Carbondale and Edwardsville

Feffer & Simons, Inc.
London and Amsterdam

K612f

Library of Congress Cataloging in Publication Data

Kirstein, Lincoln
  Flesh is heir.

   Reprint of the ed. published by Brewer, Warren & Putnam, New York.
   I. Title.
PZ3.K6415F5 [PS3521.I74] 813'.5'2   75-9584
ISBN 0-8093-0730-8

This edition printed by offset lithography in the
United States of America
Designed by Gary Gore

For E. S.
September
1930

TABLE OF CONTENTS

Flesh is Fear

Art-magicianis and astrologis,
Rethoris, logicianis, and theologis,
Them help is no conclusionis slee
Timor mortis conturbat me.

1922

1

Roger was sitting on the big table in the Common Room, piled and littered with magazines, the accumulation of the summer's vacation. It was the opening day of school and Roger was one of the first to return. He had been up to his corridor and unpacked his bags. The trunks hadn't been sent up yet from the village. A few new boys kept sticking their heads tentatively through the open arches of the Common Room and then passed on down the hall. Roger was reading *Punch*. He came on a picture of a waiter in a smart hotel. A lady and gentleman had just finished dinner. The waiter absent-mindedly had thrust his hand under the lady's cloak and with his other he was making as if to pull down and straighten her dress. He had forgotten she was a lady. Roger laughed out loud to himself. His laugh rattled around the big airy room, and the suddenness and isolation of its sound, his own laugh to be sure, but somehow isolated from himself, made him look up. Before him were the figures of Mr. Tonson, his English teacher, and another boy, a new boy.

" Hello, Roger," said Mr. Tonson. " You're back in plenty of time, aren't you? "

Roger put down his *Punch*. " Hello," he said. " When did you get back? "

" This morning " — Tonson smiled — " Did you have a good summer? "

" Yes " said Roger — " I've been down to the shore."

" Fine," said Mr. Tonson. " You'll be able to write me
some good themes then about it." He indicated the boy
at his side, " I want you to meet a new boy who is also
interested in things. This is Andrew Stone, Roger
Baum."

The two boys shook hands and looked at each other.
Andrew Stone was taller than Roger. He had a curious
gourd-like head and his face, while not fat was fleshy;
when he smiled rolls of flesh arched around the corners
of his mouth. He had a slightly leaning stance and a
humorous and kindly expression in his mouth and eyes.

Tonson went off on some business, to look up lists
for the headmaster or something. Roger and Andrew
Stone were left talking.

" How long have you been at Wood-and-Stream? "
asked Andrew.

" I've been here two years," said Roger.

" Do you like it very much? " Andrew's eyes wandered
all over the room and ended up on Roger.

" It's all right," said Roger, easily, for a starter.

" Have you been to many other schools? " asked
Andrew.

" Why no," said Roger. " Have you? "

" Lots and lots," smiled Andrew. " This is my
fifth — "

" You've been going to prep school for five years? "
asked Roger in astonishment. The other boy couldn't
be more than fourteen.

" Oh no," said he. " I've only been going for two
years."

" Didn't you like them? " asked Roger.

" They were all right," said Andrew Stone.

" Well, what was the matter then? " — Roger considered that he had a most curious face.

" They didn't like me," said Andrew. He smiled.

" Oh," said Roger and looked over at the magazine covers spread all around him —

" You were laughing when we came into the room," said Andrew.

" Why, yes," Roger looked at him — " Anything wrong in that? "

" Was the joke so very funny? " asked Andrew.

Roger fumbled with *Punch* and found it for him. He laughed again and gave him the magazine.

" Oh," said Andrew, " is that it? "

" Why yes," said Roger — " Don't you think it's funny? "

" I like your laugh better," said Andrew —

" My laugh " echoed Roger.

" Yes, your laugh. When we came into the room — " Andrew looked stolidly at him, " There was no one in the room and yet you laughed out loud — "

" Don't you ever laugh when there's no one around? " asked Roger.

" Very seldom," said Andrew — " Almost never."

As chance had it Andrew's room was on Roger's corridor and they presently went upstairs to investigate. Roger told the new boy about the corridor system and explained to him how much or rather how little he could expect to get away with, at first. Roger's corridor was on the top floor of the newest school building. The rooms were all small, all gabled and the hipped roof cut away half the square of ceiling. The beds were usually placed under the eaves to save room. There were about twenty boys to a corridor, each one having his own room, his bed, a table, chair, a bureau and a window looking out onto the rolling country or the sheltering hillside. All the studying was done downstairs, either in the study

hall or in the library. The lavatory was at the far end
of the corridor and opposite it was the master's room.
He had his own bath. Wood-and-Stream was not a strict
school, as strict boys' schools go. That is, there was no
rigid enforcement of tiresome rules. Instead the routine
was so full and so monotonous that one never had a
moment to oneself and consequently not much time to
break rules. One could of course be late to a class or an
" activity," and break the routine that way. But the
pressure behind the routine was so great, made turgid
with such a fatness of moral obligation that one scarcely
ever broke it. If you smoked or drank alcoholic liquors
you were expelled. But you were usually put on probation first. No, it wasn't really a strict school.

The boys on Roger and Andrew's corridor were very
much like the boys on every other corridor and in every
other school for that matter. There were Slims, and
Rustys; and Buds and Leftys and Tubbys and Curlys.
They were all good-hearted and nicer, insomuch as they
were at least more physically active and appealing, than
they ever would be in their lives again. Roger had some
old friends on the corridor, relics of last year and the
year before. Mainly, these were Dusty Rhodes and
Tubby Turner. Dusty Rhodes was a small, slight
freckled boy of thirteen who wrote a good deal of non
sense verse. His great work was a tragedy called th
" Purple Laugh," in which all the characters were
Smiles, Snickers, Snirts, etc. Tubby Turner was of cours
fat. He had a typewriter and spent all the spare time,
some fifteen minutes a day, either just after lunch or
just before bed, in copying out the Declaration of Inde
pendence on his Corona, to the beat of a metronome, .
improve his fingering. He wrote home to his par ms
every Sunday afternoon and signed his name on the type-

writer as well. It was a habit with him. Once Roger and
Dusty Rhodes had come into his room and found a
very sad letter half-written, to his mother. Usually these
epistles were sent to both parents at once, but Tubby
had been having acute indigestion, football had been
going badly, and he was low in his marks. No one else
was near the room, so Roger and Dusty quickly tapped
out a finish to the letter and signed it. They said among
other things that Tubby had a passion for a large choc-
late cake, four dozen razor blades (none of them shaved
yet) and the softest toilet paper she could find.

Roger began to see as much of Andrew Stone as he
did his old friends Tubby and Dusty. Roger was fascinated by Andy's probing, prowling curiosity. Before
Andy appeared he had accepted everything for granted.
Now under his insidious tutelage, he too wanted reasons.
Why does Mr. Kendall the corridor master never bathe
with the rest of the boys in the corridor lavatory. Probably, answered Roger, because he has his own. No. Andy
was sure it was because he had some unthinkable de-
formity.

2

Andy made friends too, but not readily. He had one
particular friend, or servant or slave. Gerry Bates was
a well set up, attractive, appallingly servile child. All he
wanted was to do things for people. It was better now
since his servility was localized onto Andy. He made
Andy's bed, he rearranged Andy's bureau drawers, he
would go down, unasked, to the housekeepers and bring
back Andy's laundry. He was silent and inoffensive and
Andy seemed to be fond of him. At least Gerry Bates
was allowed to traipse along after him wherever he went,
like a willing shadow.

Andy liked Roger, but he hated Roger's friends. He admired the way Roger rose to his teachings, to the inculcations of his subtle curiosity. But what he could see in Dusty Rhodes or Tubby Turner was beyond him. Roger liked them because they were old friends of his, and because they were easily led and would go on any adventure. Saturdays were half holidays when there was no football game to attend. Roger, Tubby and Dusty would explore the immediate vicinity of the countryside. Once they were walking across a piece of land that was pitted and hillocked with bumps and depressions of fir-covered earth and they came across a hole in the ground. Investigation showed that there was a distinct widening of the cavity below the surface, on the inside. Roger was thrilled — a cave! Roger decided that it was the start of a dried-up underground river. Visions of shimmering stalactites and stalagmites leading down into the earth's core overwhelmed him. He swore Tubby and Dusty to secrecy and didn't even tell Andy. They would come out two or three times a month with tin cans and dig at the hole in the ground. They were careful to carry the excavated dirt far away from the hole because they didn't want anyone to find signs of digging, and besides the roof of earth was not strong enough to carry much weight. One afternoon they were all digging happily at the cave. Roger had been outlining to his enthusiastic aids the idea for an octagonal room they would build in the centre of the cave — a kind of inner sanctum lined with mirrors. Suddenly there were voices on the hillock above their cave. They dropped their spades and lay down flat on the ground. But at that moment, the foxy features of Andy Stone appeared over the ridge, with his shadow Gerry Bates, and saw them.

" Why, look who's here " — said Andy vacuously.

Roger stared at him angrily but said nothing.

" What are the little boys digging for? " asked Andy
— " Buried treasure? "

" None of your damned business," said Tubby Turner
and glowered.

" Shut up," said Roger to his lieutenant.

" It must be hard work for the little boys to dig holes
in the ground," pursued Andy.

" Why don't you try it? " Dusty Rhodes started to
hate Andy.

" Shut up," said Roger.

" Anything to keep the boys out of mischief," said
Andy and came over to inspect the hole.

" No one asked you to come here," said Roger slowly.

" That's why we came," answered Andy. Gerry Bates
snickered.

" I don't like to go places I'm not wanted," said Roger.
More snickers from Gerry.

" How do I know I'm not wanted until I come," said
Andy peering into the hole they had dug, and kicking
a little dirt from the side down in.

" Well, you know now," said Dusty Rhodes.

Roger was silent.

" I know what? " asked Andy. " No one's asked me to
go — "

Roger said slowly: " I ask you to go, now." Dusty and
Tubby picked up their shovels; they weren't going to
lose any more time.

" What happens if I don't? " asked Andy. Gerry Bates
danced around him.

Roger was at a loss — " Well, if I ask you to go —
You will, won't you? "

Andy persisted — " But suppose I don't? "

At this point Dusty and Tubby brandished their shovels ineffectually. They were clumsy weapons — " We'll make you," said Tubby breathlessly.

" Yes," cried Dusty, " get out of here — "

" Yes," said Roger suddenly, " get out — both of you." Gerry Bates drew back.

" Oho," said Andy stiffly. " Boy scouts."

" We are not boy scouts," said Roger — and as if to prove it — " Now you get the hell out of here before we make you." Tubby and Dusty were tense; they advanced.

" Come along," said Gerry Bates.

" I will not " said Andy. Roger didn't speak —

" O come on, the sissies " said Gerry Bates. Then Andy turned his back suddenly and walked up the knoll; Gerry scuttled after. As he gained the top, he faced around and directed on Roger a glance of concentrated malevolence that was actually frightening. Then they disappeared. The boys went on digging and curiously enough, as by mutual understanding, they never once referred to the incident all that afternoon —

The malevolence of Andy's stare stayed like a shadow on Roger. He felt that he really had been terribly rude to Andy. He felt guilty and ashamed. But he knew that all this was a mask to hide his real feelings, for somewhere, somehow he was frightened of Andy Stone, and he knew it.

That night he decided to apologize to Andy for his rudeness. He looked in his room for him but he wasn't there. He looked in the library but he wasn't there. Not until bedtime when the boys were brushing their teeth in the lavatory did Roger come upon him. Roger walked over to him, nervously drying his tooth brush on his pyjama top.

"I say, Andy," Roger lowered his head. "I say I'm frightfully sorry about —"

Andy turned away, and went on brushing his teeth. He pretended to laugh at a joke one of the other boys cracked at that time. It was so patently a pretense. Andy never laughed at other people's jokes.

"I say, Andy," Roger looked at him, "I'm most frightfully sorry about this afternoon." Andy screwed on the top of his tooth paste and ignoring Roger completely, walked out of the lavatory, down the corridor into his room. Roger finished brushing his teeth, looked out of the window, where the panes were frosted and walked slowly down the corridor. He had intended to stop in at Andy's room and make a complete apology but he saw two or three other boys there, looking at one of Andy's books. This surprised him a little as Andy didn't usually entertain. As he paused on the threshold — the corridor bell rang: two minutes before lights out. The corridor master controlled the switch for the whole double line of rooms. Everyone scuttled off to bed. Roger opened his window, kicked off his slippers and drew up the covers. The lights went out. But Roger couldn't sleep; he couldn't even rest. He kept thinking about the afternoon, about Andy. He had been rude, he shouldn't have lost his temper. He shouldn't have let Tubby and Dusty behave that way, and underneath his shame and guilt like a tiny corkscrew flame of briars and crumbs in bed, twisted the recognition that somehow in some unsuspected way he was frightened of Andy Stone. . . .

Roger threw off his covers, and searched with his feet for his slippers. He listened by the side of the door and quietly opened it. Corridor running was extremely dangerous. If you were caught you got four demerits. You might even get put on probation. It all rested with the corridor master and Kendall was no good friend of Roger's. Corridor running was accomplished by running from room to room, quickly and quietly, waiting until you were sure you could go on into another room, and so on down the corridor until you reached your objective. Roger leaned his head out into the hall to see if Kendall's door was open. As it faced the lavatory door, and the light there burned all night, Roger couldn't tell if his door was open or shut. If he waited a little while he could pretend he had to go to the lavatory. There would be no excuse now so soon after lights out. But Roger was afraid by that time Andy would be asleep and he didn't want to risk waking him, so he went on. He slipped quietly down the hall and opened Tubby Turner's door, and shut it silently. Tubby jumped up in bed —

"Who is it?" he asked breathlessly.

"It's Roger — I want to get down the hall — "

"What for — ?" Tubby whispered quickly.

"I want to talk to Andy" said Roger.

"Well give him hell for me, too," said Tubby and went back under the covers.

Finally Roger got inside Andy's room. Andy rustled in bed. The spring under the mattress tingled. He saw it was Roger but he didn't speak. He rolled over on his side, his back to Roger and began a soft parody of snoring.

"I say Andy," whispered Roger, "I'm terribly sorry about this afternoon — I want to apologize — I know I was rude."

No answer.

"I want to be friends with you" went on Roger — The snoring kept up. "I hate not to behave like a gentleman — " he stopped. No answer.

"I'm very sorry really, Andy — Tubby and Dusty are, too. We want you to come dig with us next time — "
Snores, snoring. Roger had failed and it had scared him. He could feel Andy smiling through his snores —

No use going on, thought Roger, I'd better go back. Then — "I wish you'd say something, Andy," — snores — "I'm really sorry."

Roger went over to the door and felt for the knob. "Very well" he said weakly, "good night. My apology doesn't apply to your friend Bates" said Roger. He whispered the last louder to sound more convincing — "Your friend Bates" only snoring replied.

Roger went out of the room and shut the door. He looked for a moment down the hall and started for his room. Then the corridor-master's door opened. He was caught.

"Well," said Kendall — "Where have you been?"

"Down to the can" said Roger, "I got stuck."

"You did not," said Kendall — "I never heard you go in — "

"If you don't believe me" said Roger limply —

"Come around in the morning and get your de-merits" said Kendall — "Now get on with you and go to bed — "

"Good night, sir" said Roger and walked noisily down the hall. He didn't give a damn. He should worry.

3

But he got the four demerits, and the four demerits made him stay in study hall all of the next Saturday after-noon. So Tubby Turner and Dusty Rhodes had to go out digging alone, and it was really hard to bear be-cause the days were getting very much shorter; winter wouldn't let them dig much more. But finally study

hall was over and Roger went to find if his friends had
come back.

They were up in his room sitting on his bed, waiting
for him. Their faces were set. He looked at them and
something told him to brace himself. He paused, set his
books down on the table and said " Well — what did
you do? "

" Nothing — " said Tubby Turner —

" What do you mean? " asked Roger.

" We did nothing " said Dusty Rhodes —

" Why, what happened — ? "

" We got out there " said Tubby, " and it was all
bitched — Everything was smashed — Someone," and
he paused significantly, " had crashed the whole cave
in — "

" My God," cried Roger, " Who could it have been? "

" Who indeed " said Dusty — " I wonder where Andy
is — ? "

" Andy? " gasped Roger, " Andy, not him! "

" Who else? " said Dusty, " You bet it was Andy."

" And he's going to pay for it too," said Tubby Turner, " You bet your life — "

Then they considered plans for revenge, every con-
ceivable sort of plan. They were in deadly earnest and
they went slowly and surely, with the incredible in-
genuity of young boys they were determined to effect
only that one plan which was sure to give Andy Stone
the most pain. At first they thought of threading wires
through his mattress and attaching them to the lights in
the hall so he would be badly shocked. They thought
of putting dead things in his drawers, in his bed. But
these were all rejected as being too physical, too transi-
tory in their effect. Finally Roger had the brilliant idea
that they would somehow attack Gerry Bates. A blow at

his personal slave would hurt Andy more than anything
else he could think of. And Roger knew Andy's tem-
perament pretty well. The others agreed. There was a
good deal of laughter when they decided what to do.
Somewhere, sometime soon they would get him without
any clothes on and shave all the hair off his belly. They
knew how dearly hair on boys that age is prized. It is
the badge that shows they'll soon be men, and anyone
as unsure of his sex as Gerry Bates would feel ten times
as badly to lose it as a member of the football team. But
then, thought Roger, it would be pretty hard to hold
a member of the team down long enough. But the three
friends were agreed and they were happy and satisfied in
the course of their intended action.

Roger, to his great chagrin, was not in at the death.
It was hard to get all of the three together and find Gerry
Bates with his pants down. But Tubby and Dusty
Rhodes happened to be in the locker room with Gerry
after track, and the three of them were the last ones
dressing. With a demoniac leer Tubby reached into his
coat pocket for his razor. He'd been carrying it around
for days. Dusty shut the locker room door. . . .

There were some screams, though Dusty rammed his
fist into Gerry Bates' mouth. He kicked too. If he hadn't
have, there would have been no blood. Even so they
didn't cut him very badly. Tubby wiped his razor triumphantly, like a surgeon, he thought. He and Dusty
dressed speedily and went off to tell Roger. Gerry Bates
was left sobbing on one of the benches, but he stopped
his tears as soon as they had gone out of the room.

4

Nothing seemed to happen. Roger was amazed, a week passed — and no results. Andy had, for no good reason, turned very friendly, friendlier than ever before. He made plans with Roger to get control of the school paper. He wrote stories furiously. He read two of the best ones to Roger. One of them was about a society of priests who lived in a temple of brass. They stood in a circle all day long worshipping the sun. Silver pipes, let in to their veins, connected them so that a single life stream coursed through the whole brotherhood. There was no point to the story. The other was about a girl called Emma who had a child by looking at a star. She looked at the star until it made the moon jealous and then the child died.

Soon after Roger was walking out in front of the building about five minutes before lunch. He was looking over the great roll and flow of hills dappled in the hollows with snow. The day was bright and he looked forward to lunch and an afternoon on the hockey rinks. As if from nowhere a very large and expensive looking automobile came up the drive and stopped at Roger's very feet. The chauffeur put on the brakes and helped the passenger out. It was a lady. A tall overbearing lady with an elaborate flower basket of a hat. No hat for the winter, thought Roger, particularly the winter in the country.

The lady looked at Roger; " This is the Wood-and-Stream School, isn't it? "

" Yes " said Roger " This is it."

" Do you know Gerald Bates? " she asked. There was a drop on the end of her nose.

" Yes," said Roger in wonder. " I do."

" Are you a friend of his? "

" Well," admitted Roger, " I know him."

" I thought so." She paused and used her handker-chief — " I'm Mrs. Bates."

" Gerry's mother," said Roger brightly.

" Ah " she said, " You see the resemblance, too." She looked at the chauffeur who was folding up the motor robe.

" Well " said Roger, " Shall I take you to see the head-master? "

" Where is he? " asked Mrs. Bates.

Roger suddenly thought. " Why at lunch, I guess. I'm late myself."

" So much the better," said Mrs. Bates, " I want to look around."

" But there's no one to take you," said Roger. He'd got to get to lunch.

She looked appraisingly at him. " You'll take me," she said, and he did.

She said she wanted to see everything. She wanted to know just how Gerry lived. Roger wished to get back to lunch, however late he would be.

" Now " said Mrs. Bates, " this is fine. Now show me the bathrooms."

" The bathrooms " Roger was horrified. " Why do you want to see those? "

" I want to know if there are adequate facilities " she said.

" But supposing someone came in " said Roger, " sup-posing somebody was there."

" I wouldn't mind " said Mrs. Bates, " come along now."

Roger followed her until he was tired, tired from her and from the irony of being absent from lunch without excuse. Several times he thought of bolting but her masterful eye held him.

" And now " she said, " I suppose you wonder why I have come here, this way."

" Well . . ." said Roger.

Then she opened her purse and took out a piece of paper.

" Read that, young man," she said. " Read that."

Trembling, Roger took the paper —

" *Dear Mummy,*" he read — " *I am well. My English is lower than last week but Latin is better (67). I have taken many long walks — The weather is very good here now and some snow. Thank you so very much for the chocolates — All of the boys on the corridor enjoyed them too and thank you too. Two boys held me down and shaved me all over not on my head, mummy, if you understand. I fought. They cut me. I do not tell anyone for fear of telling. One should not tell.* (Roger was amazed — the God damn little fool — then why did he have to tell *her*) *Please write soon and send me my snowshoes —*

Your loving son

Gerald "

Mrs. Bates snatched the letter out of his passive hands. " So you see " she said, " now, why I wanted to see the bathrooms! "

Then she went off to the headmaster. Then Roger went off to get lunch. He was pretty late and could think of no adequate excuse to offer. The others got up from the table and left him still eating. He remained quietly buttering pieces of thick baker's bread in the great empty dining hall. He looked out the high windows on to the snow-specked hills. A few winter-bound flies buzzed around the butter and the sugar bowl. He wandered up to his corridor to get his clothes for hockey.

He saw Tubby and Dusty Rhodes and told them about
Mrs. Bates and the bathroom. They were suitably
amused.

Roger came back from hockey about quarter past four
and he was surprised to hear the bell in the study hall
ringing. At first he thought it was the fire alarm. But no,
it was the study hall bell. Other boys stopped midway
in their walking and asked each other what the matter
could be. There was only one thing to do, obviously, for
the bell meant only one thing, and that was to go into
the study hall, and sit down at one's desk. Gradually
everyone did so. The room filled up. All the desks, except those occupied by the boys on the first hockey team
were filled. They were still down at the gymnasium.
There was a low buzz of conversation in the room.
Everyone, of course, wondered what on earth was the
matter.

Suddenly the door opened in the side wall and the
headmaster came into the room. His leonine grey and
white head was bowed pensively. He tossed back some
mutterings at the train of undermasters who followed
him. Roger saw that they must have been having a
faculty meeting. What on earth could be the matter.
Had someone died —?

The headmaster Mr. Stark was indeed a lion or he
looked like a noble grey-headed beast of some sort.
There he sat at the master's desk at the end of the study
hall, fumbling with the black satin cord of his pince-nez.
His skin was pink and healthy and curiously corru-
gated. Wonderful photographs were taken of him every
year to be included in the senior class album. He always
looked slightly inadequate in comparison with the
photographs; there was the likeness to be sure, but it
seemed always to one who had seen them both, that Mr.

Stark today, the day one saw him, was looking poorly; —
it was an off day with him.

But there he sat dangling his pince-nez from his black
satin ribbon. His brows beetling, his latent nervousness
filling every fold of his light grey tweed suit. The junior
and the senior masters were ranged around him, shifting from foot to foot, or their hands in their pockets,
or talking in low tones to each other. The air was humid
with suspense. The school could see Mr. Stark was waiting for the hockey team. What was this incident of such
great moment that demanded the attention of the entire
school at such an unaccustomed hour? Roger wondered
if the two or three boys up at the infirmary would be
brought in on stretchers. Presently the hockey team
came in, smoothing their hair, still wet from the showers,
looking eagerly at every face for some information, and
took their places. A silence. Even the flies ceased to buzz.
One of the masters inadvertently coughed. Mr. Stark
glared at him. He too was silent. Roger, for one, was
hypnotized by expectation.

" I have summoned the school, thus," began Mr. Stark
in his most awful voice, (if God spoke, thought Roger,
thus would God speak) " in the matter of the first importance. Something has happened that threatens to
attack the very vitals of that system that makes Wood-
and-Stream what you, what I, what we have come to
know, to love, and to respect. I have been teaching
boys," Mr. Stark's voice was definite — his eyes sought
the memories of his full, dedicated years, " for almost
half a century. They have never once let me down. I
hope I have never let them down. I try to choose boys
for Wood-and-Stream who are Wood-and-Stream boys,
and I hope we all know what that means. If we don't, and
I'm sure we do — " he indicated the masters ranged

round him like a court — " those of us who care about
teaching and about boys have failed — "

Roger wondered if the Gettysburg Address fell
on the ears of its first audience as did this great
diction.

" Not two hours ago a woman came to me, troubled
to the extreme in her soul. One that she had loved, one
that she had entrusted to our keeping, one whom I,
up to two hours ago, was personally responsible for, had
in some way been grievously hurt. I said in some way.
In what way I do not know. I cannot tell. I cannot
guess. That poor mother did not have the strength to
tell me what happened to her boy."

Roger wondered how Tubby Turner and Dusty
Rhodes were feeling. For himself he was bursting with
fright and amusement.

" That mother has withdrawn her boy from Wood-
and-Stream. I have as I have said, no exact reason as
to why she felt called upon to take such a drastic action.
I know from her grief and from her sincerity that there
was no other way open for her. I must admit to all of
you here, that it is a very sad day for me when a mother
recalls her trust. I feel, in a measure I have failed — "
A pause, — to allow a hundred and fifty boys to silently
say No — No — Mr. Stark. No. No. " This poor mother
has taken her son from us, and left us a warning — a
warning that strikes to the very vitals of that system that
makes Wood-and-Stream — what you and I — what
we — " Mr. Stark checked himself and coughed. " She
said " — it was the lord justice summing up before the
council of his peers — " She said that either I must find
out the cancer gnawing at the root of our system —
myself — and I feel she was right — or forever forfeit
the right to be called a good schoolmaster — and a good

schoolmaster, a friend and a master of boys is all that I have ever wanted to be."

He had wound himself up to the verge of tears; presently even the hockey team would be sobbing.

"Now" said Mr. Stark " I want those boys who were in any way implicated in the incident to which I have referred to stay here in the hall and make a thorough confession. I have the names of all those boys, nor did the unfortunate boy who has left tattle on his mates. Nevertheless I know who his persecutors are, and they will be dealt with more gently, I assure them if they come to me of their own accord. I would prefer none of you to talk of this among yourselves and I feel that there is no necessity of arousing the fears of your parents by communicating the details to them. Wood-and-Stream could only be harmed by misunderstanding—" Mr. Stark looked around him. " Those who have no further business in this room at this time are dismissed."

The masters filed out. The senior prefect walked out of the room followed by the student council and four members of the sixth form. Two members of the hockey squad got up and walked out. To Roger's amazement no one else moved. Not a soul stirred. Nor spoke. Nor by the grace of God— laughed. There they all sat paralyzed by Mr. Stark's phillipic. None of them but three knew what he had been talking about, yet all of them were rendered immobile through their overwhelming sense of guilt. They each of them no doubt had done something to be ashamed of. There they all sat like scared rabbits. The confusion of the situation dawned on Mr. Stark. He cleared his throat and all his school was at attention.

"I had not intended to intimidate the school into unnecessary confessions," he said, " only those boys who

are directly implicated in this painful incident have
anything to fear. The rest can leave." Clearly, Mr. Stark
was at a loss.

The same idea flashed at the same moment on the only
three boys in the room who had any idea what Mr. Stark
was talking about. They suddenly realized that he had
no idea whomsoever was actually implicated in the
painful incident. At least Gerry Bates had not tattled.
Slowly, at least an inkling of this idea trickled into the
consciousness of the rest of the boys. Slowly, by twos and
threes they left the room. Dusty and Tubby and Roger
passed unnoticed in the general exodus. Soon Mr. Stark
was left alone in the study hall, and asking the hundred
and fifty vacant desks what was the cancer gnawing at
the root of Wood-and-Stream, and at the system he had
created, and respected, and so on. . . .

5

Andy for one had no idea why his shadow had been
suddenly seized from his side. If he suspected Roger's
hand in it, he never by any word or sign showed it. On
the contrary a greater intimacy sprang up between them,
and Roger was seeing more of Andy than of Tubby and
Dusty, mainly because he was full of such fascinating
information.

They would take walks down the firm snow-packed
road when the state plow had cleared enough away to
allow you to go without sinking up to your hips where
the wind had made the sliding drifts.

" And some stones " said Andy, " have magic prop-
erties too — "

" What sort of stones? " asked Roger.

" Precious stones, diamonds, rubies. . . ."

" How do they get that way? " asked Roger.

" By staying a long time in the same family." Andy
knew lots about magic. " Egyptian scarabs are often
haunted; people in tombs get blood poisoning. People
will never learn not to fool with ghosts."

" But ghosts " said Roger, " Really, when I was a kid."

" I don't mean sheets with pumpkins, hallowe'en; I
mean ghosts. Ghosts under the influence of the moon,
real ghosts."

" Did you ever see one? " asked Roger " Really."

" Yes and no " said Andy, " I know how they
work — "

" How do they work? " asked Roger crunching snow-
balls between his mittens.

" They work by haunts and by charms; often by
charms."

" What kind of charms? " said Roger. He was learn-
ing a lot, " Things you say? "

" Yes, and things you do. For instance, a Scotch prince
wanted to be king instead of the real prince so he got a
bird, I guess it was a nightingale and cut its heart out.
Then every moonlit night for seven nights he said his
enemy's name over it. On the seventh night, he took his
dagger and stabbed the heart. The next morning the
other prince was dead."

" But I can't see the connections," said Roger, " It's
not logical."

" That's where the charm comes in " said Andy finally.

" Well," said Roger, " what other charms? "

" If you want to get rid of a man," Andy's information welled out in a resistless stream, " supposing he's
a blonde. Well, get a lock of his hair and pin it onto a
black oak or a black birch. Then cut the tree down and
he'll die."

" I can't believe that " said Roger.

" Or stand in a circle," continued Andy, " drawn to the twelve points of the Zodiac and invoke the moon to burn your enemy."

" The moon to burn? " echoed Roger.

" The sun burns," said Andy finally, " why could not the moon be made to, too? "

" Do you ever do charms? " asked Roger.

" Sometimes," said Andy significantly.

" Any luck? " asked Roger, kicking the snow before him.

" Luck," said Andy, almost hurt, " sometimes I am successful."

"You are? " Roger stopped short. " Tell me."

" I once looked at a boy in a school. I didn't do anything else. Sometimes when the moon was up I'd look at it and say the boy's name. But I really only looked at him, for a long time. His mother came," said Andy proudly, " and begged me to stop it. But I wouldn't. I looked right at him. They moved away."

" They did? " asked Roger. " What happened to the boy? "

" He died," said Andy, and picked up a handful of snow.

" But why did you do that? " asked Roger.

" I was told to! " said Andy.

" Who told you? " asked Roger.

" My own" said Andy significantly, and then: " I've said enough for today."

The two boys turned and started back walking down the road to school. It was getting grey in the sky and colder on the land. The line of fir trees on the hills' horizon with snow for epaulettes marched up the roadway and the boys followed after.

As they turned the corner by the stone gate leading up the road, Andy stopped to tie his shoe lace which had come undone. Roger went on walking up towards the school. The lights in the dining room twinkled vaguely through the fuzz of bare trees. The maids were setting the tables for dinner. Suddenly he was thrown flat on his back. Andy had tripped him up. He was so completely caught by surprise that he couldn't make even a verbal resistance. He lay on the road in the snow with Andy sitting on his stomach. He looked up at him.

" So you will, will you? " asked Andy fiercely.

" Will what? " Roger had no idea. . . .

" Run away from me," Andy's eyes sparkled brilliantly.

" I was just walking ahead " said Roger, " get off me."

" So you will, will you? " said Andy, " But you won't."

" What the hell do you mean? " said Roger. " Get off me."

Andy then took some snow and threw it in Roger's face. Roger started to struggle, half-heartedly at first, then more so, then desperately. The two boys fought hard in the growing dark. They really fought hard. They scratched and bit and Roger was starting to get scared. He managed to hit Andy behind the ear. The pain paralyzed him for a second and he fell off. Roger stood up and breathlessly brushed his coat. Then Andy got up and faced him.

" Let's go back," said Roger. " We'll be late."

" Sure," said Andy, " What were we fighting about anyway? "

" Fighting about? " asked Roger, " I thought it was a roughhouse."

" A roughhouse." Andy paused. " No," he said, " that wasn't a roughhouse."

6

December snowed itself thoroughly into the hillside and Wood-and-Stream carried on its routine activities like a community of snowbound moles under the white, clean dry blanket of cold and crystal. Vacation emptied the halls for the holidays and was a pleasant, a necessary break. Before vacation the stream of constant companionship became insufferable. Some boys weren't speaking to each other for some reason of fancied slights. Acute attacks of homesickness spread its epidemic nostalgia over the lower forms. And however many tired boys, and coughs, and measles they brought back with them after New Years, vacation was a necessary evil.

Andy and Roger were comparing vacation notes in the corridor, the second day after they had gotten back. Roger had told him the plots of all the plays and movies he had seen; the parties he had been to, of his Christmas presents, and showed him his new books. Andy had gone down to Florida to be with his parents and he had met a girl.

" We went skating one day in a roller-skating rink. I'd only seen her once before in my life. We had hardly ever spoken. I watched her all along. She was so tall and wonderful looking and she never talked at all. I was determined to get to know her somehow. Our skates were fastened on by little chains bound under our shoes. I watched her bend over to adjust her skate and I saw she wasn't noticing what she was doing. So I bent down and fixed the chain around a bar running along the floor which a sliding gate ran on. When she got up and started to go across the floor, she fell. So I got down and helped her take her skates off and we went out and I went to a stream to bathe her head in some water and

then I carried her to a wonderful mossy bank all covered
with flowers, lilies of the valley, and I took off all my
clothes and she had hers off already, and we lay there
with sun shining. . . ."

" In the broad daylight," said Roger horrified. " How
could you? "

" Oh, the sun's all right," said Andy, " when you know
how to treat it."

" But this girl," said Roger. " What will happen to
her? "

" I'm going to send her a check for a hundred dollars," said Andy, " for her to buy books with."

" But what will happen to her? " asked Roger.

" She will be provided for," said Andy with authority.

Roger was puzzled as in the case of many of Andy's
stories. He wasn't sure whether to believe it or not. It
did not somehow sound right and yet it always seemed
almost sacrilege to Roger to disbelieve Andy's stories,
they were so much more interesting than anyone else's.

Roger told Dusty Rhodes the story. Not that Dusty
was particularly a man of the world. He confessed that
he had only kissed one girl in his life and then she had
kissed him first. But he inclined to believe Andy's story,
as told by Roger. So Roger told Tubby Turner. He believed it too. Roger was puzzled. This concurrence of
opinion was surprising. Roger decided that they just
wanted to believe it, that somehow they wanted to identify themselves with Andy and the girl. The boys on
the corridor liked Andy. To be sure they thought him
curious. His strange fleshy fox face, his small curved eyes,
his questing nose. But he carried an air of authority, he
had a cruel and somehow wistful sense of humor and he
thought up very excellent pranks. It was he who had
the idea of clipping out all the coupons in popular

mechanics and sending the sex books in plain wrappers to members of the faculty. He even went to the expense of paying a deposit on a baby grand piano and having it delivered to the football coach. It was he who spread all the seats of the cars parked in front of the school for the fall dance with shredded wheat, and whenever the seats scrunched, he would rush down in the dark along the line of cars, and point an accusing finger at the startled pair and say in his ridiculous high flat voice, " Whatcha doin'? " They even admired his spirit of opposition. When he came down late to a football game one bright day dressed in an old rain coat, carrying an umbrella and delivered a little cheer with the late Gerry Bates, " Goody goody for our side and pooh bah for yours," he got away with it mainly because he wasn't afraid, mainly because he assumed an intellectual authority over the rest of them, and was contemptuous.

7

Andy was only afraid of one boy and that was Hollis Morton. He played hockey and football. He was extremely stupid, so stupid that he had to stay two years in every form. Consequently he had been longer in the school than anyone else. His face was constantly jellied into a loose grin. His stupidity expressed itself variously but mainly in his bullying. He was an incorrigible and brutal bully. His cruelty was never restrained by the traditional bully's cowardice or a horrible guilty conscience. He mainly tortured young boys, but for some curious reason he had taken a violent dislike to Andy. The mere sight of him would make him furious. If he sat back of Andy in chapel for example he would spend his entire time trying to hurt him, pinch him, tickle

him, so he would cause a disturbance. His brute stupidity made such a powerful effect on Andy that he
could never find it possible for himself to make the
slightest resistance or give the least indication that he
was being persecuted. And Hollis Morton had absolutely no notion of his power over Andy. He only knew
he hated him, and he expressed his hate pretty directly
and immediately, whenever convenient.

Roger was passing Andy's room one Sunday afternoon
and heard scuffling. The door was half shut and Roger
opened it and walked in. There was Hollis Morton
holding Andy's neck in both of his great raw fleshy
hands, shoving Andy's head into an open drawer. He
was working pretty hard and his victim as usual was
making no sound, but Roger saw at once how much it
must have hurt. He stood for a second watching the
punishment and then with some courage kicked Hollis
Morton in the tail. Morton looked up with his blank
baby face inscribed with his cruel grin, and laughed but
he kept grinding Andy's head into the drawer. Surely,
thought Roger, soon either one or the other will break.
Roger kicked Hollis again and gripped his waist in his
hands. Only when Roger made such exertions did he
realize how ridiculously weak he was, how incapable of
self-defense. He went on tugging at Hollis. But it didn't
seem to have much effect. Suddenly the bully gave a
pull and a shake to rid himself of Roger and the drawer
came out of the bureau. The three boys fell on to the
floor in a heap. This had the desired effect. Roger
scrambled up and out of the room and Hollis Morton
lumbered after him. Andy was left shivering on the
floor with suppressed anger, terror and impotence.

Roger ducked down the hall, but there was little
necessity for flight. Hollis didn't trouble to follow him.

He ambled off and was soon in search of some other amusement. Roger went to his room. Sunday afternoon was generally free time, and Roger was using it to the best of his advantage. He was finishing up the portrait of a man, a fantastic courtier of some sort in a turban. He had made the back of the drawing all opaque except for the features so when you held it up to the light the features glowed. He got his paints out, his brushes and went off to the bathroom to get some water. On his way back he met Andy. One would never have known that anything had happened to him.

" Whatsa matter," said Andy looking at the glass of water. " Thirsty? "

" No," said Roger walking on down to his room — " I'm going to paint."

Andy followed him. Roger busied himself with his work. He painted very slowly with a fine tiny brush. If he had used a bigger brush that he had he could have worked faster, but he preferred the fun of niggling work. Andy sat down on the bed and watched him.

" You'll never be a decent painter," said Andy.

" Why not? " murmured Roger, deeply absorbed.

" You don't know enough," said Andy.

" I can learn." Roger licked his brush.

" Don't do that," said Andy, " you'll get poisoned."

" No, I won't," said Roger, " these paints aren't poisonous."

Andy laughed irrelevantly and went on. " Who are you painting that for? "

" Myself," said Roger.

" Pretty damn selfish, aren't you? " Andy was looking at him.

" Might give it to my sister," said Roger.

"She wouldn't know what it was all about," said Andy.

"How do you know?" asked Roger looking up at him. "You've never met her."

"I've seen her picture," said Andy looking over on Roger's bureau. "She looks stupid."

Roger said nothing. "She looks stupid," repeated Andy. "Is she?"

"I don't know," said Roger.

"Well," said Andy, "I don't like her looks."

"Don't then," said Roger, unperturbed.

"Gee, you're painting that badly," said Andy.

"Well stop joggling me then." Roger drew his work away.

Andy laughed. "You know," he said, "you're almost as ugly as your sister."

Roger kept right on with his painting, "You're uglier than your sister — God, with your face . . ." said Andy and stopped short. He paused, then, "God, I bet your family is awful looking." No answer. "Are all Jews awful looking?" No answer. "I asked if all Jews were awful looking." Silence, "Do all Jews smell as bad as you?" asked Andy. "Do they smell? Do they stink?" Roger went delicately on with his work.

"God," said Andy suddenly. "I hate your face."

Roger looked up at him, and turned his eyes quickly down to the painting.

"I really hate you," said Andy, "and your whole family."

Roger felt that under no circumstances must he speak. Then said Andy, "Give me that drawing, you're drawing." Roger looked up. . . .

"It's not finished," he said.

"Give it to me anyway," said Andy.

" It's not for you," said Roger. " It's for my sister."

" Your sister," said Andy contemptuously, " your sister."

Roger went on painting, as if there had been no talk.

" I want that drawing," said Andy, " and I'm going
to get it."

" You are not," said Roger.

" I tell you I'm going to get that drawing. I'm going
to get it."

" You are not," said Roger.

" I bet you anything you say I'll get it," said Andy,
" anything you want."

" I won't bet on a sure thing," said Roger.

" Why don't you stick up for the Jews," said Andy,
" are you all afraid? "

Roger was silent.

" Why don't you stick up for your family? " asked
Andy. " I thought Jews did that."

No answer.

" Give me that drawing," said Andy. " Either you give
it to me or I'll rip it up."

But at that moment the bell rang for chapel. They
had five minutes before prayers. Roger immediately
protected the drawing and started to put his paints
away, somehow more methodically than usual, as if the
logical slowness of his order was, in a way, a defense
against Andy.

" Why don't you stick up for yourself," said Andy.
" Why don't you answer me? " Roger put his paint box
in the table drawer, " Why don't you answer me you
son of a bitch? "

Roger stood up and looked at him. His mouth trem-
bled. " Why don't I answer you? " He asked. " Because
I know you don't mean a single word you're saying."

Andy was dumbfounded. He looked at Roger with
wide empty eyes. It was the first time Roger had ever
seen him actually defenseless, and it was dreadful. He
seemed caught in the act, discovered; the skin was off
his face and there was only a frightened fox beneath.
Roger shoved the chair next to the table and prepared
to leave the room for chapel. But there Andy stood, his
eyes fixed straight ahead and with a rising tide of mois-
ture on the verge of welling over his eyes. Roger hoped
he wouldn't cry. Then the last bell for chapel rang and
Andy turned and walked out of the room. Roger hesitated for a moment, and pulled his drawing out from
under his blotter. He ran and overtook Andy, going
downstairs.

"Here," said Roger, "here is the drawing you
wanted."

Andy looked at him savagely. "You'd better," he said
and snatched it from him. Roger followed him downstairs to chapel. Andy was laughing.

8

Roger decided that he was seeing too much of Andy.
He had begun to be frightened by him. He hated to admit it but he knew he was really scared of him. He was
so scared of him that he decided he must not make too
decided a break with Andy, or he would notice it, and
in some way retaliate. So he systematically saw more and
more of Tubby and Dusty and less and less of Andy. He
wouldn't ask Andy to do things with him as much as
formerly. On those rare occasions when Andy took the
initiative Roger found himself always occupied. The
worst of it was, Roger knew that Andy felt it and this
frightened him too. So Roger saw less of Tubby and

Dusty. He kept to himself for the most part. He hoped
Andy saw how much he kept to himself. Andy only saw
how he never went around with him.

Roger was sitting on the window seat of the school
library. It was hot sitting there, since the radiator had
a vent, and a thin streak of cold air hit him from a
crack in a window, but it was nice to sit reading, and
whenever one wanted, to look out the window and the
smoky valley. Roger was reading *The Research Magnificent*. It was all about the necessity for having courage, about a boy who couldn't face jumping across an
easy but tricky looking chasm. Roger read it with considerable conscious concentration as if it were a technical treatise, a textbook, almost a Latin grammar. He
was alone in the room and his mind kept wandering
aimlessly about the landscape outdoors.

The door at the end of the library creaked and Andy
came in. He walked slowly over to Roger, who pretended he was still reading his book.

" Roger," said Andy gravely, " I want to talk to you."

" Well," said Roger as pleasantly as he could, " What
do you want? "

" I want you to do something for me."

" Sure," said Roger, " what is it? "

" It is very important," said Andy, " a great deal depends on it."

" Well," said Roger, " what is it? "

Andy took a long thin pair of scissors out of his
pocket, opened it and shut it.

" I want you to give me a lock of your hair," said
Andy.

" What for? " asked Roger quickly.

" You know very well what for," said Andy.

" I do not," said Roger. " What for? "

"Will you or won't you?" said Andy, clicking the shears.

"I will not," said Roger.

"Yes you will," said Andy.

"What if I won't?" asked Roger.

"Then I'll have to cut it myself," said Andy. "I don't want to do that."

Roger was silent for a moment. Then an idea came to him. He looked at Andy.

"I'm sorry about Gerry Bates," he said, "I really am, I'm sorry we got him fired that way."

"Gerry Bates is nothing to me," said Andy, "you didn't get him fired."

"It was a lousy trick," continued Roger. "I'm sorry we did it."

"You didn't do it," said Andy. "Turner and Rhodes did it."

"It was just as much my fault as it was theirs," said Roger with emphasis. "I put them up to doing it."

"Are you going to cut me a piece of your hair or not?" asked Andy.

"I am not," said Roger.

"Then I'll have to do it myself." Andy bent down and cut off a sliver of Roger's curly black hair. Roger kept very still. He was really frightened that Andy might cut him and it wouldn't make much difference whether it were by mistake or not.

"Thank you," said Andy bitingly, "very much."

Roger paused. "You're welcome," he answered weakly.

Andy left the room silently. Roger could hear the scissors clink in his pocket. The door creaked close. Roger turned his eyes again onto *The Research Magnificent*. Except the print had split. It had become two

or three different sets of print and it shifted sickly all
over the page. Roger shut the book.

9

Roger was more and more alone. Somehow he thought
it would please Andy more. He became morose. He
wrote home more seldom. He became ridiculously sus-
picious about his health and he haunted the infirmary.
Nothing physical was the matter with him and he knew
it. Andy hardly spoke to him at all. When he did it was
on the most trivial occasions. At meals Andy would ask
him to pass the bread, if he happened to be sitting next
to him, or he would show him where the lesson was if
Andy were late to class. The very insignificance and
familiarity of these communications terrified Roger.
They seemed swollen out of all proportion by the implied overtones of Andy's malevolence. Roger frightened himself by his resistance, by his cocky attitude of
opposition against any of Andy's insignificant insinua-
tions. Roger could feel Andy casting a spell over him.
He was getting ready for anything.

The suspense was the worst thing. Roger would walk
down the hall expecting at every step to be encountered
by Andy. Every corner he took hid the possibility of
Andy meeting him, and in the meeting one of these
quiet terrifying battles. Their eyes would fight. Their
smiles would wrestle. Roger kept more and more to himself. He began considering all possible contingencies.
He told himself he wouldn't be surprised if Andy would
come through the ceiling down on him or through the
floor up at him. He wouldn't be astonished if Andy
would appear from the open air, or spring out of a
tree trunk or emerge from the book shelves. He took to

looking under his bed every night before he went to
sleep and in his closet. When he opened his window,
he would investigate the eaves. He made pretenses to
go in and look at the boy's room next door and the boys'
rooms facing his across the hall. He was snappish to his
old friends. The suspense was ruining his studies.

One Sunday night two or three weeks later Roger was
sitting at table. He had folded his napkin, finished with
eating. He was waiting for the others to get through.
He had had a busy, comparatively happy day. He had
partially forgotten Andy's existence. He was feeling full
of food and tired. There was a shuffling at the far end
of the dining hall. The headmaster had risen. This was
the signal for a general thunder of feet and chairs all
over the room. Everyone got up. After dinner on Sunday evenings the school gathered in the common room
to sing two or three hymns and sing the one school song.
There was always a rush to stand at the very back of the
room so as to be close to the table where all the magazines were piled. Those in front could hide anybody
behind who preferred to read rather than to sing. Some
boys tried to curry a little innocent favor by boldly
standing in the front line where there was no possible
question of deception. Roger tonight felt the necessity,
somehow for a little moral support. So he placed himself firmly in front of Mr. Stark. The headmaster smiled
pleasantly at Roger, a kindly anonymous Wood-and-
Stream smile. Suddenly Roger was attracted by Andy's
eye. It was mocking. He knew very well why Roger was
standing in the front line. Roger saw it, and felt his
heart beating faster. He made a gesture of pretext, of
excuse and walked slowly over to the edge of the room.
Some other boy took his place. Roger gradually worked
his way to the back of the room, behind the rest of the

school, next to the magazine table. He deliberately took
up a copy of *Punch*. He had seen it before, but then he
wasn't going to do much reading. The necessity for this
much defiance frightened Roger considerably. Why
must he make all this fuss? Why not keep calm? The
singing started.

" Jesus calls us o'er the tumult of life's dark fitful
sea. . . ." Roger wasn't singing. He wasn't even listening. " Saying Christian follow me." Good lord — he
thought, what can possibly happen to me anyway? Then
they sang " Wood-and-Stream, hail school of ours."
Then they bowed their heads and said the Lord's
prayer — " sssss as we have forgiven our tresspasssesss "
— The S's always sounded like a whisper out loud;
there was a second of silence before everyone went off
to their rooms. Suddenly Roger felt Andy at his side.
He didn't look at him. He held himself perfectly rigid.
Keep calm, thought Roger, keep calm.

" When the moon is full," said Andy, in his regular
voice, " I'm going to kill you."

Andy moved away. Roger stayed still for a second,
and joined the rest of the boys who were going up the
corridor.

" So that's it," said Roger to himself. He was glad to
know so definitely.

He went upstairs, took off his clothes, deciding to
get a little extra sleep. But the boys on the corridor
made so much noise that he couldn't sleep at all.

Yet there didn't seem to be much difference in Roger's
life. School went on. He ate and bathed and slept. He
even passed Andy on the corridor. They didn't speak of
course but Andy didn't seem to be inimical. There was
nothing unnatural about him. Yet Roger had no doubt
that Andy meant what he said. That when the moon was

full he would kill him. Why not tell someone? Why
not try to stop him? Roger, in the first place, couldn't
believe anybody would listen to him. It was too pre-
posterous, the whole story, and he had absolutely no
evidence. There was nothing in Andy's actions, or
speech that could be interpreted as damning evidence.
And strangely enough Roger knew he wouldn't have
told anyone, even if they would have believed him.
Somehow it was strictly between them. It was their game,
their lives and their death.

Several curious things did happen to Roger however,
and showed him things were not quite the same.
Strangely enough he stopped getting letters from home.
Perhaps the letters were lost. Perhaps Roger's never
reached his home. He never knew, except this very
precious link with reality was taken away and although
Roger could never be sure there was an intention behind it, nevertheless it gave him an uneasy, hunted
feeling to go down for the mail and know that his box
would be empty. Then, a day or two later he came up
to his room and found all the arrangement of the furniture changed. His bed was swung around the other side
of the room. His bureau was put at the head of his bed.
His table was set under the window. It wasn't even
inconvenient only it was different, disturbing, and yet
whenever he saw Andy there was only the mask of innocence. He joked and laughed with the other boys on the
corridor exactly as before. Then Roger began missing
things. First his toothbrush and soap, little things that
he thought he had misplaced. Then papers of his, notes.
Then handkerchiefs, a single shoe — a single overshoe.
Roger never thought of looking in Andy's room for
these losses. He knew so very well that he would find
nothing. He didn't tell the corridor master of the thefts

because they were so insignificant, so valueless. Who
would want to steal a single golosh, or a shoe? They
must be misplaced. But Roger knew they were not misplaced and it upset him. The terrible thing was that he
could never raise the slightest resentment, of hatred, or
resistance against Andy. He didn't hate him; he liked
him. He tried to think that it was not really Andy who
was killing him but a kind of Andy raised to third, or
fourth or nth power, like a coefficient in algebra, and all
the time Andy cast a spell over him, soporific, devitaliz-
ing, spiritually torturing enchantment, that left Roger
open to any possible attack, and yet at the same time
guaranteed to Andy that he would never tell anyone,
or in any way betray him.

10

One night after Roger had gone to bed, it must have
been quite a long time for he was almost asleep, his
door softly opened and a shape came in. The door
closed. Roger had been so nearly asleep that he couldn't
tell who it was that had come into the room. He raised
himself up on his elbows and his eyes searched the dark
for this presence. But the shadow hid it perfectly. He
couldn't possibly tell without getting out of bed and
making it move over to the light. Why didn't Roger
speak? Why didn't he say something? Why didn't he
ask who it was? He soon got cold with his arms and chest
exposed, so he pulled up the covers and lay on his side,
looking into the dark. How could he be sure? thought
Roger. How could he be sure?

Roger must have fallen asleep for when he woke up
in the morning there was no one else in the room. Perhaps he had dreamt it. Perhaps there was no one there

at all. He jumped out of bed and went quickly to the lavatory. He wanted to look into Andy's face, to see if there was anything there to tell him whether or not it was he. But Andy's face told him nothing. It was just like Andy's face. Perhaps it wasn't Andy at all, thought Roger. Perhaps it really wasn't Andy — that is, even Andy raised to the nth power. Perhaps, thought Roger, perhaps it was . . .

The next night Roger didn't go to sleep so quickly. He waited a long time making a strong effort against sleep. But as no one came, gradually he went to sleep. Sometime later he woke. He woke naturally, he afterwards decided. He heard nothing to disturb him. When he opened his eyes he did not move. If he had moved a quarter of an inch he would have struck with his own head a face, a white amorphous characterless face. But he didn't move. He shut his eyes. Through his shut eyes he felt the formlessness of this face above him. Everything in existence resolved itself down to the question of whether he could open his eyes again or not. He couldn't, and in the morning he woke again and went through the same formality of telling himself it was all a dream, or that it wasn't Andy or that it wasn't really Andy.

Roger was profoundly frightened. The month was drawing on. He couldn't tell about the progress of the moon because most days were overcast and snowy. He made futile attempts to look at daily papers or almanacs. But he didn't want to know really. He was so frightened he barely spoke. All daily operations merged in a misty activity of hands and feet. School was not real. People lost their identity. All except the great unidentified and unidentifiable force, the loose, vague power that was sapping every ounce of Roger's spirit, that was extract-

ing the bones from his body, painlessly through his flesh
and skin and that would leave him a disinherited spirit
with no territory in which to exist, except as in the constant squirrel cage of a horrible nightmare that increased
as the night went on.

Roger thought of putting his bureau up against his
door, of piling up his furniture as a barricade. But what
good would that do. It didn't bother with bureaus. It
wasn't stopped by barricades. It passed through key-
holes. It came in through crevices in the plaster. It was
all around him always, waiting to be polarized into a
power by the electric shocks of his piercing fear.

The next night as Roger was coming back from the
lavatory having brushed his teeth and settled himself
for the night he stopped for a second in Tubby Turner's
room. There were four or five boys in there, talking. He
felt the need of a sustaining contact with his fellows.

" Anyway," said Tubby, " it's a rotten shame."

" Whatsa matter," asked Roger. " What's a shame? "

" Haven't you heard about Morton? "

" About who? " Roger looked at the other sympatheti-
cally resentful faces.

" Hollis Morton. Stark fired him after study hall
tonight."

Hollis Morton — Andy's bully. " Fired him? " asked
Roger quickly. " Why did he do that? "

" He was on pro, anyway. Then some lousy bum on
the council got him with a lit butt behind the kitchen."

" Gee, that's a shame," said Roger.

" You're God damned right," said another boy.

" This *is* a lousy school," said Tubby.

" Gee, that's a damned shame," said Roger dumbly.

" Yeah," Tubby looked at him. " Even if he was a
God damned bully."

" A God damned shame," said Roger, considering.

" I didn't know he was any friend of yours." Tubby
looked hard at Roger. When Roger passed by Andy's
room, he saw him bent over his bed fixing his shoes
together, and he thought that the curve of his great elevated hips were reared up in a most sly obscene trium-
phant grin.

Then Roger went to sleep, or so he thought, at once.
He was determined not to open his eyes even if he woke,
until the morning came. The morning, even if there was
no sun, somehow dispersed the terrors. These grew more
powerful around noon because night was nearer. Roger
lay in bed sleeping. His eyes and ears were shut. He was
sleeping. He wasn't thinking about anything. He heard
nothing. How could he be awake if he didn't hear anything. Then he knew it was there. He felt it in the room.
He felt its presence as strongly as if he had opened his
eyes and found the room flooded in light and seen it. It
was definitely there. Roger felt his heart like a piston
mounting up into his neck. His eyes kept closed. He
wet his lips. They stuck together. His tongue finally
pierced through. He could feel the wet under his arm-
pits. He wanted to throw off the covers that kept him
hot but he was paralyzed by the fear of what would become of him if he tried to and found he couldn't move.
He lay there with little indissoluble crystals of horror
freezing the blood in his veins.

And suddenly a detached voice. A voice that had no
body behind it, that existed and was motivated only by
the sound it made for itself.

" Do not fear," said the voice. " It will not hurt."

Everything in Roger stopped at once. He could feel
all his mechanisms stop, and himself go off from them,
as if he were on a ship and watched the dock move away.

He wondered how far the separation could get without something breaking. It got thinner and thinner like a pulled-out thread of molasses. When it broke Roger found himself asleep, or what passed for sleep.

The next morning, however, spilled as usual. Roger was in a coma of fear. He could not concentrate even on passing the sugar at breakfast. He put some fruit in his mouth and felt nauseated. He asked to be excused from table. He walked quickly to the lavatory, hoping that he could throw up and gain some measure of relief from that. But he hadn't eaten for twelve hours. There was nothing in his stomach.

Somehow he got through his classes. It was much less real than his dreams. Every so often a bold and bullying thought came to him that he had invented the entire structure of his fear, that there was no truth to the persecution at all. Surely there was no physical basis for it. No one had hurt him or touched him even. But he quickly banished there from his mind as almost traitorous impulses to harbour against the tremendous malign benignity, the gracious, caressing horror that ranged him round.

11

He was walking back from the gymnasium alone. Dusty Rhodes had asked if he were going up to school and Roger deliberately lied. He went out by the side door alone. He hadn't gone very far when Dusty overtook him.

" I thought you weren't going up," he said.

" I changed my mind," said Roger.

" What's the matter with you these days? " asked Dusty. " You're so blue."

" I'm busy thinking," said Roger.

" What are you thinking about? " asked Dusty.

" Ideas," said Roger, " ideas for plays and stories."

" That's swell," said Dusty unenthusiastically, " what sort of stories? "

" Mystery stories," said Roger impatiently, wishing he'd go away.

" Gee," said Dusty, " tell us about it."

Roger thought for a moment. He could risk nothing by telling Dusty. He would betray no one. He wouldn't mention any names. He would tell it leaving himself out of it. The two boys walked on up to the school.

" One of them's about a student at a girl's boarding school," said Roger.

" Oh," said Dusty laughing, " sexy! "

" No," said Roger, " it's not. Another girl gets sore at her and tries to get her in dutch all the time. The first girl gets scared . . . and . . . and goes home —." He paused. " Then the other girl gets a gun and shoots her."

" Hell," said Dusty. " That's not much of a story. Where does the mystery come in? "

Roger was silent. Dusty was right. It wasn't much of a story.

That night Roger slept better than he had in a week. He didn't sense anything in his room at all. He woke up feeling extremely fit and refreshed. To be sure, he thought of several troubling things. For example he had been missing the key ring having his locker key, his own home door key, and a charm on it. This morning he found it on his bureau. He knew it wasn't there last night. It was Saturday and Roger cleared up most of his work so as to be free for the afternoon. He even thought of taking a walk with Dusty or Tubby Turner. He went down to the lavatory and took a shower and brushed his teeth. He felt fine. He wondered why on earth this cloud had been over him for so long. When he got back to his room Andy was seated on the unmade bed, looking at the floor.

" Hello," said Andy, " How are you? "

" Fine," said Roger. These were the first words they had spoken to each other in Roger didn't remember how long.

" What are you doing this afternoon? " asked Andy.

" Nothing," said Roger, " what are you? "

" Nothing," said Andy. " Want to take a walk this afternoon; snowshoes? "

" Sure," said Roger. Not until Andy had gotten up and walked out of the room did Roger realize he had never once lifted his eyes from the floor.

Roger thought of writing various notes for people. Farewell notes. People usually did that sort of thing. " Dear Mother," for example. " When you find this note, I will be no longer here. I want to send my love." Roger stopped the automaton that had served him now for so long as a mind. He decided he couldn't write any notes. It wouldn't want him to. It would be dishonest somehow to it. It would be too easy. Roger made a list. Father, mother, his sister's name, his nurse who was now looking after some young cousins, the names of the young cousins, Tubby Turner, Dusty Rhodes. He numbered each one and then scratched it all out. Then he scrunched up the paper in his hand and threw it into his desk. He thought of how much the same as today it would be tomorrow, although he would not be necessarily here to see how much the same it was.

Roger and Andy walked down the road past the gymnasium, their snowshoes on their backs. When they came to a break in the stone wall that ran along the road they stopped and put on the webs and struck out into the open country. The day was fine and a brisk wind blew any presumptive cloud out of the sky. The boys didn't talk much, but there was no apparent strain in their casual conversation.

"Well," said Andy, "it's been a pretty good year."

"Yes," said Roger, relieved to be able to talk freely. "I've enjoyed it."

"School's not such a bad place," said Andy. "I'm glad I came."

"Yes," said Roger. "I'm glad I came too."

"Even the masters," said Andy, "they're not so bad."

"Tonson was awfully nice," said Roger, "and interesting."

"You liked Tonson," said Andy, "didn't you?"

"Very much," said Roger. "You never had him did you?"

"No," said Andy.

"The boys too," said Roger, "they were nice too."

"Some of them," said Andy.

"I liked Dusty and Tubby a lot," said Roger.

"I don't know them," said Andy.

"You would have liked them, if you'd know them," said Roger.

"Perhaps," said Andy, striding ahead of Roger.

"What's the hurry?" asked Roger.

"We have a long way to go," said Andy.

"The country is great," said Roger, "isn't it?"

"The country is the best part of school," said Andy.

"Well," said Roger, "I'm glad to have had the chance to have come up here."

"It was better to have come," said Andy.

The boys walked on and the snow sifted in powdery veils through the thongs of the snowshoes. Andy was leading. Roger talked on and thought about nothing in particular.

" Do you know what happens to lights when they go out? " said Andy.

" No," said Roger, " what happens to them? "

" They go out," said Andy. " Then they come on again in the dark."

" In the dark? " Roger was puzzled. " What dark? "

" Do you remember the first time I ever saw you? " said Andy.

" No," said Roger, " when was that? "

" You were sitting in the common room reading *Punch*."

" I remember." Roger remembered.

" When I came into the room you were laughing out loud," said Andy.

" Was I? " asked Roger.

" The joke wasn't very funny either," said Andy.

" I thought it was awfully funny," said Roger.

" I can see that it was, now," said Andy. " Let's stop here."

" No," said Roger, " let's go on."

" Let's stop here," said Andy. He stopped.

Roger went on walking ahead. His feet were rather tired with the weight of the snowshoes.

" I said let's stop here," said Andy in a loud voice. Roger didn't look around. He kicked off his snowshoes to be freer and started to run across the field of snow. The crust was slightly frozen and as his ankles went through the crust they were recurrently cut by the knife edge of snow ice.

Andy was after him in a second. Roger ran desperately, hopelessly in a large wide-flung arc back to the direction of the road to school. He could hear Andy

behind him, but he wasn't afraid. He ran pretty fast
and was holding his own distance when he stumbled and
fell close to a stone wall. He saw anyways that even if he
hadn't fallen he couldn't have got across the stone wall
without Andy having overtaken him.

Andy was on top of him in a second. He didn't feel
very heavy either. Roger lay quietly in the snow and
Andy carefully arranged himself so that Roger was
practically helpless, his legs, his arms close together
and pinned by Andy's weight. Roger felt helpless of
course, but he never even wondered why it was impossible to make any physical resistance. The moral,
the overwhelming spiritual emanation from Andy
had bound his soul so fully that he didn't want to
resist.

" Shall I choke you," said Andy, " or bash your head
in with a rock? " He looked at the stone wall. Roger said
nothing. His terror had worked itself up into a sixth
sense, like sight or smell. But Andy made no move. He
was careful to keep Roger pinioned..

" What do you want to kill me for? " asked Roger. " I
never did you any harm."

" What has that got to do with it? " asked Andy.

" You'll be caught," said Roger. " They'll kill you."

" I will never be caught," said Andy. " I'll hide your
body in the snow."

" They'll look for me," said Roger.

" What of that," said Andy. " Then you'll be dead."

Dead, thought Roger. Dead. The being dead I won't
mind, nothing. It will be nothing. But the passage into
the nothing, the discovery of the nothing, that nothing
is really nothing.

" Let me up," Roger squirmed. " You're hurting me."

" I mean to," said Andy. " I will kill you soon."

" Why do you wait," said Roger. " I'm getting cold."
His bare neck was fast against the snow.

" I'm waiting," said Andy. " I'm making sure."

" But why do you kill me," asked Roger. " Why? "

" You ask me that! " said Andy darkly.

Roger had often wondered how people died. The
frame of the actuality of their death, the immediate
mortality of the act obsessed him. Now he was in that
frame. This was the death of Roger Baum, his own
private, unique and separate death.

" You're frightened," said Andy. He smiled kindly.

" I'm not," said Roger.

" I won't hurt you," said Andy. " It won't hurt." He
sounded like a surgeon. Roger's spirit swooned with
the sickly anticipation of ether, the black veil, the cloak
of death. He started to make one last violent struggle.
He almost caught Andy off his guard. But this made
him furious and he planted his knee heavily into the
pit of Roger's stomach. It hurt terribly. He felt his
insides pressing against each other. The fear of death
was directly on him like a spotlight catching him in the
dark on a stage in any empty theatre. He felt it. It was
cold and clammy and he hated it.

" Let me up," gasped Roger.

" I'm going to kill you now," said Andy.

What do people do, thought Roger, do they pray? He
couldn't pray. He waited. Andy's knee gouged into him
just below his breast bone. He hoped he wouldn't break
his ribs. He felt a churning inside. He knew his stomach
was turning over.

" If you don't get off me," said Roger in a grey far-
away voice, " I'll throw up."

Andy looked at him and saw he was green. With a
look of disgust he got up and straddled Roger. He looked

down at him and smiled. Roger coughed and turned his head away. The snow was cold on his face. Andy stepped delicately over his body and went off to look for his snowshoes. Roger lay on the ground listening for his heart to come back. The line strung between his two ear drums was humming so loud that he couldn't hear it.

Finally Roger got up and staggered over to the stone wall. He blew his nose and spat the phlegm out of his mouth. Andy was off there retracing his steps to find the place where his snowshoes had been kicked off. Roger rested on the fence. His whole body was filled with the most curious nauseous lassitude. There was no time nor place for him. He felt like a creature deprived of every faculty, shorn of every sensibility but the capacity for nausea. Presently Andy came back. He came up to Roger and looked at him.

" Let me help you," he said.

" No," Roger moaned. " Go away."

" I'll help you home," said Andy and made as if to put his arm on his shoulder.

" Go away," Roger was past any more fear.

" I can really help you," said Andy sweetly. " You may as well let me."

Roger let him and he finally got home. He started crying when they were about half way there. He had no handkerchief. Mucus started from his nostrils. He was wretched and undone. He wept on heedless of the tears falling or his running nose, heedless of shame. Before they got up to the dormitory Andy looked at him and gave him a handkerchief. He couldn't go up to the corridor looking like that. Roger got up to his room and threw himself on his bed. He couldn't cry any more. He looked at the cracks on the floor and vaguely wondered

how soon supper would be. He thought of washing his
face and hands and changing his clothes. He got up and
looked at the mirror. His eyes were hideously bloodshot.
He hoped there wouldn't be anybody in the lavatory.

When he got back to his room there was a small bottle
of a yellow liquid on his bureau. A note beside it
said, *Drink a little of this. It will restore you.* Andy had
put poison there. For a moment he thought of swallow-
ing the bottle in a single gulp. Then he put the note
down and was interested to see his hand tremble of its
own accord. It really was trembling, thought Roger, as
a gauge to convince himself of the depth of his own
terror. It is honestly trembling.

But he got through supper and was surprised to find
how hungry he was. He ate ravenously, greedily finishing everything before anyone else at his table, so that
he would be ready for seconds and thirds on the help-
ings. After that he ate bread and drank a lot of water.
He felt considerably better. Before eating he had
thought of asking to be excused from the usual Saturday night entertainment, but with his sated hunger he
felt considerably better and was prepared to enjoy the
movies. How did he feel towards Andy, he asked himself
precariously. Could he hate him yet? No, he couldn't.
Could he resist him yet? No, he couldn't. Was he still
frightened of him . . . ? He couldn't tell. The stars
snapped above him in the crisp February night and his
shoes snapped the thin covering of ice on the boardwalk down to the gymnasium where the movies were to
be shown. Was he still afraid . . . ? He couldn't tell,
but he was beginning to think about not being afraid;
perhaps this afternoon was the death. Perhaps Andy
wouldn't try any more. Roger went in to the movies
with the rest of the boys. When he came out he was

feeling terribly tired, tired and worn. For the first time
in his life he felt old. That is, the perspective of his life
spread out behind him. It seemed all past. There was
nothing ahead. There were people he saw around him
actually younger than he was. He was almost too tired
to question himself further. There were traces of fear
still left in his heart, like dust in the corners of an ill-
swept room.

After the movie Roger walked back to his room. The
stars seemed to converge into a point of brighter light
wherever he fixed his gaze on them. He turned away
and closed his eyes for a second but he still seemed to
see the stars. He walked on and up the stairs. There
didn't seem to be anyone else back on the corridor yet.
He stepped into his room and hung up his coat on a
hook; then he went over to his bureau and looked in
the mirror. He started to brush his hair for no reason
at all. Then he saw a piece of paper on the bureau cover.
It was all folded up in small folds. He looked at it
for a moment before opening it. He thought he knew.
He undid all the creases and went over to the light by
the window to read it. It was written in pencil — on an
uneven surface so that some parts were darker than
others.

" *This is the end. No noose, nor dagger nor poison.
That bottle was not poison it was brandy. It would have
revived you. The end is an end. Something falling into
the ocean, the ship sails on. This really the end. Every
tree in the forest tonight will break and all the houses
fall to pieces. Even the stars would pity you if they knew,
but they are beyond the ring of the moon and may not.*"

Roger stopped his eyes as the writing stopped and
looked out the window. Indeed the moon was quite full.
It fell on the lead and slate of the roofs like pale liques-

cent metallic enamel, a putrescent vitriol that burned
the stone shingles. Then this was the end. He was to
really die. He was dying now. He was to be extinguished
in the pityless blackness of an influence that fitted him
like a strait-jacket. He was to be killed by omnipotence,
by omniscience, by an unknown enemy which inocu-
lated him with the poison of non-resistance, like a spi-
der anesthesizes its prospective victim. Dying. . . . He
could feel all the inner fixtures of his body detach
themselves from their anchorage. They started turning
slowly like a conglomeration of raw ball bearings.
Wherever the surfaces touched it burnt him inside,
and he could taste the smell of the burning coming up
the inside of his throat. Fear, no longer. It was the
start of a loathing, a strong hate of corruption, the
hatred of what his body would turn to after it had ceased
to be his.

The hatred grew stronger and stronger. It seemed to
be localized as a pain in his head and in his stomach.
It grew like two opposing tumors inside him and they
seemed to have a connection in resistance; they pulled
against each other. Roger was standing perfectly rigid
waiting for the something to snap inside him. The cords
drew tightly and twisted closer together.

When it did snap he started coughing. He coughed
and coughed. He thought he was coughing blood. He
gripped his throat in his hands and his hands seemed to
go right through the flesh and meet each other on the
other side. He started running very fast and stopped
quickly to find he had not moved at all.

Then he walked out of his room and to the stairs.
Dusty Rhodes was coming up from the movies. He
looked at Roger and was about to speak. Roger seemed
not to notice him. He went on walking downstairs

and up the next corridor. He beat on a door at the end
of the corridor. It was Tonson's, the English master's
room. The door opened and it was Tonson.

" Why, Roger," he said, " come in." Roger looked
around. Andy wasn't there.

Roger walked over to a sofa and sat down. A fire
was burning on the hearth.

" Well, Roger," said Mr. Tonson. " It's nearly bedtime, isn't it? " Then Tonson looked at him and said
suddenly, " Why, Roger, what's the matter? "

Roger looked up to say something. The words came
out in a whisper. He listened for the sound of the
whisper. But he could hear nothing. Tonson came over
to look at him more closely. Roger tried to speak again.
He felt terribly tired, drowsy and cold, freezing. Then
he started sweating. Then he swayed and fell on to the
sofa for his heart missed a beat.

When he came to he felt a little sick. He found he
was not in his own bed. He seemed to be alive. When his
eyes were accustomed to the light he discovered he was
in a high bed in the school infirmary. The faint smell
of iodine or lysol seemed to cling around the antiseptic
white iron pipes of the beds and tables. He called for
the nurse, and she came in, clean and smiling, bearing a
thermometer.

" Well," said the nurse, " — this is a lovely day."

" Yes," Roger looked at her uneasily.

"You just put this under your tongue," she said,
shaking the glass tube — " and I'll get you some breakfast."

" Thanks," said Roger, taking the thermometer. " I'm
as hungry as hell — "

" Oh dear," laughed the nurse, " — all you can have
is some orange juice — "

" Why? What's the matter with me? " Roger felt suddenly unhappy.

" We don't know yet," said the nurse — " just put this under your tongue."

" But I'm all right," said Roger, taking the thermometer from her clean hands, " — there's nothing wrong with me."

She smiled, saw that the thermometer was awkwardly settled under his tongue and withdrew to find the orange juice.

Roger swallowed it. The taste kept recurring even after he had brushed his teeth and washed his mouth out.

When he came back from the bath room, she said suddenly — " There's a friend of yours here to see you."

" To see me? " Roger considered — " Who is it? "

" It's a boy," said the nurse. She smiled. " He said it was important — but he wouldn't tell me who it was."

" I know who it is," Roger looked at her closely.

" Well," the nurse waited, " do you want to see him? "

" Oh, yes," said Roger. " Thank you very much."

Andy came in, smiling. He stood, his arms akimbo at the base of Roger's bed.

" Well," he said, " You're looking fine."

" What do you want? " asked Roger.

" So you tried to tell — didn't you? " Andy was not sure.

" Yes, I did," said Roger. " What the hell did you think I'd do? "

" Nothing," said Andy. " It makes no difference anyway."

There was a pause — which gave Roger time enough to feel he was not in the least upset or frightened or amused by Andy.

" **I'm** leaving . . . ," Andy continued, ". . . school."

" You're leaving? "

" Yes," said Andy. " I'm fed up."

" You're going," said Roger, thinking fast.

" I'm going this morning. . . ."

" But how can you? " asked Roger. " The term's not up."

" What of it? " Andy turned his head.

" Well, what will Stark say? " Roger smiled questioningly.

" I don't give a damn what Stark says."

" All right," said Roger. " All right."

" I won't even ask him," Andy considered.

" You're not going to skip? " Roger could feel the old excitement as Andy's temerity slowly warmed him.

" And why not? " Andy shuffled his feet.

" Just skip out — not leave a word? " Roger was pleased.

" I'm going now," Andy decided it was a sure thing.

" What'll I tell . . . people? " Roger asked shyly.

" Why do you have to tell them anything? " Andy started to glare at him. Roger sat farther up in bed and started to glare back —

" I don't," said Roger. " I was only asking."

" Tell them anything you want," said Andy. " Goodbye." As he turned to go, Roger felt the necessity of some final dismissing gesture — . . .

" Where will I write to you — . . ." he asked. " Where will you be? "

" Why should you write? " Andy looked vaguely out the window, turned and withdrew. Roger heard the door slam at the far end of the outer corridor. He sat in bed waiting, and shoved the pillow back up behind him. The nurse came in.

" Did you see your friend? " she asked.

" What friend? " asked Roger, almost startled.

"Hasn't someone called to see you? " she said.

" Why — no," said Roger. He looked up at the nurse's medical curiosity and winced inside. He paused and said with some trace of guilt — " Oh — he; — well, — he went away."

Flesh is Work

When my mother died I was very young,
And my father sold me while yet my tongue
Could scarcely cry " Weep! weep! weep! weep! "
So your chimneys I sweep, and in soot I sleep.

There's little Tom Dacre, who cried when his head,
That curled like a lamb's back, was shaved; so I said,
" Hush, Tom! never mind it, for, when your head's bare,
You know that the soot cannot spoil your white hair."

1924

1

Roger was through with school but his father decided that he was too young to go to college. Instead he would work at something or other for the year between. Roger would have preferred to work by himself, to draw when he cared to, to wander around in an easy enjoyment of the lack of school discipline which had for the last four years become an imposed rhythm on his pleasure in existence. But his father was right, he ought to go to work at something.

For two or three weeks he ventured into the lofts of architectural sculptors, artisans who made plaster models of churches and country clubs and monuments, and sign painters. The atmosphere of craft, the idea of men creating an expression of living outside of themselves fascinated him. He preferred their being craftsmen rather than creative workers because they worked with their hands and their directed effort implied no competition on any basis of talent. He could learn what they learned. Time and practice was all that was necessary. Materials, the smell of wet paste, plaster, sheets of white cardboard and drawing papers, bottles of colored inks, various sizes of scissors were all a potential alchemist's paraphernalia; finally the manager of a stained glass company said that Roger could work there if he liked. It was a privilege to enter his guild. And of course there would be, at first, no thought of pay.

Roger was delighted that he had landed the occupation. His parents were. pleased that he had found something to amuse him and they gave orders that he should be called from now on at seven o'clock.

McDermott's stained glass shop was on the top floor of a loft building that had been made around 1870. The ceilings were lofty. Steep flights of dusty creaking wooden stairs fanned around a series of landings that opened into job-printers with the constant rush and muffled crash of small presses, carpentry shops and a laundry. One walked up four flights and at a turn in the stair found a stained glass panel set in the corner of a landing. It was illuminated from behind by electric lights. It showed a young girl as an angel with a basket of grapes. It was heavily seamed with leading, holding the bits of glass together, and Roger could see that it had been there a long time for the weight of the glass had caused the lower portion of the panel to crack and buckle. Roger went on up to the double door that read " McDermott Stained Glass Shop " in heavy gothic characters, partially chipped away on the glass. All around were large charcoal cartoons of Christs and angels tacked upon the wall.

He knocked and entered. The girl at a desk told him, when he asked for Mr. McDermott, to wait. He sat down in a pew that was set against the wall of the outer office and looked up at more stained glass panels. He was somewhat nervous. Roger was never sure what people expected of him and he usually felt inadequate and expressed it by being too grateful. He was preparing speeches of gratitude for Mr. McDermott, when voices came out of the inner room.

" So for all of me I can quit now," a harsh voice.

" You know very well how often I've asked you to reconsider," a soft voice.

" You don't mean a god damn word of it," the harsh voice louder.

" Remember there are other people around us," the soft voice, softer.

" I don't give a damn who hears me, and I'm good and fed up."

" I am sorry but I can say nothing further " exasperation, even embarrassment Roger thought.

" All right then, Mr. McDermott," came the harsh voice deliberately, " I quit right now." Silence. Roger shifted uneasily. He knew he ought not to be overhearing this conversation. But they talked so that he couldn't help hearing, and it would be too obvious if he got up and went out into the hall. He looked over at the secretary. She was smiling. He turned quickly away to hear the harsh voice continue.

" And before I go I want to tell you a few things, Mr. McDermott."

" Why," came the genial softness, " I think that's hardly necessary."

" No — well you're going to hear 'em anyway. I'll be god damned if I don't get some satisfaction of this lousy joint. McDermott, you're a thief and you know it. You're a lousy stinking rotten Irish skinflint and you can have the fun of knowing that your whole god damned gang of crippled . . ."

" Come now," said McDermott quickly, "you get out of here quick — that's about all I'll take from you." There was a noise of shuffling chairs and feet on the floor inside.

" O. K.," said the other man quietly. " You're right. I'll go." A tall dark, fierce man of about thirty came quickly out of the inside room and made for the door. As he passed he gave Roger a swift, abstracted stare.

Roger couldn't connect the face with the voice. The
door slammed. Mr. McDermott came out of the inside
office and paused on the threshold. Roger saw him turn
to the secretary and smile. She winked at him, looked
over at Roger with the wink still in her eyes, to indicate
that the boy waited, and quickly resumed her typing.

"Ah," said Mr. McDermott, "I had no idea you'd
be so prompt. I'm very glad to see you. Come. I'll show
you around the shop." Mr. McDermott led the way
past several small draughting rooms where various men
and boys were at work at cartoons for windows tacked
upon the wall. They passed into a very large and tall
loft with a great gabled roof which was gloomy and
dusty. A smell of burning sugar and some pungent acid
blew through when a door opened and shut. At the far
end of the room a huge rose window let in the light.
Roger thought it more beautiful than anything he had
ever seen. It was so close to its creators, so tangible, so
large and with such an infinite variety of jewels and
colors. Mr. McDermott noted with pleasure the impres-
sion this made on Roger.

"That is the top light for St. Anthony's in Dallas,"
he explained. "I've just had it stuck up there so that
the architect can see what it looks like."

Roger was overwhelmed with admiration and a gratitude buttered with humility. He wanted to tell Mr. Mc-
Dermott how very much he appreciated being allowed to
work in his shop. The older man smiled and brushed
him aside, "Not at all, we like to have young men here
always." Here . . . here . . . Roger looked around at
the great tables covered with frames of the cut glass.
There was a mediaeval atmosphere of concentration,
devotion, almost a religious, consecrated glow. Roger
was fascinated. Far in the corner of the large loft a man's

head was stooped over some work. He stopped and put
a record on the phonograph at his side, an orchestra-
tion of a Bach prelude and fugue. Roger knew that he
had hit the most lucky place to work in the world and
he was breathless with anticipation for the tour of inspection to begin, so that he should be given some work
to do, at once, and become a part of the devotion.

Mr. McDermott's kindly smile noticed everything. He
was, Roger saw, big enough not to demand any explanation of feelings, as a flattery. He said only, " It's
really pretty fine, isn't it? "

" I should say so," said Roger, " what shall I do? "

" Well, I'll take you around and meet the men; then
you tell me what you want to do."

Roger saw the furnace tended by an old man, bald
and heavily unshaven. A small boy flickered around the
fire shoving trays of white plaster and glass into the
heat. The furnace door clanked shut. The boy faded
away. By a long row of plate glass windows set against
a north light men in smocks stuck pieces of colored glass
upon transparent frames of glass bound in wood. They
squinted at each piece, adjusted it, took it out, replaced it by another, squinted, bent over long pine
tables and stared out the windows. Opposite the benches
were the glass racks full of huge sheets of every con-
ceivable color and gradation and texture of colored
glass.

McDermott smiled at the men, said Roger was to
work in the shop, passed on. The men paid little attention to either of them. They seemed far too absorbed in
their work. After the tour of inspection they ended up
back in McDermott's office. Roger suddenly thought of
the conversation he had overheard as he came in. McDermott seemed to be so kind, so understanding that for a

moment Roger's great curiosity almost made him ask for
an explanation of that harsh-voiced violence. In the in-
terval of silence, it seemed as if McDermott sensed his
intention, for he turned brusquely to Roger and said,
" I think you can clean the frames for a while. That's as
good a way to start as any." He turned to his secretary
with a sheaf of letters. As Roger turned to find the
foreman he saw her smile again, whether at him or
McDermott he couldn't tell.

2

Gibson, the foreman, was an iron-grey man of fifty.
His face had the stamp of dignity, a nobility and a curious subservience that unsettled Roger. He explained to
him how to wash the heavy frames of glass that were
used to stick the glass upon and pointed to a large pile
of them in a rack. Gibson was thorough and amiable
in his explanation but after he had gone about his
own business, Roger hesitated before he took up the hot
water and brushes. There was a tone patronizing him, in
the foreman's voice, as if perhaps he was explaining a
new game to a boy like Roger, which was something
more than a game to a workman like himself.

At all events washing the frames was no game. Roger
enthusiastically set about scraping off the black lines and
wax from the plate glass slabs. A mixture of sugar and
lamp black warmed up to flow easily, simulated the
lead lines of the finished glass, through all the process
of creation. Dabs of beeswax at the junctures of every
angle held the glass in place. When the window was
finished and sent down to be finally braced and leaded
the glasses were cleaned up again to be reused. The
sugar and lamp black was a powerful glue and resisted

the heaviest scraping. Hot water was necessary and the combination of constant scraping of beeswax and the sugar black, dirty water and friction quickly macerated Roger's hands which were unaccustomed to any effort more than gripping the handle bars of his bicycle. He displayed his cracked and raw fingers proudly to his parents. It was a badge of honour. They were suitably impressed. However he was quick to hide them from Gibson or any of the other men whose palms were thick enough in which to quench cigarette butts. Roger went on diligently scraping down the frames. As in all such manual work there was a technique that could be quickly developed so that the various processes in the cleaning could be accomplished with the greatest vigor and economy. Too quickly for Roger the technique was discovered, for at first he was never bored; each glass presented a new problem. But presently when he got facile enough to find each glass was exactly the same he lost any curiosity or interest; he became hideously bored. For his hands were constantly employed in the mechanism of cleaning. All of his nervous energy was thus automatically liberated and concentrated, but his mind, which was ten times as nervous as his body, had nothing with which to occupy itself. He couldn't finish the glasses quickly enough to absorb himself in counting them as they piled up. Repetitions of numerals rattled around in his head. He was an absolute outsider as yet in the shop. People were friendly in a distant way. They approved of his thoroughness but made no gestures as to intimacy. His curiosity in their direction was greatly piqued. He was chained to the glass yet his eyes roved about trying to discover things which would suggest food for consideration and still he went on pouring the hot water over his raw fingers, scraping and polishing the slabs, becoming more and more jumpy, as if a second Roger were inside his exterior shell trying to burst the bounds of this oppressive, exhausting ennui. This went on for two or three weeks. Roger became doggedly depressed. Everybody else in the place seemed to be doing what they wanted to do, were creating, while he was cleaning glass. He knew he must stick to it. He couldn't really ask them to change his job since they were so graciously allowing him to be there at all. He scraped on and his body sweated and his mind sweated and he felt that his lack of a focus for his imagination was what people mean when they spoke of going crazy.

One morning he was standing up a particularly large frame, polishing off the final touches of Bon Ami in large, desperate, professional strokes when one of the draughtsmen came up to speak to him. His name was Jan and he seemed to be Danish or Norwegian.

" You've learned to do that pretty well," said Jan; he looked appraisingly at the size of the frame and at Roger's wild restless eyes.

" It's not very hard to do, you know," said Roger. He felt as if he would like to explain just how he felt, but he didn't.

" Are your hands sore? " asked Jan.

" Mine. Why, no not at all."

" Well, mine were good and sore. I did this job for six months once."

Roger's heart fell into his stomach. " Six months? "

" Yes, six months, but," and Jan laughed, " I was paid for it."

Roger averted his eyes and went on polishing. He'd keep his mouth shut from now on. But Jan as if to apologize for his dig at Roger's insecure pride went on, " Do you like polishing the frames? "

"Did you?" asked Roger with dignity.

"About as much as you do. I'll give you a word of advice," said Jan. "Tell Gibson you're fed up with this lousy work. He'll change you."

"Gee," said Roger, "I wouldn't dare do that . . . I've just come."

"Yes?" said Jan, "Well, if you don't, you'll be at it for six months and then I suppose you'll be going to college."

"Who told you that?" asked Roger.

"Oh, we know all about you," said Jan. We, the rest of the shop. They might at least be a little decent about him, Roger thought. He was working as hard as he could. "Nevertheless," went on Jan in a perfectly kindly way, "if you want to have any hands left I'd ask Gibson to give you a change." A silence.

Roger finished the frame, took it from the bench, set it down on the floor and carried it to the rack. On the way over he decided it was really very nice of Jan to have troubled himself with him at all. He went back to thank him, but by that time Jan had gone into the draughting room. Roger hoped he wouldn't think he was stuck up for his silence, and went to look for Gibson.

3

The foreman lifted his iron-grey bullet head up from a bench where he was sorting large pieces of the fired glass. Roger stood sheepishly at his side wishing he'd never come. Before he could speak Gibson looked up.

"Tired of your job, eh?"

"No," said Roger. "I'm not in the least tired of it."

"Not in the least?" said Gibson and laughed. "Most

of us have that job for two months." Accent on the months.

" I'm not complaining," said Roger, and tried to re- member how one acted in similar circumstances. But all of his previous preparation in reading success stories and commercial adventure failed him. He was socially embarrassed.

" I suppose you'd be sore," said Gibson to the boy, " if I shifted you to the draughting room."

" Oh, that's just what I wanted," said Roger, and started to thank him.

" I thought you were satisfied." Roger saw that Gib- son's smile was really frank, really good. After he had cleaned up his own job he presented himself in the draughting room. Jan was alone in front of the lower part of a colossal Christ. He was fixing the sandals and kept on at his job after Roger had come in.

" Mr. Gibson said I could work in here from now on," said Roger.

" Did he? " said Jan. " You seem to be getting on."

From polishing glass frames Roger was promoted to do lettering on the borders of the finished cartoons. It was difficult to make the spaces come out right and the Gothic cast of the letters was as tricky as it was ugly. " In Blessed Memory of Jonathan Grey Stevens " the " In Blessed Memory of " would come out all right on one line but the name wouldn't fit. He erased and re- erased until the paper was grey with the rubbed-in smooch.

" You don't seem to be doing very well," said Jan, " shall I give you a hand? "

" No, thanks," said Roger scrubbing away, " I'll come out all right."

" You keep to yourself a lot, don't you," said Jan.

"Why no," said Roger, "I only thought all of you having been here so long."

"All of us?" laughed Jan, "All of us; that is the people who work here."

Roger was silent. His silence indicated that he felt he worked there too.

"Oh, I know what you mean," said Jan. "You're all right. We've just been watching you."

"Have I passed inspection?" Roger didn't feel jocular. He felt strained.

"Why, yes and no — I think you're O. K."

"What does Mr. McDermott think," Roger looked up from his work.

"Oh," said Jan. "I'm sure he thinks you're fine."

The word "fine" somehow stood by itself. Jan gave it too much emphasis.

"Well," said Roger, "that's good. I hope Gibson thinks I scrubbed the glasses well." Jan smiled. "I don't know anyone else here."

"They know you," said Jan. "They talk about you."

"Oh," said Roger. He was really surprised. "What do they say?"

At that moment another of the draughtsmen came back from lunch. His name was Firs Martens. He was also a Dane and he lived with Jan. Roger was introduced.

Firs started sketching in a sheaf of grain and grapes and lilies, idly, with one hand free on a cigarette. The three were silent, suddenly Firs turned to Jan, "Gibson's sore at me again. He blew up before lunch."

"If you get here every morning about noon," answered Jan, "no wonder."

"God! I'd like to leave this lousy job. A man has some rights."

" Yes," said Jan quietly, " got another job somewhere? "

" You know damn well I haven't. But I can get one
whenever I want."

" So you always say. I wish you'd either put up or
shut up."

" I didn't expect much sympathy from you," said
Firs.

" You don't get much either, do you? " Jan answered.

Firs suddenly looked at Roger, then back at Jan,
" Guess I oughtn't to be talking that way in front of
the kid."

" I don't see what the hell that's got to do with it,"
said Jan. " The kid's all right. He won't tell Gibson
you're crabbing." Firs smiled in the direction of Roger
who was careful to be intent on his lettering.

" Sometimes, Firs, you give me a pain in the neck,"
Jan left the room with a roll of cartoons to show the
boss. There was a busy, a forced silence. Firs could see
Roger was not actually so intent on his work as he
seemed.

" Jan is a queer customer," he said.

" Yes," agreed Roger fatuously. " Do you know him
well? "

" Know him well." Firs was delighted at the opening.
" Say, boy, he's my oldest friend. We've lived together
for four years."

" Oh," said Roger.

" Yes, sir," Firs put down his charcoal to give all his
attention to Roger, who was against his will, interested.
He maintained, however, his independence to the extent
of going on with his work. " Yes, sir," pursued Firs, " I
met Jan when I was soda jerking. You know what I
mean? " Roger wished Firs wouldn't look at him with

that trace of doubt which ruined any equality. " Of course," said Roger.

" I was soda jerking one whole winter. I'd left art school. It wasn't a bad job and I met a lot of interesting people."

" What sort of people? " Roger kept his eyes on his drawings.

" Oh, all sorts of bums . . . bruisers and pugs and some real nice girls, too. You'd be surprised."

" Yes," said Roger.

" Yes, they got sort of used to come into the drug store and I knew pretty quick what they all had and often I could tell when they were coming in so I had it ready waiting for them, sandwiches, sodas, you know."

" Sure," said Roger.

" I had a real nice girl then, a model I met in the Normal Art. I saw her all the time. Then one day Jan came into the store for a drink. We got talking. I found out he was Dane, too. Our family lived practically in the next towns in the old country."

" Wasn't that extraordinary? " said Roger. He felt the necessity of an acquiescent interest to keep Firs going.

" Extraordinary? " said Firs. " Why, yes. I guess it was. Except that Jan and I got to be friends. He asked me to room with him. Two together is cheaper."

" Much cheaper? " Roger should really shut up. Yet he felt he must show a real, practical knowledge to back up his interest.

" Not much cheaper. We got a good room for two for seven-fifty a week, while both alone would be — " But Firs felt the assumed interest of Roger's question, and he quickly went on with his narrative. " Jan and I lived together. I used to have my girl around a lot. She was

a real nice girl. As soon as she got her eyes on Jan she
fell for him. She left me cool. She used to come up into
my room, into our room every night and wait for him.
Then they'd both sit there and stare me out of the room.
God, I felt guilty if I came into my own bed. I used
to walk up and down the god damned street all night,
waiting for her to go home."

" Gee," said Roger with great feeling. " I think it's
wonderful you two are still friends."

" Friends, hell," said Firs. " I hate his rotten guts."

" But you live with him, don't you? "

" Sure I live with him," said Firs, " didn't I tell you
two living together is cheaper? " Then Jan came back
into the room and by his eyes Roger guessed that he
knew what they were talking about.

" Well," said Firs, " I guess I'll get something to drink.
I'm thirsty."

" What's that rat been filling you up with? " asked
Jan after he'd left.

" Well, we were really talking about you." Roger
smiled sheepishly.

" If he hates my guts, I hate his. And he knows it.
You can't have any use for a lousy coward." Jan spoke
personally, and frankly to Roger. " Can you? " Roger
shook his head. " Well, Firs Martens is the worst coward
I ever met, always talking about leaving his job, and
how much he hates me. What I done to him. Christ. Do
you really want to know what I done to him? " Roger
was about to say he really would, and to add that Jan
could count on him, when Mr. Lansing came into the
room. Mr. Lansing was McDermott's assistant, his right
hand man. He did some designing but he was mainly
used as a liaison officer between the shop, between the
men and McDermott. He was thirty-seven or eight;

going bald with a fat belly rolling from under his watch
chain, and two small fat bellies rolling under his eyes.
His nose was stubby and his jaw was faintly blue. His
eyes were like the small glazed eyes of a roast boar's
head. His manner was affable, and he had come to see
how Roger was getting on.

"Well, hello Jan," Lansing called the men by their
first names. They called him Mr. Lansing. "How is
our young friend getting on?"

"Let him tell you," said Jan.

Roger left his work and said, "Oh, I'm getting along
very well, thanks."

"Lettering?" asked Mr. Lansing. "Well, you're coming right along. How about a little vacation? I'll take
you around and see the painters." Roger was overjoyed,
but somehow as he left the room behind Mr. Lansing he
averted his eyes from Jan, instinctively.

"What are your first impressions of our shop?" asked
Mr. Lansing.

"Oh, I think it's wonderful," said Roger. "Everybody
seems so —."

"Just so," said Mr. Lansing. "It's refreshing for
someone as young as you to feel the dignity of what
we do."

"I don't see how anyone could fail to feel that," said
Roger. He was looking at the recently stuck-up series of
evangelists that McDermott had made for a college me-
morial chapel. The convention of hieratic byzantine
stiffness, the steady glow of color really moved him.

"To be sure," said Lansing. From the corner of the
room the phonograph ground out Tristan's love death.
"Do you like music?"

"Oh, yes," said Roger, "very much indeed. That is
Wagner, isn't it?"

"Wagner," said Mr. Lansing, "to be sure. Do the men like the music?"

"Why, yes," said Roger. "I think they play it a lot, don't they?"

"Yes," said Mr. Lansing. "Do you think the music is a good influence on the men?"

"Why, yes. I don't see how it could help but be a good influence."

"Oh, I think so," said Mr. Lansing as if someone else didn't. Roger felt himself being drawn into a conversation, into a situation, in which, he was amazed to find, he had something to lose.

"Do you think the men are satisfied?" resumed Lansing.

"Satisfied?" echoed Roger vaguely.

"Yes, do you think the men are content?" Roger looked surprised.

"Why, I can't tell, I haven't been here long enough. I can't say." Roger was amazed and somehow horrified that he should have been thus taken into Mr. Lansing's confidence, as young as he was and having only just got this job. "Over here," said Mr. Lansing, pointing to the back of a man seated in front of a window, "is the cleverest glass painter we've ever had." They made their way over to his side.

The glass painter did not look up, though he must have heard the two draw up to his bench. "I was just telling our new man Baum," said Mr. Lansing,, "what an excellent worker you are, Peter."

"Yes," grunted the man. Lansing continued, "Baum, Roger," he smiled, "I want you to meet Peter Foster. He can teach you all there is to know about painting glass. And there is a great deal to know," he added vaguely, pulled up a chair next to Foster's, indicated that Roger should sit down and watch, and then went off.

For a long time neither spoke. Roger was fascinated at the skill with which the man traced the cartoons onto the glass with a fine brush dipped in a thick solution of iron oxide. Often the line of the cartoon was uneven. But Foster's traced work was as mechanically perfect, as an engraved copy of Spencerian penmanship, and as impersonally. Finally Foster looked up from his work, sideways at Roger.

" You are the new boy? " he said. Roger said he was.

" Do you want to be a glass painter? " asked Foster.

" Why, yes," Roger considered, " but I'd rather be a designer."

" A designer," Foster paused, " then a painter is not good enough for you? "

" Not at all," said Roger, " only I like to draw."

" Ah," said Foster, " to draw, to express yourself."

" Yes," answered Roger uncomfortably, " that was my idea."

" You have never tried to paint on glass at all? " asked Foster.

" No," said Roger, " can I try? "

" Here is a piece I spoiled," said Foster. " Try on that." He filled his brush and gave it to Roger. Roger tried to sign his name. He barely could draw the recalcitrant sticky medium across the glass plate. He kept dipping it again and again in the solution.

" That is not the way," said Foster. " The brush is already full." Roger looked vainly at the way he held his fingers, and the fingers that gripped the brush. But the knack of the thing baffled him. " The only way to learn to paint on glass is to paint constantly." Roger took up the brush again and managed to sign in a faltering splotchy way, " Roger Baum."

" Roger Baum," mused Foster. " Baum is a German name. I am German too. My real name is Forschster. I am Prussian — "

" My grandparents were Germans," said Roger. " My mother and father were born in this country."

" A Jew, too," Foster looked at him. He nodded, " and rich? "

Roger shook his head, and asked, " How long did it take you to learn? "

" It has taken me all my life," said Foster, " I had to learn to do it well. It makes my living — "

Roger was determined to ignore the aggressive personal allusions of Foster. "And would you rather be a glass painter than a designer? " he asked.

Foster laughed. " I will tell you, my friend. I, too, am a designer. I am a very good designer. After the war I went to Brazil and had my own shop there. The country is full of Catholic churches. I designed very many windows, all my own, I was very successful — "

" Why did you come here? " asked Roger.

" My partner made off with all our money. I have nothing. So I came to North America and I am now — you heard Mr. Lansing say, one of the best glass painters he knows — "

" He said you were the best," said Roger.

" Ah, that is only Lansing," said Foster and went on with his work.

" But I should think you would have much rather chosen to be a designer," said Roger.

" How old are you? " asked Foster.

" I am sixteen," said Roger.

" Even for that age you are very stupid." Roger knew

that this was no banter. "I am a good designer, I say.
I will not have my designs gone over and ruined and
spoiled and made rotten by these pigs here. No, I do
not — " Roger was almost frightened by the suppressed
intensity of the man, who went on savagely painting as
he talked. "No I am no designer. I am a glass painter.
I trace the bad designs of these bad designers on to glass.
Sometimes I correct them, sometimes I make them
worse, all the time I feel what pigs they are. No artist
among them." He stopped and laid down his pen. He
looked at Roger. "Are you really interested in stained
glass?" He could see the unsaid reluctant negative in
Roger's eye. "No, well that is just as well. For if you
had been interested in the glass painting I could have
shown you many interesting things. As it is you'd better
go back to your designing — "

"I'm only doing lettering now," said Roger, to show
that he was genuinely humble, and somehow apprecia-
tive of the confidence.

"Well, you'd better go back to your lettering. Lansing does not like the new men to talk to me too much,"
and he laughed, as Roger thought, in a very Prussian
way, and proudly.

4

Roger went back to the draughting room. When he
got inside the door he found the two Danes, Firs and
Jan with a boy of about twenty or twenty-two, anyway
he was older than Roger and yet he seemed young. They
didn't trouble to introduce Roger so he went back to
his inscription and his eraser.

"You know some day you'll get killed that way," said
Firs to the boy.

" Oh, I can take care of myself all right," he answered in a curious cracked voice.

" Don't you never trust no sailors," said Jan. " They're bastards."

" Say," said the boy. Roger thought the crack in his speech sounded like the occasional twangy chord a phonograph sometimes makes — the same split note. " If you've known as many as I have you know how to treat 'em."

" Sammy," said Firs, " you know I don't like that attitude of yours. It's not respectful." He winked at Roger.

" Sammy is getting very fresh," said Jan, " I think he needs to be spanked."

" Oh, now, go away with you," said Sammy. " I've got four trays of glass now and they'll be all melted while I've been talking here with you."

" You can't go until you apologize," laughed Firs.

" And now for what? " Sammy's voice went up into a little scream and cracked again. " Just me telling you I know more about sailors than you boys."

" You bastard," laughed Jan, " I should hope you did."

" Just the same I'd like to sock you," said Firs.

" But I done nothing," said Sammy, " I got to get back to my trays."

" You ought to get socked just to put some sense in you. You talked too much," said Jan.

" But for Christ's sake, you was asking me," said Sammy. Roger couldn't tell whether he was frightened of the two men, or it was all a game they were playing that he did not understand.

" You're too fresh," said Firs and hit Sammy on the nose with his fist. How hard Roger couldn't tell. Sammy

made for the door. Jan caught him, pulled him back
into the room and Firs came over to help. They started
to pull his pants off, laughing uproariously and punch-
ing him whenever he squirmed. Roger was disturbed.
Obviously Sammy wasn't enjoying it. Something should
be done, so Roger became boldly deceptive. He pretended somebody was outside, somebody important, perhaps Lansing, perhaps McDermott himself was outside.
He coughed and pointed his thumb over his shoulder,
to draw Firs' and Jan's attention. The ruse worked.
They immediately straightened up and Sammy did up
his trousers and escaped out the door to his furnace. As
he passed Roger looked at him to see whether or not
he was really hurt. Only the determination, the des-
peration of his never looking back and the speed of his
flight made Roger suspect he really was frightened.
When no one was obviously coming in to interrupt
them, and Firs and Jan were at work on their drawings,
Roger asked who Sammy was.

" Oh, Sammy," said Firs, " he's the furnace monkey.
He cleans up around the place. He does all the dirty
work. He's funny as hell."

" Why do you roughhouse with him that way? " asked
Roger.

" Roughhouse? " Jan paused. " Oh, that. His old man
beats hell out of him all the time and we just like to
make him feel at home."

" But isn't it bad for him? " Roger was insistent.

" Bad for him. Hell, no. Young kids oughtn't to be
too damn fresh."

Roger was pointedly silent, but Firs went on to explain, " O, hell, no, we just kid with him. It seems rough
to you, but it really isn't. You see he makes a living
bumming off them bums. They're rough as hell, so

we've just got to keep him in training. Because we like
the kid." The two Danes laughed uproariously.

5

Gradually Roger got to know everyone in the shop.
Every one of them had a curious and different history,
compounded of the same bitter ingredients of hatred,
frustration, disappointment, and a terror of poverty in
old age. Yet there they were all bound together in a
singular confederation linked only by the common
bonds of their uneasy despair. Roger's sympathy was
exhausted. He could only listen. Strangely enough the
men talked to him without reserve. He was absolutely
no part of their world but his youth and his frankness
made it possible for them to be intimate with him,
almost to confess to him with no fear of betrayal either
to their fellows or their superiors. To be sure they were
not all discontented. There was Palmer for example.
Palmer had gone to art school, like most of the draughtsmen. He had an easy facility with the crayon which had
started by finding he was able to copy cartoons in the
daily papers. Then he did illustration work for magazines, and now he had ended up at McDermott's as a
reliable repeater of details; every so often he would
turn out a Christ or a saint for a small window. The
features were always properly identical, reflecting his
own goodlooking, slightly wasted ordinary face. Roger
naively thought he shaved too much, for his face seemed
perpetually raw as if the outer fine layer of epidermis
were constantly removed. Roger was doing some printing for him, labelling saints' names in Latin at the side
of a biggish cartoon which he was finishing.

" Then this woman," continued Palmer, " got to be

crazy about me. She wanted me around her all the time. She was goodlooking, too, and had more money than she knew what to do with."

" But what about her husband? " asked Roger, accepting the convention of worldly easy curiosity a good deal better than he could have three weeks ago.

" Oh, hell, he didn't give us much trouble." Palmer laughed and set down his crayon. " She used to let me know whenever he was away and then I used to go up and stay all night."

" Gee," said Roger enthusiastically as possible, " that must have been great."

" Sure," said Palmer, continuing quickly. " But one night he came back suddenly, and we had a hell of a time. I had to get in among her clothes and stay there the rest of the night, frightened out of my skin."

" How did you get out? " asked Roger. All the time he felt he had either been told this story, or read it somewhere or seen it acted somewhere, all years before. Nor did he exactly doubt Palmer.

" Hell, I slept standing up. I waited until he'd gone off to his office. Then I spent the rest of the day with her. I wasn't seen in the shop for two days. I was pooped out."

" How long after did you get married? " asked Roger.

" I'd been married about six months then," said Palmer gravely. "You see, I gave this other girl up as soon as I could without hurting her feelings."

" How long did that take? "

" Oh, it took some time. She was crazy about me."

" Have you known a lot of women? " asked Roger, absorbed.

" I have." Palmer was deliberate. " I started early."

Palmer's saga fascinated Roger and the man could

feel the boy's preoccupation with all the practical details of the mechanisms of his love affairs. He was preoccupied with them himself and indulged in a welter of realistic information. He was so emphatic, so thorough that after the first shock of the excitement in his physicality wore off, Roger was amazed to find himself admitting that every story Palmer told was the same story. All the women were the same woman. But Roger would rather be talked to than not and whenever Palmer was around he would ask for more stories and they would always be readily forthcoming. The monotony of their relation somehow quieted both Roger and Palmer. It was a kind of convention, a formal exchange of friendly contact. Roger was surprised to find that soon he preferred the stories just as something to listen to, rather than as stimulating subject matter. Palmer exhausted the possibilities of variation pretty quickly.

"I'd never had a virgin before that," Palmer would say, "except for that kid I told you about the other day." Roger would nod. "Well, I'll tell you it was damned hard going. She was a nice kid and absolutely crazy about me."

On such an occasion Firs came into the room disgusted.

"Good Christ," he said. "I can't stand this lousy joint much longer."

"What's the matter?" asked Palmer. "Gibson get your goat again?"

"You said it," said Firs. "You know he just lays for me all the time now."

Roger went diligently on with his drawing. At all times when complaints against the superiors were being made he felt obligated to stay strictly clear of anything,

almost righteously so. Since there was not much interest
aroused in his crabbing, Firs continued.

" God, it wouldn't be as if I'd bitched something. Why
he picks on me and I don't do nothing at all."

" Perhaps that's it," said Palmer brightly.

" Say, boy," said Firs, " I work just as hard as any of
the rest of these lousy loafers around here. None of us
get ourselves in much of a sweat."

" You ought to get married," said Palmer. " You need
a woman around to quiet you."

" Yeah? " Firs laughed. " Got any extras? "

" But," said Palmer seriously, " you ought to see more
girls."

At that point Jan came in with a roll of cartoons.
He listened. He was amused for Firs had not noticed
him come in.

" Yes," Palmer continued. " I'll try and fix you up.
Know a damn nice girl. She's a nice kid and she was
crazy about me."

" Good work," cried Jan. " Firs is fine with girls. He
is strong. They like him, too."

Firs whipped around. " Yes," he snapped. " Why I
hate girls is they like rats like you. A man wouldn't
work in a lousy place like this. I'm going to quit right
now."

" I've heard that before, too, haven't I? " Jan quickly
lit a cigarette. " We'd all like to quit, wouldn't we? Yes,
indeed we would. Even you, so quiet down."

Roger kept quiet.

" Yes, we'd all like to quit but we can't and we won't
and we know it."

" If," said Gibson coming in the door, how long he
had been listening none of them knew, " if there was
a little less gab going on here there might be a little more

work. Not much more, but maybe enough to make it worth McDermott keeping you on his payroll." Gibson was not surly; he spoke easily but with conviction. After he left, indeed, there was a general resumption of occupation.

Later on Roger went out to lunch. He was in the washroom rinsing his hands when Sammy, the furnace boy, came in with his face covered with soot. He went over doggedly to the basin, shoved Roger out of the way and snatched at the mechanics' soap. Roger stood out of the way, as amused at his rudeness as he was amazed. Then Sammy saw it was Roger.

" Gees," he said, " I didn't see it was you."

" Well," laughed Roger, " what difference would that have made? "

" You got to fight for what you want around this place," said Sammy.

" Yes," said Roger non-committally.

" I mean I got to fight," said Sammy, and savagely massaged his face.

" Oh, hell," said Roger adventurously, " you seem to enjoy yourself."

" Yeah? " came through the lather of soap.

" I mean you roughhouse, and have a pretty good time? " Roger wanted to know how much he liked it.

" You mean with them two Swedes? " Sammy stood still.

" Jan and Firs are Danes," said Roger.

" Them Danes," said Sammy equivocally and reached for a towel. " Them Danes is O. K., you bet," he went on unenthusiastically. " They're all right."

" They're strong as hell, aren't they? " pursued Roger. Sammy was about to answer. Instead he looked furtively at Roger, tossed his towel on the rack and went out of the washroom slamming the door.

6

When Roger went home from work that night he had a lot to think about. He was puzzled at the unanimous emotional and moral dilemma he found himself to be in, for the first time in his life. Working without pay in McDermott's shop had given him a curious advantage. He worked hard and did not play for favor so the men trusted his integrity and felt free to say whatever they pleased in front of him, although they never asked him any personal questions. Lansing, Gibson and McDermott smiled on him when he passed, and felt somehow vaguely and snobbishly that his gentility was a refining influence on the men. Roger was pleased that he was accepted at least on a partial basis of equality with the workmen, and the aloofness of his position gave him delusions of power. He quickly decided he wanted to help the men better their conditions. He was a good deal better off himself than they were and he had been in the shop long enough to see how with slight trouble to the boss they could be made a great deal happier. The more he thought about it the more strongly he felt his mission. At first he decided that he would foment a strike. He saw himself in the rôle of a fearless young labor agitator. He would demand for the men more free time, less close surveillance, that they could carry through all the designs that they had created from start to finish, and no longer make the draughtsmen submit to the humiliating castration of their slightest original impulse, in any way a deviation from the traditional style mechanized and reduced to stencils by McDermott.

He would make McDermott see that these men could do better work if left more on their own. But a strike, a strike was serious business. He ruefully remembered that in a strike that he had considered fomenting he would be the only one who had nothing to lose. No, a strike was impossible. What other means then? He could talk to Gibson. He could ask Gibson to tell Lansing and then it would get to McDermott. Or anyway he would think about it, he would accomplish something. He owed it to the men and incidentally, he decided, to himself. But the more he thought about it the more difficult it seemed. What course of action could he take? There seemed absolutely no tiny loophole, no cranny into which he could thrust his pitying wedge.

Some days later Roger was coming back from lunch. He strayed into the great loft room where a new great oriole window had been stuck up. He half shut his eyes and the vibration of color into the darkness, the phonograph as usual turning out Tristan in a corner overwhelmed him with the possibilities, the overwhelming potentialities of this place. He flung back his head, and opened his nostrils to drink in the air of determination, of increased endeavor. But, since the windows could never be open, his lungs were only slightly pricked by the tang of acid, sugar and beeswax. Undaunted, he strode back and past the furnace area. The door was wide open and he saw the gas of molten heat, an intense inferno, burning so brightly there was no variation in its light. The furnace door was wide open, but he assumed that somebody would quickly come to close it, or he would have done so himself for at that moment he would have greatly enjoyed the co-operative gesture, the slight aid in helping carry on someone else's job, the common job of the shop. As he turned away from

the blaze he walked on down the corridor that led into
his own draughting room, but before he could get into
the door he was startled by two piercing shrieks. He
stopped, almost frightened. A series of shrieks made him
dash into the room.

There on the floor lay Sammy. Firs had a hold of one
leg and Jan of another. In one horrified moment Roger
saw that they were tearing him apart. As soon as they
saw him they dropped Sammy, and sheepishly turned
aside. Roger ran over and knelt down by the agonized
boy. His face was tight drawn and his eyes were shrunk
with pain and fright. He said nothing. Roger was so
angered and indignant, so shocked at what seemed to
be wanton, brutal torture that he was impotent. He
could do nothing but feel hot tears well up behind his
eyes and he hoped to Christ he wouldn't start crying
himself. But at that moment the foreman came in and
absolved him from any necessity of action.

" What the hell is all this roughhouse? " asked Gibson.

" Martens and I were only kidding," said Jan. Roger
looked away.

" You kid too goddamn much," said Gibson. Then to
Sammy, " Why in hell are you here? "

" They called me here, honest Mr. Gibson. They
try — ," then Sammy shut up. He was sitting on the
floor with his hands pressed on his crotch.

" What's the matter, now? " asked Gibson peremp-
torily of Roger.

" I don't know, sir," said Roger. " I just came from
lunch."

" Very well," said Gibson. He was good and angry.
" This is the last time this will happen. Sammy, you're
fired. You've ruined a whole furnace load of glass. The

door was open when I came by. As for you two," he
turned savagely towards the draughtsmen, " you'd better watch your step." He looked at Roger and was silent.
Then, " Well, is there anything you want to say? "
Sammy hung his head, and after a moment Gibson
turned and went out of the room. The sound of his
shoes turned the corner and died away before anyone
spoke.

" Christ," said Firs, " some day I'm going to tell that
son of a bitch what I think of him."

" Yeah? " asked Jan. " There was a good chance just
now."

Firs laughed boldly and picked up a piece of crayon,
started whetting it. Sammy started to rise, stumbled and
fell, and then he walked stiffly out of the room. Roger
was literally on fire. He felt that all his kneecaps and
funny-bones had been hit at once. He was tingling and
overflowing with enough confused emotions and reso-
lutions and intentions to make twenty men in twenty
situations do the only one wrong ill-considered thing.
He went straight to McDermott's office. He told the
secretary he must see McDermott at once. The secretary
smiled and said he was busy. Well, how soon will he
be through? Is it so very important? Yes, it is very important. Well then he could wait — he waited.

He must have waited for fifteen minutes. He told
himself he must think straight. The chief thing was to
think straight. How could he talk straight if he didn't
think straight. But he couldn't. His mind was full of
cog wheels, lights and sounds hummed behind his ears.
He felt very much as if he were about to have a surgical
operation, the expectancy of ether, of enforced restraint
of a terrifying power greater than he was, and yet himself as obliged, himself as dependent. The secretary's

smile, somehow attached to her voice came to him. He
could go in now. Just as he was passing into the threshold of Mr. McDermott's office he bumped into Lansing.
Lansing was going in too. Roger was outraged.

Then McDermott said, " Did you want to see me? "

" Yes," said Roger, " I've got to see you." McDermott
looked over at Lansing.

" Oh, I can wait," laughed Lansing and turned to go.

" No," cried Roger, " you can hear this too."

" Oh? " said Lansing. McDermott looked up and
smiled.

" It's terribly important," said Roger. He said it
again because as yet he had no idea how to start in.

" Won't you sit down? " said Mr. McDermott.

" Oh, thank you," said Roger. This unsettled him. He
had not counted on courtesy.

" Well? " said Mr. McDermott. Lansing twiddled
with the chain that looped his belly in. He looked
gravely out of the window.

" It's about Sammy," said Roger breathlessly. " The
furnace boy — Mr. Gibson just fired him."

" At last," said Lansing relieved.

" But Mr. McDermott," went on Roger, " It wasn't
his fault. He should not have been fired."

" Whose fault was it? " asked Lansing, interested.

Roger stopped short. This is not what he had meant
to say at all.

" I don't mean that, really," he went on breathlessly.
" It's about the men."

" Just what do you mean? " said Lansing.

" I'm talking to Mr. McDermott," said Roger savagely.

" Go on," said Mr. McDermott.

" You've got to forgive me, Mr. McDermott. It was

very nice of you to let me work here this way. I know I'm not very experienced. I've not been here a very long time but I feel I've got to tell you some things I've seen."

" Surely," said McDermott. " I understand, go on."

" Aren't the men satisfied? " asked Lansing.

" No, they are not," cried Roger. Then as if to correct himself, " Well, maybe they are, only they could be so much more so. They're all so unhappy. They get on so badly with each other. They could be made so much happier. It wouldn't cost you a cent."

" What would you suggest? " said McDermott.

" Oh, take more of an interest in them. Make them feel," Roger felt at last he had a good idea. " Make them feel you personally cared about them."

" But," said Mr. Lansing smiling, " either Mr. Mc-Dermott or myself go over every single piece of work they do — with our own hands."

" That's just the trouble." Roger wound himself up. " You take whatever guts they have in a drawing out of it. You just break their spirits that way."

" But," said Mr. McDermott, " I thought we should take an interest."

" Yes," said Roger, " but not that way. You, er, you ought." He felt the ground slip from under him. He was perilously near having nothing more to say.

But Mr. McDermott said, " Oh quite so. I see very well what you mean. And don't mistake me. I'm very glad, very proud that you're interested."

" I don't mean to blame anyone," said Roger.

" Of course not," said Lansing, " we understand perfectly."

" You see," said Mr. McDermott, " we're up against a very difficult proposition. It's not as if these men were responsible."

" Why, what do you mean? " said Roger.

" Can't you understand? " said McDermott, and paused. " Of course you can't, you haven't been in this place for twenty years. You haven't seen men come and go like I have. You don't know that to make a cent I've got to constantly drive these men, drive them as hard as we can. It's no joke."

" But don't drive them," said Roger. " Make them want to work! "

" Who wants to work? " said McDermott, disgustedly. " I never met one yet who wanted to work. They want to eat. They want to play and drink but they won't work unless I make 'em and I know how to make 'em."

" But you've lost touch," pleaded Roger, " you forget they're actually people, each one is different each one — "

" Which ones," said McDermott. " Name me a few names."

" Well, there's Firs and Jan," said Roger. Lansing looked at him closely and he wished he hadn't been such a fool as to name these first.

" Well," said McDermott, " as fine a pair of loafers as ever I paid. They're bullies, dishonest, loafers, both of them."

" But Palmer," said Roger, " surely Palmer — "

" You know, I have a funny feeling always about him," said McDermott. " I hate to let him draw me a virgin — I'm afraid of what will become of her."

Lansing laughed. " But," said Roger, " he's a good draughtsman."

" Good — good," McDermott snorted. " Why he's the worst of the lot. He's not even a competent copyist. If he'd keep his mind above his belt he'd discover how women really looked."

" But, Foster," said Roger, and he felt that the worst
verdict was reserved for him.

" Foster," echoed Lansing with a sneer.

" Foster," said Mr. McDermott, " is an excellent ma-
chine. We pay him well for work that one day will be
done by stencils."

" But my god," cried Roger, " you're supposed to do
the best glass in the country."

" And we do," said McDermott, " we do indeed."

Roger was frightened. He felt that his audience was
coming to an end. It had gained neither himself nor
the men anything. McDermott was tapping with some
papers on the desk.

Then said Lansing, " Well, is that all you have to say
to Mr. McDermott? "

Roger paused, " Why, yes. I guess so." And suddenly,
" but it's not all I've got to say to you." He hoped his
temerity did not sound as ridiculous to them as it did
to him. " You're the reason everything's so terrible,"
said Roger.

" I am? " said Lansing astonished.

" Yes, you are," Roger clasped and unclasped his
hands doggedly. " Yes, you go on sneaking around the
shop, trying to overhear conversations, spying, cribbing,
stealing — "

" Why really," said Mr. McDermott.

" Yes, and you're always there," Roger was breathless, " calling everybody by their first names."

" By their first names," Lansing was puzzled.

" Oh, can't you see, Mr. McDermott," Roger was desperate, " he goes on around all over calling us by our
first names! "

Then Roger went out of the room and he could feel
the iron smiles on the faces of the two men behind him

settle about their mouths with a logical and reasonable triumph.

Roger did not work any more that day. He walked home in a daze of failure, of disappointment, frustration and doubt. Now what on earth should he do? Could he go on working at McDermott's any longer? After all he had told Lansing and McDermott? Would they fire him? Fire him. He laughed to himself. Probably not. They would let him play on their cartoons. It cost nothing and by the morning they would have probably forgotten everything he said anyway. He freely admitted to himself that he was wrong. He never should have spoken at all. He would never seem to learn. Perhaps if he went back and never referred to it again they would ignore it. It would be the same as before.

The next morning he came in to the draughting room. He happened to be a little late. Palmer, Firs and Jans were there. He said hello, good morning, and went to attack one of his interminable inscriptions.

" You did not come back yesterday afternoon," said Firs.

" No," said Roger. " I took the half day off."

" You were very fortunate to have the little holiday," laughed Jan.

Roger said nothing. He scrunched his eraser up into a tighter ball.

" Did you have a pretty good talk with the boss? " said Palmer suddenly.

Roger was surprised. " Why, what do you mean? "

" He means did you have a pretty good talk with the boss," said Firs.

Roger looked up at him uneasily. " Why, yes," he said.

"It must have been interesting," said Jan. "McDermott's quite a boy."

"Always open to new ideas," said Palmer, "openminded."

"What do you mean?" said Roger. He was frightened sick.

"Nothing," said Palmer. "I hear Sammy's left us."

"Poor Sammy," said Firs.

"I don't know what you mean," said Roger.

"Sammy wasn't such a bad little louse," said Jan.

"If you think I told McDermott, it was you and Firs, about Sammy, you're crazy," said Roger.

"Oh," lilted Palmer. "You don't know what we mean."

"I did not," said Roger. "I never said a word."

"So Lansing said," said Firs. "Trust him."

"Lansing," Roger jumped up to face them. "Lansing. Why I gave the bastard hell right in front of McDermott's face."

The three others laughed, not uproariously, nor quietly, merely the convinced laughs of irrevocable disbelief. Then they worked on in silence. Roger felt horribly abused, misunderstood, guilty and powerless to speak.

"Why, you'll be going to college soon," said Palmer. Roger looked up but said nothing.

"Send us a postcard from the big city," said Jan. "Don't forget your old friends."

"Any clothes you don't want you might let the chauffeur bring down to us," Firs slowly considered his final imaginative dismissal. "It'll be a cold winter for the poor."

Roger finished the little work left to do, set down his tools and slowly walked out of the room. He went down

the aisle where the men were bent over their benches.
They all seemed very busy, intent. He looked up and
down for one answering eye. Maybe they really were
busy, and yet — . He passed into the great raftered loft.
The oriole-jeweled hymn was still singing the praise of
color. Lights fell in pools on the trays of glass and on
the floor. Suddenly Peter Foster was at his side.

" I hear there has been trouble in the draughting
room," the German said.

" I don't know anything about it," said Roger firmly.

" I didn't suppose you would," Foster smiled and
paused.

Roger uneasily stared up at the shining oriole again.

" Sammy was not a very steady worker, perhaps," said
Foster, " but he was not a bad boy."

" No," said Roger, " I never said he was. Who said
he was? "

" You know," said Foster blandly; Roger could have
killed him. " I think McDermott got you in here to spy
on us."

" You knew very goddamn well he did not," said
Roger, and yet through the cruel curve of Peter Foster's
smile, standing in the gloomy parody of a cathedral,
with the subdued signs of work, of doors shut and opening, of glass being moved from the shelves, and yet,
thought Roger, and yet —

" Perhaps," said Foster, " I am wrong, all things are
possible."

Roger turned away from him. There was little enough
left to do. He supposed he should really say goodbye to
Mr. McDermott. He should try to behave as well as he
could, as he knew, as he felt he was supposed to, from
now on. McDermott's secretary looked up at him, as if
to say, " What — again? "

" Can I see Mr. McDermott? " said Roger.

" You can if you wait," she said. " He's busy."

Roger sat down. Then a man opened the outer door
of the office, bowed to the secretary, smiled at Roger
and sat down next to him. Roger noticed that he had
rather a fine old face, sensitively moulded with cavern-
ous eyes and fine lines penetrating from his cheeks, like
erosive valleys down to the rim of his mouth. His eyes
were vague and grey green. He wore a large floppy black
tie, pinned back with a small silver crown of thorns.
He nodded indulgently at Roger. Roger returned the
nod.

" Do you work here? " a kind almost feminine voice.

" Yes," said Roger.

" For long? " asked the man.

" Not very," answered Roger.

" It must be a fine thing for boy to grow up here,"
he said. " I always think of McDermott's as a piece
out of the middle ages. The last guild in the world,"
he continued, " to think . . . the last guild in the
world."

" What do you do? " asked Roger.

" I am a builder," said the man. " I build prayers of
stone."

" Prayers of stone," Roger was almost pointedly ob-
tuse.

" Nowadays they call us architects . . . I build cathe-
drals."

" Big ones? " asked Roger.

" I am building the greatest Gothic monument in
the new world," said the man; he laughed impulsively,
" I like to think of myself as the new Abbé Suger."

" Abbé Suger? " asked Roger.

" He built Chartres," said the architect.

" Chartres? Oh," said Roger, " then McDermott does your glass? "

" A bright boy," said the architect with a merry laugh.

" Did you want to see Mr. McDermott? " said the secretary to Roger. " He's free to see you now." Roger looked at the architect and then at the secretary.

" No," said Roger. " I guess I don't." He got up and went out the outer door and closed it quietly after him.

Flesh is Jail

Then hate me when thou wilt; if ever, now;
Now, while the world is bent my deeds to cross,
Join with the spite of fortune, make me bow,
And do not drop in for an after-loss:
Ah, do not, when my heart hath 'scaped this sorrow,
Come in the rearward of a conquered woe;
Give not a rainy night a windy morrow,
To linger out a purposed overthrow.

1925

1

He was told to meet Graham at a Soho restaurant called Claudia's. It was behind Dean Street and he should be there at a quarter of eight. Claudia's was full. As he came into the door the hum and chatter seemed to swell in his ears and he hesitated a second before he took the plunge. Graham was suddenly at his side.

"Oh," said he, "we'd given you up for good." He was led over to a table at the end of the room where half a dozen people turned up their faces at him.

"This," said Graham, "is my American friend Roger Baum. Miss Dennison, Mr. Cochran, Mr. Blair, Mr. Fisher, Mr. Stevens and this is Miss von Krazen — or Madame von Krazen or Kythe." The names flitted so swiftly over the succession of heads that Roger's interest landed with an accumulated rush on the last one. Kythe von Krazen was Welsh and German. She looked about seventeen. Her ash-blonde hair covered her head like a boy's. She wore a mannish black velvet tailored suit — a white carnation was in her buttonhole and her black tie was fixed with a biggish gold hunting crop. She seemed unusually bent over her food.

"I'm sure we're all very glad you've come," she smiled graciously in Roger's direction. The conversation that the introduction had interrupted gradually resumed itself. To make up for lack of familiarity she turned to Roger and said, "We've all been talking

about what one had better do when one's money gives
out."

"Oh, yes," answered Roger. His money had never
given out.

"Bobby," she pointed at the name Cochran, "is
very broke. He's always hard up, but now the bailiffs
are after him."

"Dear me," answered Roger inadequately.

"We think he'd better go to jail and give us a rest,"
said Graham.

"Come now, don't be horrid," said Cochran.

"I'm not horrid, if you were in jail, it would be perfectly clean there and you'd be out of mischief."

Cochran turned with an idiotic supplication to
Madame von Krazen.

"Darling, you're not going to be tiresome, too, and
let them take me off."

"I'm sure you roundly deserve it," said she. She
seemed to mean it.

Cochran looked at Roger, "Ever been in jail, my
boy?"

"Why, no, I can't say as I have." Roger really
couldn't help it.

"No," said Cochran, "I suppose not. Well, it's not
much fun."

"I bet it isn't," said Roger warmly. He must maintain his connection with these strangers somehow.

"Oh, come, come," cried Madame von Krazen, "what
possible interest can this all have to him. Order some
dessert all of you, and let's talk about something else."

"It can't help interest him now," said Graham,
"you've gone too far in it. I shall explain. Cochran here
is a painter. I don't know why, but people believed him,
so he ran up a lot of bills he can't pay. Now they have

stopped believing him." Graham paused and raised his
right hand. "And either," he continued generously,
"Miss Dennison, Mr. Blair, Mr. Fisher, Mr. Stevens,
Miss von Krazen, or myself will be obliged to pay up."

"Oh rot," said Cochran, "that's not fair."

The boy called Blair, considerably younger than the
rest and pleasant looking spoke up, "I can't see any
point in your continually picking on Bobby, Graham.
He never hurt you."

Graham drew his hand over his face and said, "Oh,
let's drop it."

Roger was bored and embarrassed, but to make a decent face of it he smiled at Cochran in a friendly way.

"I may as well be frank with you," said Cochran.
Why? thought Roger. Why? "I don't owe much, a
mere matter of ten pounds. If I had that I could finish
this silly thing, this picture I've had in my head all
winter."

Roger looked blank but Cochran continued, "Yet
where to get it? There must be a lot of money in the
world?"

Madame von Krazen clapped her hands. "Enough,"
she said, "I'm going home. Blair darling, you take me."
The boy fumbled with a curious stick and handed it
to her. When she got up Roger was amazed to see that
she was a painfully deformed hunchback. The face of
great youth and sweetness had no connection with the
small blunt body. Roger's lips parted just a little and
the woman had the misfortune to see his astonishment
as it wiped across his face. But there was no malice in
her recognition, rather a sympathetic apology for having
caused him the painful surprise. She set her cane on the
ground and looked up at him.

"Do you like dogs?" she said.

"Why yes," answered Roger. "I love them; I have a lot myself."

"Well then, you must get Graham to bring you out to see ours," she spoke flatly, but with more than a trace of formal invitation.

"I should really love to come." She can see you mean it, thought Roger, no need to be too demonstrative.

"Graham, you must promise to bring him." The man rose and promised.

"Well, then, good night all. Bobby keep out of jail. Good night."

A shuffling echo of 'good nights' followed them away from the table. It seemed a rather flat end to the evening. But Cochran got up and called to Blair who was holding Madame von Krazen's arm.

"Dickie," he called.

"Oh, yes?" Blair looked up in surprise.

"You didn't even say good night to me."

"I'm sorry. Well, good night."

"Don't be horrid," said Cochran. "When will I see you again?"

"I'll call you up sometime." Blair looked away from Cochran at the rest of the table. They were taking this in too. Roger wanted to leave them but Graham had got him there and now he didn't seem to do anything but look disgusted.

"Oh, come on, now," said Madame von Krazen, "kiss each other good night and be done with it." Blair blushed furiously, seized her hand and the two walked out of the door. Roger saw people's heads turn and follow the tall youth and the tiny hunchback.

"Sometime," said Cochran petulantly, "Kythe is impossible."

At this point the heretofore silent Miss Dennison

spoke in a gruff heavy voice, " You're impossible all the time. You have no manners nor sense nor taste. Why do you hang around here any longer? "

" Very well," said Cochran seeming to gather his clothing around him, " I always have the sense and taste to leave when I'm not wanted." He got up to go. Roger had to step from his place to let him pass on to the floor. Cochran turned his head around to him and grinned effusively. " At least," he said, " I'm always glad to meet a gentleman." With that he strode off. Roger could only smile. He wondered why in God's name he had ever come.

" The bastard," muttered Miss Dennison, " some day he'll break his goddamned neck."

Graham turned to Roger. " Yes, I know. You should thank me for a delightful evening. Yes? You're embarrassed and you wonder who in hell all these people are. Mr. Fisher and Mr. Stevens for example, they don't talk much but they could tell a lot." Roger grinned at them. They seemed to look amazingly alike. " Mr. Fisher and Mr. Stevens are in the movies. They look alike don't they? Well, they're cousins, or something." Fisher leaned over to Roger, " Don't worry, we've got to go anyway. No one loves Kythe any more than Graham. We'll let him tell you about her." They rose to go. Stevens held the other's coat and they walked off slowly, with no more talking.

Miss Dennison left off playing with her silver and turned a wrinkled forehead to Graham, " You know, I'm worried about Kythe, Graham."

" Oh, she's perfectly all right, Jimmy. God, Cochran gets under anyone's skin. I hate his guts."

" Yes, it's Cochran. But it's mostly Dickie Blair. He's too damn young for all this."

"Kythe's a pretty good little mother you know. She's nursed him for ten years now and she knows how to take care of him."

"I suppose you're right. Well, anyway, I don't like it and the next time I see her, I'll tell her so." She rose to go now too. "Well," she said dismally, "I leave you two here as friends, I hope you won't spoil between now and the next time I see you."

"Trust us," grinned Graham.

"Oh, trust anybody," Miss Dennison scowled. She turned to Roger. "Yes and it wouldn't hurt you to go and see Kythe's pups. She liked you. Good night."

"Good night," said Roger.

2

But the next Sunday Graham took Roger to see Kythe von Krazen's pups. They were bull terriers and extremely unattractive. The boy Dickie Blair in a pair of old trousers and a torn bathing suit top took them out to the kennels. They met Madame von Krazen holding two puppies and rubbing their noses together.

She looked up at Roger and said, "Well, you really did come."

Graham said, "Yes, you know I promised I'd bring him."

"Well," she was really pleased, "this is delightful. Here are my dogs." She bred the prize bull terriers to give herself something to do. She kept a house mainly as a home for Richard Blair, an orphan, as long as he was at college; some place for him to bring his friends.

She sat down on the couch in her library and told Graham she was thinking of selling the house and kennels. "You see, Dickie has come down now for good.

He'll be getting a job and there's no point in my going
on with this."

Graham said, " I think it's a shame if you do. You
ought to have something to occupy yourself with. If
Dickie goes off, you ought to have it all the more."

But Dickie said, " Oh, I'll never leave Kythe, she's
all I care about; I could no more leave this house
than fly."

Kythe said, " You've got to shift for yourself sometime. I'm bored." She reached for a cigarette. " I'm
bored anyway. I want to go and really live in Paris."
When Roger went to light her cigarette he saw the same
look in her eye that he had encountered when he saw
that she was a hunchback, and he knew she hated to go
to Paris.

Dickie came over and sat down beside her. " You're
perfectly right, darling. It must be hideously tiresome
here. We'll all go to Paris." He looked up and around
at Roger and Graham. " You come, too." Graham
laughed, " I'd like to but I can't. I stay here," and he
added slowly, " with Kythe."

" No, Graham," she said quickly, " I really mean
it. I'm going to Paris. London's no life for a girl.
I'm going back to the Grande Chaumiére. I'm going
to do some real life drawing. I've wanted to for a long
time."

" Darling, if you want to, go by all means," said
Dickie, " but let me keep the house open if you want to
come home. I won't be lonely. I'll ask Bobby Cochran
to come and live here. I think he'd like to."

" I bet he'd like to," said Graham.

" Shut up," said Kythe. Roger began to decide he
really should not have come, this second time.

" O Graham, I wish you would be civil to Bobby.

He's not half bad when you know him." Dickie Blair looked nervously at Kythe and Roger. He didn't look at Graham at all.

But at that point all conversation on the subject of Bobby Cochran stopped short for that young man walked into the room.

"Hello everybody," said he gaily. He turned to Graham. "Well, fancy finding you here, and your young friend too. Well, well — and how is my angel Kythe, dear angel Kythe."

"I'm fine, Bobby, what are you up to?"

"I've just been around to see the bailiff — as luck would have it he's one of the world's most charming people."

"How fortunate," said Graham.

"Don't be horrid," said Bobby. "Anyway he won't dispossess me for a day or two."

"Then what will you do?" asked Kythe. She was looking at Dickie.

"That, lovely lady, is what I've come to ask you?" He smiled and drew up a chair to face her. Dickie came up behind him and appealed to her. "Why we have room enough here, haven't we?" Graham blew his nose violently and turned to her.

"Madame von Krazen, what is your favorite work of fiction?"

Kythe smiled and said vaguely, "I don't know — Vanity Fair, perhaps."

"Mr. Baum, what is your favorite novel?"

Roger laughed uneasily and said, "Well, I really don't know, I guess Vanity Fair is as good as any."

Dickie said, "Graham — I was asking Kythe a question."

"Oh," said Graham, "I beg your pardon. So was I."

"Kythe, can Bobby come and stay with us if he's evicted?"

Graham said to Kythe, "Now, Madame von Krazen, who is your favorite character in Vanity Fair?"

Kythe said, "Dickie, I'd love to have Bobby of course, but I've suddenly decided to sell the house. I'm going to Paris on Wednesday morning."

"My favorite character, for example, is Becky Sharpe," said Graham.

"Paris," echoed Cochran lamely, "how ripping."

"Kythe," cried Dickie, "you can't do that, so quickly. You can't leave all this . . . the kennels — you can't clear out."

"Dickie, I'm bored. I've got to go away."

"But you can't leave me, darling," Dickie was disturbed.

"You're in perfectly good hands. You're big enough to look after yourself now."

Dickie turned savagely on Graham. "Graham, you put her up to this. It's just because you don't like Bobby. Very well. Bobby and I don't like you. We can get along very well, together alone. I don't want to keep Kythe here of course, if she doesn't want to stay."

"Nor do I," said Bobby Cochran, unnecessarily.

"Oh, run away and cut out paper dolls," said Graham testily.

Later when they had left and were in the taxi on the way home, Graham turned to Roger. "You know Dickie Blair doesn't care any more about Bobby Cochran than I do. But Kythe has told him he's so grown up that he feels he has to take the responsibility of something. So he takes the responsibility for that fool. Kythe hates to go to Paris, but she feels she must make him stand on his own. You see what I mean?"

" Yes," said Roger, " she's really splendid."

" She is," said Graham.

" But her friends are so awful. Those people, that night at the restaurant. I wished you had never asked me to come."

" Oh, they're all right. When you're a hunchback you don't pick and choose."

" I don't see what that's got to do with it," said Roger stiffly.

" I don't mean to be cruel. I only mean that if you're young and beautiful, and Kythe is beautiful, and if you're a hunchback your life is somewhat ruined. That is, men are not generally attracted to you."

" But I think she's marvelous," said Roger.

" So do I," said Graham, " but I don't want to marry her."

" Has she ever asked you to? " asked Roger shortly.

" Oh, no, she never has, and you're quite right. She doesn't like men. She hates them and I don't blame her."

" But she likes you, Graham."

" Yes. She likes me well enough. But I treat her as if she were a woman, not as if I would be afraid to touch her. But she hates most men."

" And women too."

" Not so much," Graham paused. " Some women like her a lot. But she's not very fond of them. They upset her too much."

" Why? " asked Roger blankly.

" Think it over," said Graham. He paused. " No, she doesn't like anybody but silly little girls like Bobby Cochran or those two dim ferns Fisher and Stevens. They tell her all their troubles and she knows damn well they never worry about her physical deformities or anything else."

" She must be frightfully lonely," said Roger brightly.

" She is. Get her to tell you about it some time."

" No, I don't mean that, but she's so sweet and so damn pitiful."

" Well, up to the present she's had Dickie Blair to mother. He's all right but with his newly developed sense of obligation, she may lose him yet." Graham looked at Roger, " Oh, it's all right. Don't get messed up in other people's business. It doesn't pay."

" But I am messed up in this now. I mean I like Madame von Krazen."

" You've seen her twice in your life. You may never see her again."

" But I want to. I really want to help her."

" All right," said Graham, " suit yourself. But I do hope she goes to Paris and if that son of a bitch Bobby Cochran was out of trouble, Dickie Blair could take her and she'd get a change and it would be a lot better."

" Do you think so? " said Roger.

" Of course I think so," said Graham and paid for the taxi.

3

Roger had some difficulty in discovering Bobby Cochran's lodging house without letting anyone know about it. Bobby had covered his own tracks pretty thoroughly. Not even the American Express knew where to reach him.

The automobile drew up at the last house but one of a long line of dismal dwellings in an Earl's Court mews. He prayed that Cochran was out because if he helped him once there would of course be no end to future appeals. He got down from the taxi and told the man to wait. He walked up the three steps of the stoop and rang the bell. Some time afterwards a maid with a cloth around her head leaned out of a window. She said, " Please? "

" Is Mr. Robert Cochran in? " asked Roger.

" Is it Mr. Cochran you want? " she called.

" Yes," said Roger, wishing she wouldn't call so loud. Presently she came down and opened the door. " Well, if it's Mr. Cochran you want, he's not in now."

" That's fine," said Roger.

" But you wanted to see him," said the maid.

" Not really," said Roger. " I'm a friend of his. I've come to pay his bill."

" Well that's a blessing," said the girl. " The madam thought she'd never see the color of his cash."

" Will you please find out how much he owes quickly. I'm in a hurry."

The girl flew off. Through the open door Roger smelled the fumes of boiled beef and vegetable marrow; a dead plant stood on the newel post of the banister.

Soon she came back. " The madam says she'd be down only she's bathing herself. Here's the account."

Roger paid it and said, " You must promise me you'll never never tell him who paid." He shyly gave her a shilling.

" But I don't know your name, sir."

" Well, when he asks, say it was a young stoop-shouldered girl."

Roger shut the taxi door.

4

Kythe left for Paris. She gave Roger the address of her hotel, Segovie, in a street off the Rue de la Grande Chaumiére. She asked him to stop there. She said she practically owned the place, all of her friends always stayed there to be near her. It was their club. Roger promised to call on her though he was frightened by the thought of the hotel as a place where everybody knew everybody else except him. Two or three weeks later he was in Paris and one noon he took a taxi over to the Segovie.

It was a perfectly nice third class small hotel with the one public room generally occupied by the concierge's family; a sunny court with the bedding sunning out the windows and a large square key-rack next to the staircase. He asked for Madame von Krazen. The concierge gave him a key and told him to go up, " Elle dort encore."

" Alors je ne monte pas."

" Montez," said the concierge. " Il est midi et demi. Il faut qu'elle se reveille."

He knocked on the door softly. No answer.

He knocked again — louder. No answer.

He knocked again. " Who's there? "

" It's Roger Baum to see Madame von Krazen."

" Roger who? "

" It's Graham's friend, Roger Baum." Now he knew he shouldn't have come.

" Oh, the American. Have you a key."

He stuck it in the door.

" Well then come in."

Kythe lay in a large low double bed. She looked like a child with her fine yellow hair spread over her pillow and her face fresh on waking with no trace of the soil of sleep. Bottle green light fell on the counterpane, through the Venetian blinds.

"It's very nice to see you," she said, "if you don't mind the way I look."

"I think you look lovely," he answered and went over to close the window. She reached for a shawl and pressed the button at her side. "I suppose you've had breakfast." He nodded and sat awkwardly on the front of a chair. She seemed very bright and edgey. Her boy's face and her incredibly young eyes seemed gayer and more nervous than in London. "Well," said she, "what have you been doing?"

"Well," he smiled, thinking of London and of how little of what he did could possibly amuse her, "I saw Graham. He's working very hard."

"Dear Graham," said Kythe, "you like him very much."

"Yes," said Roger, "I've known him a long time."

"Is he your best friend?" she asked.

"Why," he was surprised, "I'd hardly say that. I mean he's very nice to me . . . he's always known me."

"To be sure," she broke in, "and whom else have you seen?"

"Well, no one really." He felt he must say this, "that you know. I suppose you know Cochran left London."

"Do I know it? I should say I do know it. God, if I ever learn who got him out of going to jail, I'll kill him."

"Oh," said Roger weakly.

"He's practically ruined my vacation. My one idea was to get Dickie set up for himself, put him on his own . . . away from me, you know: Graham must have told you."

" Yes, but I thought if Cochran got out of jail then Dickie could come over here with you."

" Yes? " said Kythe. " Well, so did they. Dickie gave him enough money to pay his bills, and so did some other goddamn fool. So, between them they had enough to come here together."

" Are they here now? " asked Roger with a feeling of hideous guilt.

" Yes, indeed. I should say so. Dickie is being shown the town and I'm not doing the showing."

" Gee," said Roger, " I'm awfully sorry."

" You are? " Kythe looked at him steadily, " that's awfully sweet of you. It doesn't make much difference as you know. I often have very good plans for my friends and they always turn out badly. But here's my frightful rolls and coffee."

Roger got up to make way for the maid and tray. She couldn't possibly think, he thought, I've been here all night. Then he was ashamed of his thought.

" You're not staying here, are you, at the Segovie."

" No," said Roger. " I've got a place nearer the Louvre."

" Then you really want to be a painter," she smiled.

" Well, I think so. But I only meant it's more convenient."

" I'd hoped to have had you near us." She said this with just the trace of a hurt presumption. Roger was amazed that she seemed to consider him at all. Then there was a knock on the door.

Kythe brightened up perceptibly. Roger rose to open the door.

" Oh, don't bother," said Kythe, " they all have their keys. Come in, come in."

The door opened and in walked a very curious young

man. He was tall and blonde. He wore no hat and his
yellow hair conformed to a wig-like pattern as in a
Pisanello medal. The high collar of his top coat went
up to his ears. A blue silk handkerchief rolled out from
his neck. He took off his white kid gloves and strode
gravely to the side of the bed. He bent down and took
both of Kythe's little upstretched hands and touched
them to his lips.

"And how is my big husband today?" said he.

"Very well, darling, and how is my little wife," she
smiled knowingly at Roger.

"Always the happier for being nearer my mate." The
accent must belong to a Russian thought Roger.

"This," said she, presenting Roger, "is a great friend
of mine. Mr. Baum, meet Prince Alexis Napovitch."

"An American," said Alexis. "Dear husband," he
said hoosband, "dear husband, your stamp collection is
complete. Now in your album is two English pink and
grey, or pink and pink." He turned to Roger, "You
know Mr. Fisher and Mr. Stevens?" Roger nodded.
"And your Roumanians and your Germans . . . they
how do you say it, cancel each other. Then there is the
Spaniard. He is somewhat damaged, but if placed in
conjunction with a good Frenchman," Kythe laughed,
"maybe they are worth saving. I am Russian. You will
meet my Swiss friend Georg. He is a three-cornered
aerial stamp. He is a mechanic. And what sort of a
stamp are you, Mr. Baum?"

"I guess I'm just a plain American two-cent stamp
with a picture of George Washington on it," answered
Roger.

"Oh," said Alexis, surprised at the fullness of his
reply. Then as an afterthought, "You will enjoy be-
longing to Kythe's collection."

Before Roger had time to agree, Alexis sat down on the bed and started to stroke Kythe's hair. " Shall I bathe my great big husband," he said with considerable tenderness. For one horrible moment Roger thought he really would and he felt they wouldn't mind his being there either. In fact they would like it. Before he could think he had risen and seized his hat.

" Don't be afraid, Roger Baum," said Madame von Krazen quickly, " my wife here is only joking," and Roger turned his head for fear he would see again on the hunchback's face the terrible recognition of her own trap. Roger cursed himself for playing the fool again. He swore that no matter what happened he could, he would, he must stand by her. Fortunately no explanations were necessary for a knock on the door settled their tension.

" Come in," said Kythe. A key rattled in the lock and two small dark men or boys slipped in, and over to her bed.

" Prinzess," said one, " Die Sonne scheint für Sie — and you waste it in bed."

" Ma Reine," said the other, " embrassez moi." She embraced him.

" Mr. Titulescu and Mr. von Papen."

The Roumanian stamp and the German stamp, surmised Roger. Alexis guessed his thought and laughed, " Yes," said he, " and if you can wait they will cancel each other."

Roger looked at him, but could not smile back. He stared over to the bed where Kythe held one hand of each of her friends.

" Mariano is so stupid, dear Princess," said the German. He raised his hands in an elegant deprecatory gesture. " He is so indiscreet. He will be the death of me."

" Cherie," answered the Roumanian, " Heinrich is so demanding. He asks so much. I give him all I can but if I tell people how much I love him, he hates me."

" Now what's the matter with you two silly children? " Roger saw her eager, happy interest.

" Nothing as usual," snapped von Papen. " At the Cigale last night who should come by but that bitch Florent Bryce. He went right up to Mariano as if he'd never seen me before, as cool as that, and asked him whom he was with."

" And what did he say? " grinned Kythe.

" He said he was with me," von Papen laughed and slapped his thigh.

" But, ma belle, what else could I say? " implored the Roumanian.

Kythe exploded with gaiety. She nodded sweetly to Roger and her lower lip went up, as if to say . . . I'll tell you all about it later. Roger did his best to make his grin seem more than automatic.

" Personally," said Kythe, " I think I should spank both of you."

" Oh, no," cried Alexis, " they'd like it too much."

Mariano Titulescu was irritated but he turned graciously to Alexis and said, " And where, mon Prince, is your Swiss garage hand? "

" Georg is not a garage hand," snapped Alexis. " He is an aviation mechanic."

" And a very sweet boy, too," said Kythe. The German and the Roumanian winked at each other. A key rattled in the door again and no knock announced the entrance of Bobby Cochran and Dickie Blair.

Kythe leaned forward in the bed. " Dickie," she cried,

" Dickie, I thought you weren't ever coming to see me any more."

" Dickie has been very busy, my dear," broke in Cochran. " You know he's never been to Paris before and I've been showing him the sights."

" I'm sorry, Kythe. But I really have been busy." Roger saw he was sulky.

Kythe looked at Dickie quickly. " You might at least give me a hello kiss." Dickie pecked her forehead. " Well now you might tell your old aunt what you've seen."

" Dear lady," said Cochran, " he's been in the most excellent hands. He has seen the Arch of Triumph erected by Napoleon the first."

" Which one? " snapped Alexis.

" You might let Dickie tell me," said Kythe to Cochran.

" He means the Etoile," said Dickie savagely to Alexis. Then more softly to Kythe, " Oh, we've seen the Louvre and the Luxembourg. You know, the usual things."

" Oh, the ungrateful child," cried Cochran, " I've shown him everything."

The German and the Roumanian edged forward. " Dear lady, although we have not met your delightful new friends," he bowed to Dickie Blair and Cochran, " we must take up our crosses again. Adieu, till the next petit léver."

" Oh, it's only Dickie Blair," said Kythe sweetly. " You know, I've told you, I brought him up. Rather we brought each other."

" Pas d'excuses, Madame." Titulescu minced toward the door. " We leave, we are not hurt, we would be charmed." He grinned at Dickie Blair and bowed to

Cochran. The door shut behind the German and the
Roumanian postage stamps.

" Who were those adorable people? " asked Cochran.
" You might at least have introduced me."

" Shut up, Bobby," said Kythe, " you know it's hard
enough for me to bear you around as it is." Dickie Blair
got up and looked out the window. Kythe noticed this
and centered her attention on him. Alexis turned to
Cochran and pointedly asked him to lunch. They left.
Dickie still stayed by the window, his back to the bed.
Roger got up and reached for his hat. He really was
going.

" It was too lovely to see you again, Madame von
Krazen."

" I hope it was. When you see me again call me
Kythe." She was relieved, Roger thought, to have them
go and she was so disarmingly sweet in her eagerness to
be alone with Dickie.

" Can I have lunch with you? " said Dickie suddenly
wheeling around to face Roger flatly.

" Why, yes," Roger snapped his head up. " Only I
thought — ."

" I'll see you later, Kythe," said Dickie. He kissed the
top of her head and pushed Roger out of the room. It
was all done so quickly that Roger was very glad afterwards he did not have to refuse to look at Kythe's face
again.

Dickie and Roger went downstairs and out into the
sunshine and up the street and to the avenue past the
picture shops and framers' shops to the Closerie des
Lilas. They sat down and ordered lunch. No one else
was there and Dickie was completely silent. He was so
silent that Roger felt like breaking it with some extraordinary question to compete with the silence, for in-

stance; Why did you feel the necessity of asking me to
lunch? But he knew why. Instead he said shyly, " Mr.
Cochran said you'd been to the Louvre a lot? "

" Oh yes," said Dickie flatly, " I don't know about a
lot. We saw a lot of pictures."

" Did you like them? " Roger forced himself to go on.

" Did I like them? Yes, I liked them." He poured
some red wine from the carafe into Roger's glass. " You
like pictures a lot, don't you? "

" Why yes," said Roger, " I want to be a painter."
(Don't worry about it, thought Roger, I won't go on
and tell you about it if you don't want to hear.)

" Pictures are all right," said Dickie. " They're good.
They can't upset anybody." Roger was ready to venture
ideas, information. But Dickie looked up and laughed.
" God," he said, " aren't people terrible? "

" Some of them are," admitted Roger.

" They all are," said Dickie Blair definitely. " Except, well, except you and me." Then they both laughed.
From then on it was easier going. " You know what I
mean," said Dickie. " Those terrible people up in
Kythe's rooms. They're always there. Whenever I see
her those rats are always around her. I can't understand
it. I can't believe she likes them."

" Maybe they just seem more intimate than they
are? "

" No," said Dickie, " Bobby says she's always like
that when she gets to Paris. I can't stand it."

Roger suppressed his defense of Kythe.

" It's funny, to know a person all your life and then
find out suddenly you don't know her at all."

" I think you know her pretty well," said Roger
seriously.

" So did I, in London, but I never saw her much,

except in my holidays and we usually spent those together alone."

" I'm afraid you're making her unhappy," said Roger.

" Oh, I know it," said Dickie petulantly. " But between her beggar's court of terrible people and the way
she treats Bobby Cochran, she makes me unhappy too."

" But Bobby Cochran . . ." Roger was going to say,
was difficult you must admit, only Dickie said, " I know
what you're going to say. But it's not true. Bobby is
different from them and besides, he's an artist, and the
world owes him a lot. Kythe shouldn't be so conventional."

Roger was in it now up to his neck. He felt very badly
for having gotten Cochran over to Paris, however inadvertently, and he was determined to do something
about it, so he bravely jumped in.

" Well," he smiled up at Dickie. " What are you
going to do about it? "

Dickie was not very much surprised at Roger's presumption.

" That's just it. What will I do? Kythe's always telling
me to see for myself, to act on my own initiative. Well,
I'm going to — ."

" I think you're absolutely right," said Roger, " and
I know she does. She's told me that she hoped, that is,
she felt it would be better for you, if you stayed — if
you went back to London."

" Whoever said anything about London? " snapped
Dickie. " That's her idea, not mine. That's not my plan
at all."

" Oh," said Roger, " I thought you were happier in
London."

" Happier, no. I've never been out of England in my
life before," he laughed. " I want to see the world."

Roger finished up his omelet and felt that the situation was slipping through his grasp, and slipping from bad to worse.

" In fact," said Dickie, " I think I'll go on a walking trip through Germany with Bobby. He wants me to very much."

" Oh, I wouldn't do that," said Roger, rashly, he knew.

" Why not? " asked Dickie, and one of the nice things about him was that he didn't seem to resent these personal invasions. In fact, he was almost childishly eager to have any advice that might be offered.

" Oh, I think, I mean — I think you'd hurt Kythe terribly if you did. She worries about your future a lot."

" Well, my future won't suffer from Bobby Cochran. Besides, she says she wants me to do what I want to — to be free of her — I can't go hanging on to her all my life."

" I know, but you do owe her something — you ought to trust her that she knows best for you. After all, she knows him better than you do."

" She does not. She's just jealous of him. He's been wonderful to me. When I was at college, I did nothing. I went around with a lot of hearty people, and rowed and drank. I wasn't alive till I met him."

"Yes," said Roger. " She wants you to do what you want to do."

" Yes," said Dickie, " if it's what she wants me to do. I do love her and I always will but I can't go on being her son all my life."

" But she doesn't want you to."

" Oh yes, she does. In a way I'm all she has. I know she doesn't care about the rest of her people."

" But if you know this — "

" Oh, I know it well enough — But if she wants me
to do what I should for myself and even if — ."

5

But the conversation did come to an end, and Roger
felt very much put out and frustrated. He was left with
no strong convictions on either side. At the end of the
meal he couldn't even defend Kythe nor could he abuse
Cochran. The least he could do in the future was to
keep out of the way of these people as much as he could.
He should have listened to Graham, and minded his
own affairs. He wouldn't see any of them any more. He
was drawn to Kythe and he felt he owed her something
but he thought it would probably be better for her if
he didn't go around any more. Then there would be no
danger at least from him, of spoiling somebody's af-
fections — and finally he decided Dickie was right, pictures were best, they didn't upset anybody at least mess-
ily. He knew few people in Paris and had no way to
meet new ones except through Kythe. So he was perfectly content to spend his few remaining days in Paris
between the days in the Louvre and the nights at the
cinema.

On his last afternoon in Paris he went to say goodbye
to the gallery. He had thought of going over to the
Segovie and leaving some flowers for Kythe, but ultimately there was no point in it. Besides she would probably be hurt that he never called that morning after her
petit léver.

He was standing in front of Poussin's " Inspiration
du Poète." The picture he liked probably best of all in
the world. It was the most beautiful and touching period to place at the end of his summer. All softness of

the summer afternoon outside, of the fountains, and
the dusty bushes and the children rolling hoops and
shouting, people passing and repassing on the grand
alleys, thinned down and clarified into an intense sympathy, an unlocalized longing. Golden light defined the
gracious line of Apollo's lyre. One's eyes followed the
outstretched arm of the god on to the open book of
the poet, whose expectant eyes greeted the generous
wreath of a cupid.

"And fancy finding you here," cried the voice of
Bobby Cochran behind him. Roger turned, almost glad
to be interrupted. "Dickie insisted on coming here
today, of all things, to say goodbye to the pictures. A
month ago he'd never looked at a picture. Now who
can say I haven't educated him well?"

Roger shook hands first with Bobby, then with Dickie.

"We never could tell why you dropped us so
quickly," said Dickie.

"Kythe was particularly hurt," smiled Bobby.

"Oh, I'm sorry," said Roger. "It wasn't that I didn't
want to come."

"Busy here, I suppose," said Dickie coolly.

"Oh, not entirely," said Roger. He felt the old dis-
taste, the fear of being implicated again with these
people.

"Well, no excuses from you," said Bobby. "Not a
word. You will be quite forgiven if you come to our
party tonight."

"I don't think he wants to come," said Dickie.

"Yes, of course I do," said Roger. "What party is it?"

"It's our going away party," said Bobby. "We're
leaving for Germany in the morning. It will be such
great fun."

"But don't come if you're busy or don't want to,"

said Dickie. He was troubled in his mind Roger could
see. Bobby's insufferable gaiety found no echo in his
friend.

"I'd love to come." If I just say that, thought Roger,
simply, they may believe me. "When and where
is it?"

"Well come to the Segovie at eight. Alexis has a
friend. Oh you were there when I teased him about
his chauffeur, weren't you?" Roger nodded. "Well
anyway, he's got a colossal car for the night and we're
all going out to the Bois to dine. Such fun."

Roger promised to come and left the Louvre for good.

6

At the last minute Roger couldn't make up his mind
whether actually to go or not. But he really had nothing
to do. His bags were all packed. His bills were paid, and
if alone, he would probably only wander on the boule-
vards and go to sleep early. Yet there was plenty of
time to sleep on the boat home.

His indecision, however, made him a quarter of an
hour late. As his taxi drew up to the Segovie he saw a
big Renault touring car with polished brass fittings and
a large standard searchlight set next to the driver's seat.
The car was already full of people; thought Roger,
maybe I can't go after all.

"Well," cried Kythe, "we didn't think you'd ever
show up. You've kept us waiting for hours." And yet
she seemed glad enough to see him.

"I'm really terribly sorry. I got stuck at my place
about my bags."

"Bags, bags," laughed Kythe, "bags of honey, bags
of money."

"No," said Roger, "just bags of clothes. I'm going away tomorrow, too."

"Well, no time for excuses now," cried Cochran from the back seat — where Kythe sat between him and Dickie Blair, "hop in."

Roger was at a loss where to hop in. The back seat was full. He bowed to Mariano Titulescu and von Papen who sat on the two folding chairs. Alexis from the front seat said, "M. Baum, I want you very much to meet my friend Georges Borchardt." The driver bowed. He had a kind of chauffeur-yachting cap on and seemed agreeable.

"You'd better get in with us," said Alexis. There was plenty of room. Alexis made more room and slammed the door after Roger had settled down into the seat. The car rode easy on its springs and seemed to leave its chassis in great swings around corners, into the avenue and down across the bridge to the road that led to the Bois. The night was moonless but clear. The blackness above hung down the pin point stars as low as the branch steps. The little party gave off an air of geniality and repose. There was no forced gaiety and Roger for one was glad he had come.

"Georges here is tired," said Alexis to Roger, to bring him into the conversation. "He works at Le Bourget all day."

"Oh," said Roger, "an aviator."

"No," said Georges, "I am a mechanic, I rarely leave the ground."

"But sometimes they take you up," said Alexis, "don't they?"

"Yes," said Georges, "but they have little time to give favors."

"But you could fly if you wanted to, alone?" insisted

Alexis. Roger felt this was being carried on for his
benefit and so he turned his head, as much as he could
to be civil to Titulescu and von Papen, behind him, and
relieve Alexis of the further need of explanation.

" And do you leave also for Germany? " asked von
Papen.

" No, for America, tomorrow," said Roger.

" Why not come along with us — we've plenty of
room," called Bobby Cochran across the seats.

" Got passage booked." The car's speed and the wind
necessitated Roger to abbreviate.

" Oh, do come along," said Bobby, " such fun. We've
tried to get Kythe and she won't budge."

" Germany is a very interesting country," said von
Papen. " You should see it before you die."

Roger said he hoped to one day and turned his head
around. He was relieved in his mind that Kythe had
been kind enough to ask for no explanations of his failure to see her again, that Cochran seemed less objection-
able, and that Dickie Blair's departure was seeming to
cause no one anguish. How nice, thought Roger, my
last night in Paris spent driving in a private car, with
these sophisticated people. We will eat and drink and
years after we will remember the sweetness of this
evening of farewell.

Kythe wanted to splurge this evening. It was a
special occasion so they went to Pré Catalan. They were
seated at a large table under an awning, next to the
dance floor. Cochran ordered the food and champagne.
Kythe settled herself for enjoyment and drummed on
the table in time to the tango. Roger was warmed by her
childish smile, by her hand on the table in Dickie's
hand, by her lack of a resentment which he had gloomily anticipated. All the men were paying their homage

to her and telling her little tales to amuse her, little jokes to make her laugh.

"Ah," cried Mariano Titulescu, " dear lady — what should have happened to us yesterday? "

"What happened to you, my angel? " Kythe was delighted. She purred and her mouth smacked with a kittenish relish.

"Heinrich and I were going to tea at the Dame Blanche."

"If Mariano goes on telling that story," said Heinrich, " I am sorry but I will leave."

"Oh, but," Kythe remonstrated, " we're all such good friends here."

Cochran laughed out loud. "Go on, Mariano."

"Before Heinrich stopped me, we were going to tea at the Dame Blanche. As we entered the door, who came out but Thompson Gray-Seaton — ." General sensation.

Roger tapped his champagne glass, and then presented himself to Georges Borchardt. Any opening in a competitive conversation would be appreciated. " Is it very hard to fly, to begin to fly? " he asked.

Before Georges could answer Cochran broke in, " Thompson Gray-Seaton is a marvelous Englishman. You'd love him — such black pearls."

"He is a pig-dog," said von Papen.

"Tch, tch," said Titulescu, " he was once kind to me."

"Go on, Mariano," said Kythe, " what happened."

Alexis tried to get Georges and Roger to continue. " It is not hard at first, is it Georges? If you have good eyes — "

"And then Gray-Seaton raised his monocle — thus — you recall how — " Mariano raised his fork, " thus — "

" Yes, yes," cried Kythe.

" And walked out without ever recognizing me! "

" And quite right, too," said Dickie Blair. As far as Roger could remember, this was his first remark this evening.

" Don't be horrid, Dickie," said Bobby Cochran — and then the food arrived.

But Dickie Blair looked black. Roger could tell he had given up the evening for lost in so much as he directed all his attentions to Kythe. He deliberately absorbed himself in her and excluded himself from the slightest intercourse with anyone else. " I wish you were coming along, dear Kythe," he said.

" But why? " she laughed. " You'll be much freer without me."

" Why you can trust me, to behave myself," said Cochran inanely.

" Shut up, Bobby," said Dickie. Roger's mind snapped the reaction of his " Don't be horrid," before it left Cochran's lips. The echoes blurred.

" I think you might come a little way at least," said Dickie.

" No," answered Kythe, " I start life class tomorrow."

" You don't want to come with us."

" But Dickie, I can't always be trailing around after you? "

" No, of course not," he lowered his head, " I'm a lot of nuisance, aren't I? "

" Don't be silly, darling. Here, have something more to drink." She automatically poured more wine into his glass — never noting it was still full. The champagne splashed on to Bobby.

" I'm christened," he cried, " I'm christened, now I am off for good."

" Kythe," said Dickie, " darling, please be serious, I promise you I won't go tomorrow if you don't want me to."

" But, of course I want you to, you'll have such a good time." Roger deliberately removed his interest to the direction of the rest of the party.

Von Papen said to Titulescu, " If you eat so fast the food will all go to the bottom of your stomach in a ball and you will die."

" And will you be very sad, Mariano? "

" Sometimes," said Titulescu, " I think I will be happy."

" But," said Alexis, " if there is no future in being this way a mechanic, why do you not leave Bourget."

" Then," said Georges, " I would have no one but you to thank whether I ate or not."

" And will you be very glad to get back to America? " asked Bobby. Roger started to answer. The answer stuck on his tongue.

" If you are such a bad boy," said Titulesco, " I can only do one thing."

" I wish I'd never come to Paris with Bobby. Kythe, no matter what I do — you will love me? " Dickie's eyes never left her.

" A mechanic's job is as good a job as no job," said Georges.

" Is living really more expensive in London than New York? " asked Bobby.

" Do what you like," said Titulescu, " no one shall deceive me. No one can hurt me — no one can make a fool out of me."

" But," said Alexis, " I know a man who could use a good butler."

" I won't go," said Dickie.

"You must go," said Kythe.

"Dickie seems off his feed tonight," said Cochran to
Roger. He was becoming piqued at Dickie's insolence.
"He hates to leave his mother."

Roger looked quickly at Kythe to see if she had heard.
He guessed she hadn't. He looked at Dickie and hoped
the boy could last out the evening without crying.

"Let us dance," said Mariano, into the general circle.

"Don't be facetious," said Cochran.

"But I love to dance so," said Mariano.

Kythe moved herself back in her chair, slowly. "So
do I," she said. Roger was startled into the necessity for
action. He got up and went over to Kythe's chair. He
looked down on her hair, gilt under the lamps. He was
about to forestall an embarrassment with the fatuous
gesture of asking the hunchback to tango.

"Oh, thank you," Kythe looked up at him blankly,
"I only meant — I was reminding Mariano I do not
allow him to dance with his friend in public places."

Dickie got up too and said to Kythe, "I'm going to
be a spoil sport. I can't stand this place here, I'm going
home."

"But you must wait for me," said Bobby.

"No," said Dickie, "I'll see you in the morning."
He kissed Kythe and without a further word went
out.

"The spoiled child," said Cochran, and dashed after
him. "Good night all," he called back. The silence
responded.

"Well," said Kythe gaily, "that's that." Roger sat
down. A cold dreariness settled down over him. All his
desire to amuse her, to help her, to cheer her, froze in
impotence on his tongue. He could do nothing but wait
and suffer the small talk around him. He could not even

sustain her with a glance — for Kythe never dared look at him.

Alexis and Georges brought the car around. They were in front of course. Then Kythe and Roger sat in the back seat and Mariano and von Papen closed the doors.

" Let us," said Mariano, " go to a Par Tous. We've never been."

" A Par Tous," said von Papen, " and pray what is that? "

" They are orgies in the underbrush," said Mariano, " ask Kythe."

She turned to Roger, " Par Tous." She laughed. " You know — " He smiled negatively.

" Oh, they are parties in the Bois," she said. " Everyone goes into some remote place and they do everything. Haven't you heard? " Roger shook his head.

" Is it dangerous? " asked von Papen.

" Well," said Kythe, " you never know who's next you." They laughed.

" But how do we find out where it is," said von Papen.

" Oh," said Kythe, " ask the next gendarme we meet."

" We won't really go? " asked Roger of her alone. " Will we? " She looked at him for a moment, and said, " Of course not. It's a joke to tease you."

" You will find the Minister of the Marine there as well as Josephine Baker and André Gide."

" Is it discreet? " asked von Papen.

The car tore through the avenues in the woods of the Bois. Georges Borchardt was an excellent driver, maintaining a persistent and subtle attention in the avoidance of bumps and rattles. They seemed to flow gently through the tunnels of foliage — and the branches above swept back in a wake of dim flutterings to net the passing stars. Then Mariano discovered the big searchlight on the running board. " Ah," he said, " we will investigate the biology of the Bois." The sharp finger of light shot in among the trees but the car went too fast to permit a very thorough investigation.

" Let them play," said Kythe to Roger. "Are you quite warm? "

" Yes," said Roger, " are you? "

" I hate to have you go away and I don't even know you," said Kythe. They were both looking straight ahead.

" Well, I hate to go."

" It's so rare one meets people one likes," said Kythe.

" It is," said Roger.

" Tomorrow night I'll be having dinner with Mariano, Heinrich and Alexis — Georges can't get away in the week days."

" No? " said Roger.

" There is a Philippino and a South American that Bobby had promised to introduce me to — before he goes — He must have forgotten it."

" Why don't you remind him? "

" There must be lots of nice ·people in Paris," said Kythe.

" Yes," said Roger, " there must be."

" Where will you be tomorrow night."

" Pulling out of Cherbourg, probably."

" Mariano and Heinrich are really very kind," said Kythe, " and so amusing."

" Yes," said Roger.

" And Alexis, and Georges."

" Yes," said Roger.

"There's no reason for me to fear this winter in Paris."

"Of course not," said Roger. He drew over to her and carefully placed his arm upon the shelf of her back. She leaned her body into his.

"You would even like Bobby Cochran if you knew him," she said.

"I know I would," said Roger.

"It's funny at first — I didn't want Dickie to go with him at all."

"No," said Roger.

"I think they'll be all right, don't you?"

"Of course they'll be all right," said Roger.

"A friend of mine, a woman," said Mariano, "suddenly woke up in such a place, and behold, there was a negro."

"A negro?" said Heinrich, "an African?"

"No. It was an American negro. He played in a jazz-band."

Roger couldn't stop Kythe's sobbing. She sobbed all the way back to his hotel. She couldn't even say good-night to him.

Flesh Can Not

Oh, when I held her in my arms
I thought she had ten thousand charms
Her caresses were soft, her kisses were sweet,
Saying, " We'll get married next time we meet."

'Twas in the year of eighty-three
That A. J. Stinson hired me;
He said, " Young man, I want you to go,
And follow my herd into Mexico."

1926

1

Roger had gone to the game. He had gone to the game and it was the first Harvard-Yale game he'd ever been to. It was terribly exciting and even though he hadn't cheered as much as everyone else his throat felt hoarse and tired. He even felt too exhausted to stay up and raise hell with the rest of the Freshmen, even if tomorrow was Sunday. He simply locked his door, took off his clothes and went to bed.

Some time later he was awakened by a terrific pounding on his door. He drew himself up in bed and listened. More pounding. Roger jumped up and went to the hall door to discover that it was not being hammered, but that his fire-door was. The fire-doors were the same as the others except that they had no door knobs; only red glass-covered plates which were to be broken only in case of fire. All the rooms in the dormitory were thus partially connected. Roger went over and turned on the light. He was surprised to see his clothes spread all over the floor and he almost stooped down to pick them up. But the pressure in reiterated bangs on the door increased. He was scared they'd spring the hinges. He went over and asked what they wanted. Howls answered. More terrific bangings. Roger stepped cautiously away and leaned up against his bookcase while his fire-door was being smashed in. Then some one threw a rock through the open window. It rolled on to his desk. Then the fire-door splintered and crashed. It had been mysteriously

locked and it split away with its hinges waving, and
flopped heavily on to the floor. Roger sprang up to
muster a suitable display of outrage. A boy stood in
the open doorway. He was about six feet tall with reddish brown hair. His mouth was laughing hysterically.
It seemed to have nothing to do with the rest of his
face.

"What the hell do you think you're doing?" demanded Roger in a voice that was not quite loud enough.

"You'll pardon us, sir," said the laughing boy, "we
got to telephone."

Roger suddenly looked at him. His eyeballs were as
red as his hair and cheeks. He gripped a telephone
tightly in one hand. The wires trailed loosely at his feet.
"This phone," he said, "is out of order."

"Get the hell out of here," said Roger. He couldn't
get sore yet.

"Sir," said the boy, "we must let our parents know
how we have fared tonight." Two friends appeared behind him. Roger saw that they also carried ripped telephones by the cords.

"Get the hell out of here," said Roger indefinitely,
"before I throw you out."

The three boys stepped and staggered into the room.
One bent down and looked at the door. He wagged his
head heavily. Roger instinctively went over to stand in
front of his telephone. The boy with the reddish hair
wobbled over, guessing his purpose. He pawed for the
phone. Roger stepped aside to avoid the paw, but exposed his phone. The boy pounced on it and started
pulling. The other two gravely came to help. Roger was
laughing so hard he couldn't do anything. Finally the
phone was ripped from its moorings. Roger wondered
if they would try to telephone now. But now one of

them hurled his phone out the window. It was lucky
that the lower part of it was open. The next phone hit
the small wooden casings and glass shattered. The rest
flew out the window, their wires whipping back almost
to cut Roger's face. The boy with the red hair sank
heavily on to the sofa. One of the others tried to replace
the broken fire-door. It fell again settling crazily on him.
He allowed it to fall. Roger sprang over and opened the
hall door, hoping the light from the outside would attract them. It did. They passed into the hallway and
slid downstairs. Their friend however was sleeping stu-
pidly on the sofa. Roger shook him, saw that it was hope-
less and went into the bedroom. He was exhausted.
Even now there were still calls and screams faintly echoing from the rest of the dormitory. He drew the covers
over him and turned over. He breathed deeply and
methodically to put himself to sleep. Some time later he
woke up with his nose twitching. There was a most foul
smell somewhere about. The smell literally forced him
up. He walked into his study and it grew stronger. He
opened the door and stepped out into the bright hallway. There at the bottom of the stairs were the two
drunks burning up the telephones. They kept singeing
their fingers in the process and were cursing fiercely.
Roger opened both the windows in his study and closed
the door. He looked at the boy sleeping on the sofa. His
head hung painfully over its edge. It looked loose, a
trickle of saliva fell from the corner of his lips. His sandy
hair fell away from his head. He looked white and
drowned. Roger propped his head up on the arm of the
couch, threw his fur coat over him and went to bed. He
slept through the smell of burning rubber.

When Roger woke up the next morning he took a
bath before he went to look at the wreckage of his room.

He vaguely wondered how bad it really was, if he would
be held responsible for it or not. He wondered what
had happened to the rest of the people in the riot.
Had similar acts of violence been perpetrated in all the
freshman halls? So he considered and held his tie pin
between his teeth as he did his tie.

When he opened the door to the study he was considerably surprised to find the boy on the couch. He had
completely forgotten about him. He lay breathing regu-
larly in much the same position as when Roger left him.
His eyes only were less bloodshot. The fur coat had
fallen off on to the floor. Roger inspected the fallen fire-
door, the windows, which were not badly damaged and
then he woke the sleeper. The boy shifted himself
slightly, wet his lips and opened his eyes dizzily up to
Roger, who smiled at him.

" I guess you didn't have much of a night," said Roger.

The other boy looked around the room, " You don't
seem to have done so worse by yourself," he said and
stretched his back.

" You smashed my fire-door and a lot of telephones,"
said Roger. " You were absolutely stinko."

" I recall nothing," said the boy sitting up on the sofa,
" on the grounds that it may incriminate me." He
looked at the supine and split white door. " Ah, sir," he
said, wagging his fingers at Roger, " I only know I could
never have been the agent in such a fracas." He said
frakass.

" Well, you smashed the door and the windows."
Roger bent down and set the fire-door against the frame.
The boy bent his head down against his shoulder,
rubbed it and stood up. Aside from being sickly pale
and unshaven, he had a pleasant, humorous, open
face. " I am," he said, " yours faithfully, Alexander

Gordon Pinckney." He coughed and added, " a Boston boy."

" Are you a freshman too? " asked Roger.

" Yes, indeed," he said, " but not for long I fear."

" What's the matter," asked Roger, " are you on pro? "

" No," said Pinckney impressively, " we Gordons are not long for this world."

Roger couldn't tell if this was a joke too. Anyway they more or less picked up the room so that the maid would not have too great a shock. Roger suggested breakfast but Pinckney said he couldn't possibly face it all un-washed and in those clothes and without a pick-me-up. He asked Roger over to his room while he changed. He lived in the next hall down the row. When he unlocked his door Roger saw four or five other freshmen, none of whom he'd ever remembered having seen before. They stood looking at the opening door, in pajamas and bath towels. There was a cage with two green parrakeets in it hanging from the electric light.

" Well," said one with a towel, " our Sandy has come home to roost."

" Like a whipped dog," said another gloomily, " his tail betwixt."

" Sandy, the whoremonger," cried a third. " You louse."

" Gentlemen," said Sandy, pointing to the parrakeet cage, " there are ladies present."

" Whose sheets have you soiled? " a boy came slowly up with a toothbrush stuck into his cheek and the white traces of toothpaste on his chin. " The great Gordon with a hangover."

" This gentleman," Sandy indicated Roger, " who still has the advantage of me," Roger introduced himself,

" cradled me in the bosom of his home. Greater love
hath no man. If anyone or two of ye . . ."

" Yeah? " said one of his friends to Roger. " How
drunk was he? "

" He was pretty drunk." Roger looked around the
room. " He smashed my — "

" No tattling, sir," said Sandy gravely, " until we have
broken bread."

Sandy went into his own bedroom and took his
clothes off. Roger went up and stuck a finger in the parrakeet's cage. It was nipped. Two of the boys were having a conversation about cock-fighting, which they
thought would be a good idea to introduce. Betting.
Rake-offs. Roger asked if they had natural spurs. No.
They used sawed razor-blades. Sandy passed into the
shower room, his hands raised in benediction. The rest
of the boys got dressed and presently they all went down
to breakfast.

2

Roger got to know Sandy Pinckney very well. He
began to spend a part of every day in his room and
Sandy spent most of the evenings in Roger's. They would
try to study for examinations. Roger by sheer force of
will could concentrate on the mechanics of looking up
a German vocabulary in the back of his reader. Sandy,
with all the good intentions in the world, and a strong
start, would weary quickly and if he couldn't engage
Roger in conversation would go to sleep on the floor or
on the sofa. Roger tried the plan of doing their lessons
together; each looking up half of the words but Sandy
couldn't sustain his interest and it developed into an
unequal competition. As Roger would seem to be doing
most of the work, Sandy would then say it was unfair

and he wasn't doing his share. He'd start to do it by himself and would soon be asleep. Roger had a half-voiced interest in trying to reform him. He made him see the doctor when Sandy woke up one morning and coughed up blood. That interview restricted his drinking to the week-ends — at least.

Roger weakly remonstrated with him about his work. How he would be sure to flunk out if he wasn't careful. Sandy would make elaborate preparations for work. He would sharpen all his pencils, clear his desk of theatre programs, cigarettes and empty glasses and settle himself on his chair — for real effort. Then he would close the door and pull down the shade so he couldn't see outside. He even took the sporting prints off the wall. In fact he did everything possible to help himself except work. Sometimes Sandy and Roger would take walks before getting something to eat and going to bed. The town had a single street with a double row of noble colonial houses, white, and yellow and white, and brown and white, sleeping under the night, the long lines of the clapboards like ink rulings on their wooden façades; the arc lights from the street picking out the accents of a carved door, parts of reflecting small-paned windows or an oriole in a big coach-house, leaded like a globe of the earth. These houses were inhabited by the Tory merchants of the Revolution and they were substantially unchanged since then. The boys were talking about the sense of the past, about the possibility of people actually living, inhabiting clothes and houses a hundred years before.

" If I knew," continued Roger, " what they felt like in their clothes, if they wore underpants — and hung up their coats on coathangers or hooks — or how they washed — then maybe I'd believe they lived here."

" So hard," said Sandy, " not to think of their clothes as costumes. When do our clothes become costumes. How far back — before the war? "

" And their furniture was not antique. There must have been new books published like now. And new pictures painted."

" Were they old masters as soon as they were painted? " asked Sandy.

" I don't suppose so. But they had their old masters. Oh, I can't believe they lived here. It's only possible — perhaps they did. Every time I read about them I doubt their existence more. I never believed Washington lived — or Washington's niggers — or grooms — "

" What happened then? " asked Sandy. " Was there only your father and his father — only a world of your ancestors? "

" I don't believe in my grandfather," said Roger. " For all of me — he never —."

" I believe in the past," said Sandy. " My father taught me. His father had a diary the family kept when they first came out of Scotland. I believe in my great-grandfather just as strongly as I believe in my uncle — or my cousins. My older cousins —"

" But how," asked Roger, convinced but not satisfied.

" My great-grandfather, my mother's grandfather, had a beautiful daughter. She was as good as she was beautiful and the joy of all the countryside, that is, lower Vermont. She was a Gordon and died of grief at an early age. Her body was taken to a vault cut in the back yard of our place, six miles from the house. It rained all day and the men on the place carried her all six miles. They took turns. The minister read the " Lord gives and takes away," and my great-grandfather struck the book from his hand and wouldn't let him read any more — "

" Yes," said Roger, " that seems to have happened."

" Happened, sir? " Sandy's eyelids raised in protest. " Happened — but I have evidence." He opened the palms of his hand and slapped them smartly together.

3

Towards the second Spring there came the time of club initiations. Roger didn't know anybody in the clubby crowd but Sandy and his room-mates who happened to come to his room to get him. Roger was perfectly friendly with them, but he felt inadequate to their style. Their incessant card playing and drinking, the barrier of their special way of talking, and the fact that for five or six years they'd all been to the same school, naturally put him off. Nevertheless Sandy prevailed on the older boys from his school to get Roger into the big society that most of their gang was herded into as a matter of course. It didn't mean much if you didn't happen to get in — but if you did it was a pleasant enough place to eat — and one saw more, if possible, of the boys one saw all the time anyway. All the various large cliques in the college had such organizations, and Roger was very pleased to belong to Sandy's. They were all to be initiated on the same night and it was considered advisable to be as drunk as possible before being escorted to the clubhouse. Roger decided that the occasion demanded a terrific binge. He took about four times too much whiskey, medicinally. Together with German, Economics and Astronomy, Roger had not learned enough of liquor to pass a test in it. But anyway he kept reminding himself, anyway I'm not sick, sick. Yet, if I eat something I won't be. Yet. One of Sandy's older friends came down to meet a gang of them in his

164 Flesh is Heir

room in the freshman dormitory. Sandy was very excited. He couldn't find a pair of white duck trousers
which were the necessary initiates' costume. There was
only a pair of dirty grey ones. He stood in the room with
a glass of whiskey, appealing to his inductor to let him
go up just as he was — in a white shirt, a pair of white
socks, and sneakers —.

" That would never do," said the mentor. " You
wouldn't be let in."

" Sir, a Pinckney is never refused admittance no
matter if it were the palace." He bowed to the
company. " And gentlemen, I refer to Buckingham
itself."

" Hasn't anybody got a pair of white pants," the mentor looked around at a dozen white-clad drunken boys.
No answer. Roger began to kick himself for feeling worried but hadn't he really ought to give Sandy his own
pants, Sandy who had got him in really, and so forth,
he thought, and so forth.

" Polo pants," suggested Sandy, and struck idly at the
parrakeet cage with a cracked mallet.

" I shall ride up to the portcullis — all in white — I
shall knock twice thus," he seized the raised mallet and
struck the light out, " with my lance — I shall call for
the Castellan . . ."

" Young Lochinvar," said someone. " West."

Finally a small pair of white flannels was discovered
and they drew them on to Sandy backwards. The mentor
said it was not the regular regalia but they thought it
would do.

They eventually made their way to the clubhouse.
About twenty-five initiates were herded together in a
small ante room to be led out one at a time. There
was no precedence; whoever happened to be leaning on

to the door of the small room fell into the initiation
every time it was opened. It seemed to Roger not unlike
the Black Hole of Calcutta. It would be terrible if they
all got stuck in this room and nobody let them out.
It would be worse though in a few minutes because one
boy showed advanced symptoms of a rising nausea. Someone pushed him over on to the door so he would be the
next to fall out. The door opened. He fell. He didn't
get up though so he was dragged off. Hands took a hold
of another one and the door closed again. Roger wet his
lips and sucked his thumb. He pushed his wet thumb
into his eyes to make them cooler. It made them hotter.
A line just under his hair, all around his head seemed
to be constantly attacked by invisible electric sewing
machines. If his brain pan would detach itself finally
perhaps some of the alcohol would be burned away with
it. Some of the boys started to sing feebly. No one seemed
to know any song.

" We must sing Scotch songs," said Sandy to his little
group.

" Which songs? " asked Roger. Perhaps it was wax
melting his ears. His ears seemed to be blind. A funny
red light.

" Scotch songs," said Sandy, " The blue bells of."

" O, the bonny O. Coming through the rye," someone
hummed steadily.

" No," said Sandy, " Scotch songs. Beneath the barren rafters — "

" Beneath the barren rafters," thought Roger.
" Sandy's theme song." A funny red light. Red go, green
stop. " Here's a health to your lady's eyes."

" Lady's eyes, lady's eyes," almost a chorus —

" Here's a health to your lady's eyes — " Sandy waved
his arms.

" We have drunk to the dead already, eady, eady.
. . ." Red light went out.

" That's no Scotch song," said one interrupting.

" Scotch," said Sandy, " we have drunk to the dead
already, here's a health to the next man that dies — "

The door opened and Roger found himself seized.
The room was large. A red light neither came on nor
went out, out. Smoke hung in horizontal veils. Some
bells rang to find Roger facing a blinding light in his
eyes. People seemed dimly to be sitting around in arm
chairs. Lights out.

" Gentlemen," said a red light. " This is Mr. Baum.
You may question him." Howls. Howls. To your lady's
eyes . . .

" Mr. Baum — Baum is a funny name. What is your
favorite brassiere, Mr. Baum? "

" Do you prefer men, women or horses? " Horses. No.

" Wipe that smile off your face, Mr. Baum." Wipe?

" Can you oblige with a little leg pulling, Mr. Baum."
Oblige.

I wish that light. "What stories have you heard,
Mr. Baum. There are no ladies present." Story about the
man and the child in the pullman train — the wife
ahead giving birth to a litter of triplets — the car behind — I forgot the point. My hair grows in, in. It
tickles. Where comes now? Now.

" Give Mr. Baum the baum's rush, Mr. Secretary."
Hallejlullah — allelulia. Pit-pit. Hand on my shoulder.
A friend? rough hands. Bearing me, Baum, away. Roger
was thrown into a large tub of cold water. Really cold.
Cubes of ice floating about in it. He jumped out and
shook himself like a dog; howls of laughter. He dripped.
The water really cold. It burnt like ice. I'll take cold.
Someone thrust a glass of something hot into his hand.

Too hot. Burnt. Drop it. Drops. Dropped — ouch. Rum
punch. Good for you — Drink. Thanks. Another glass.
Here's a health to the next man. Roger felt soberer. He
shivered a little and gagged on the rum punch. Then he
sat down in an armchair. Empty. His tail was wet but
he was tired and he was going to rest. Another initiate was
brought in and questioned. Dirty questions for shame
forsooth. I know how that joke ends. Why doesn't it end?
End. Another joke perhaps. Roger got somewhat hotter
and colder. If he started to sing maybe that would warm
him — Beneath the Barren Rafters.

It was Sandy they were presently initiating. He was
being very funny. Roger laughed uproariously all over
his face. Someone hit him on the neck. Initiates aren't
supposed to laugh. Sandy was saying Sir, this and Sir,
that. His old Scotch courtesy. Sir. They were all laughing. I will not laugh, so there. They took Sandy and
Roger could see they were taking Sandy to take him to
the tub. Ice water. Roger still felt wet. His pants. His
belt tight. Wet. Some water caught in his belly button.
They took Sandy and threw him into the tub of ice
water. A terrible splash. Roger felt somehow warmer,
warmer than Sandy. No more splash. Also no more red
light. But I do remember a distinct. Sandy lay at the
bottom of the well. He didn't get up. Hurt maybe. Up.
Get up.

After a longer time than Roger imagined someone
leaned over and picked Sandy Pinckney out of the cold
tub. He was surprisingly stiff. They laid him on a table.
Roger made a very great effort to sober up although
initiates may take no part. Sandy suddenly started kicking, and thrashing out with his arms. Then he stopped.
Two or three boys went up to the table and jabbed him
softly with their fingers. Quiet, he then started to thrash

again. A loose arm hit someone who hit back. His legs
jackknifed out and stayed stiff. One of his hands bent
back in a funny way. He was raising and lowering the
middle part of his body, jerking. About six boys were
trying to hold him down. He was getting bad. Someone
said " Knock him out. Better do that." Roger tried to
get up. I ought to try to see if I can't do something. He
found he couldn't move. He chafed against his body,
his bones within the skin. He detached himself from his
flesh and went over and carried Sandy to bed. No one
would knock him out though. What about a little more
cold water. Sandy was absolutely rigid on the table.
Really stiff. The boys who were holding him took their
hands off. He was really stiff. A song being sung. Beneath the barren rafters. Roger ought to go over to help
him. He looks pretty bad. I cannot, believe it or not,
move from my chair. I am wet and tired. I really want
to help — but what can I do? Help, stand by your glasses
steady — a health to. Roger hoped that a doctor — yes
a doctor would come and do something — for as far as
he was concerned he could do nothing. Someone sang
the song about standing by your glasses steady, we have
drunk to the dead already, all the way through without
stopping. Roger wondered if the flannel pants had
shrunk much on Sandy.

4

Towards commencement Sandy and Roger saw less
of each other. There were examinations that really must
be passed. And Roger did his best to try to convince
Sandy that he was having too good a time at college to
flunk out at the end of his first year. Anyway, Roger
worked pretty hard and went to bed early. Sometimes he

went over to look for Sandy to get something to eat
before going to bed, but he was rarely in.

Sandy felt sure he would be fired. He said that this
was a great pity because now he was actually taking a
lively interest in college work. Roger could see no signs
of it but hoped it was true. When the time actually
came to the examination period Sandy saw how hope-
less it all was and stopped studying. He was going
abroad that summer and before that he was off to a
houseparty at his place in Vermont. So he wouldn't have
much chance to see Roger again. Sandy decided that
they should have a farewell gathering. He knew a girl
in town who was acting in the chorus of a musical
comedy; who was extremely nice. Sandy wanted to say
goodbye to her too and it would be a good combination.
Doubtless she had a friend. They chose a Sunday night
when the girls weren't busy. Roger had never been out
with a chorus girl before. " Chorus girl."

" I assure you, sir," said Sandy, as they drove in to
get them, " beneath their little breasts beats as gold a
heart as any deb."

" I know that," said Roger, " what do you talk to
them about? "

" What do you talk to debs about? " asked Sandy.

" Well, boys they know, or girls. I don't know any
other chorus girls."

" Never fear. When a Pinckney, sir, is on the ball
the Lord will provide."

" What's your girl like; where'd you meet her? "

" She come in in the second act, in the most beautiful
pair of little black trousers — velvet — probably; with
a white shirtwaist. I went last week with Peet Sanford
and Corey Lawson. I picked her out of the whole
troupe."

" But how did you meet her? "

" Oh, I went around afterward. Corey Lawson knows a lot of girls."

" Is she nice? "

" She's the nicest girl I ever met. Too damn nice."

They called for the girls. Marjory was really very nice. Sandy let her sit in front with Roger to get acquainted while he took her friend in the rumble.

" You're a good friend of Sandy's? " she asked.

" Yes," said Roger. " I've known him a long time."

" How long? " she asked.

" Oh, over a year," he paused and laughed. " But that's long enough."

" I've seen him twice in my life."

" But you like him? "

" Yes. I do."

" He likes you too," said Roger. " He was very enthusiastic about you."

" I guess he does," said Marjory. " Does he know lots of girls? "

" I guess you're the first actress he's known — if that's what you mean."

" Not exactly. What are the other — debutantes? "

" Sort of. He likes you better than them."

" Is he a terrible liar? " She spoke without smiling.

" I never heard him lie — Oh, well — he tells stories — you know — "

" Sure, but you can trust him."

" Oh, absolutely," said Roger. " What do you mean? "

" He asked me to marry him. He wants me to elope."

" Great Christ," said Roger, " You can't do that."

" Of course I can't. What do you think I am, a nitwit? "

" No, I didn't mean that, I meant . . ."

" All I want to know is," she broke in, " if he meant what he said."

They drove out of town to a roadhouse where they knew they could get something to drink. The other girl was called Betty something and she didn't talk very much. She wore a big cameo pin with a woman's head cut on it and there seemed to be a spot of rouge on its cheeks. Sandy paid all his attention to Marjory. He drank a great deal as if there were almost a necessity to do so.

" Then, dear Marjory," he would say, " the Colonel Jeremy Gordon, my mother's only brother, a highlander and a very great gentleman sent back the bearer of that white flag. He locked himself in his room — dismissed the servants and poured himself a highball — like I pour you now." Sandy took her hand. She was looking at him and smiling.

" Isn't she marvelous," he turned impetuously to Roger, " marvelous. I wish to Christ you could see her come in with those little black trou."

Marjory sipped some whiskey and held one of his hands in both of hers. She tried to stop him from drinking but he said he was drinking healths to all the different parts of her body. She said she had enough health as it was, but he went on drinking. He kept telling about his relations who were Indian Army officers, about his mother's rock garden. He was trying to convince Marjory to marry him.

Betty, the other girl, got a bit sick and Roger went out for a little walk with her to cool her down. Roger tried to ask her if she thought Sandy would marry Marjory. She didn't seem to know what he was talking about.

Roger drove home very fast. Betty slept in a corner

of the seat, beside him. She was more tired than drunk.
Sandy and Marjory were in each other's arms in the
rumble. When Marjory got home Sandy only said something about her little black trou. He asked her to call
him up, when she was free. He seemed vague and for-
getful. Roger shook him for fear he would offend her by
his forgetfulness but she didn't seem to mind. Roger
looked at her closely and decided she didn't really mind.
She knew Sandy.

5

Sandy flunked out of college all right. He disappeared
completely from Roger's days and nights. Roger wrote
one or two letters to which there was no answer. He
heard that Sandy was abroad, living a life of open shame
on the Bosphorus, or he had become a bull-fighter,
or again that he was a well-known young bootlegger in
southern Vermont. When Roger came back to college in
the fall he ran across Corey Lawson, but even Sandy's
friends didn't know where he was. Roger missed him a
little, but less than he had expected. Only when he
thought definitely of things they had done together,
specific things, did he regret his not being there, or
some nights when he wanted to get something to eat
before going to bed and there didn't seem to be anybody else around.

Roger had been studying history; all about the De-
fenestration of Prague. He had done his best to become
interested in the event. He tried to visualize the event
as circumstance, the robes of the defenestrated falling
about and over their heads, on the cobblestones below
the tall mullioned windows. They tried to pick themselves up and heard shouting from above, inside the hall.
The reconstruction failed, only the names Defenestra-

tion — now am I unwindowed, and "Prague" remained in the sieve of his mind. He slapped shut the history and stretched himself. He reached for his hat and went to look for something to eat. He walked up the dark alley to Arthur's and stumbled down the dingy flight of concrete steps. At the end of the cellar were silvered coffee tanks, behind, the kitchen smell of burning grease. He got a bottle of milk and a hamburg sandwich and drummed idly on the glass shelf-top. Underneath were limp pieces of custard pie and baked apples. It was midnight but he didn't feel particularly tired. He sat down on a built-in bench to eat. Other boys came in and ordered food. Fragments of their conversation, dances, crew race filtered over. Presently a body at his side nudged him as if he wanted to sit down. Roger shoved over without looking up.

"You will say: I recognize the name, but the face, sir, is not entirely familiar." Roger found Sandy Pinckney beside him, already intent on his food.

"I recognize the face," said Roger, "I forget the name."

"Alexander Gordon Pinckney; — Pinckney, Hewes & Otis; — India Wharf . . . ; in reply to yours of the last ult. would say."

"Sandy," said Roger, "where did you come from?"

"Out of the everywhere," he nodded significantly. "Dahin."

Roger felt curiously inadequate. It was just as if Sandy had never gone away. He supposed he should make a fuss about his coming back. He only said, "How long are you here for?"

"That, sir," said Sandy, "all depends on your good offices."

"What?" said Roger, "Why me?"

"A friend — any friend — You know — freund-schaft."

"Have you been in Germany? " asked Roger.

"Yes, indeed," said Sandy. "Kennst du das land? "

"But seriously why are you here? "

"Seriously I am here. Seriously. I am in trouble, boy. Grave straits."

"Yes? What's the matter," smiled Roger, "got to marry the girl? "

"What do you mean? " asked Sandy.

"Cradle-snatching. You know — big shotguns. Mar-riage."

"Perhaps," said Sandy.

"No kidding." Roger set down his empty milk glass.

"Sir," said Sandy, "all unthinking, you've struck it."

"Struck what? "

"I may get married tomorrow."

"What the hell — " Roger looked at him — "To whom? "

"Do you remember little black trou? " Roger nodded. "She's elected."

Roger was visibly impressed.

"Are you in love with her? " One asks these questions.

"No," said Sandy. "I like her very much. I got her in an awful jam. She is in an awful jam."

"What do you mean? " asked Roger. "Have you got to marry her? "

"Oh, not at all. I haven't seen her — since — Oh, almost since you have. Six months. She didn't even write to me. Betty did."

"Does she want to marry you? "

"Yes," said Sandy, simply, "she has succumbed to the Gordon charm."

"Well, what are you going to do? "

" I'm asking," said Sandy. He really was asking too.
He had no idea what to do. He looked at Roger again
to let him know he wasn't fooling.

" I was to have become a father. Picture a young lad
in kilts. The image of his bonny da'. No longer now."

" Where is she? "

" At the moment she is at a Dr. Riley's Private Home
in Harlem — I ought to go down, I suppose."

" Why are you here? "

" Oh, I came back to see about getting back into college again. I'd be a dropped sophmore on probation."

" Have you got to go to New York? "

" No, I've not got to go. She doesn't know where I am.
Except she's sick as hell and hasn't got any money."

" You'd better go," said Roger.

" I sent Betty my allowance for two months. Not
much — but it'll do — " Sandy looked at Roger. " You
think I ought to go — do you? "

" Why of course I do." Roger was almost sure.

" Yes. I guess I'd better. I'll go down and get married."

" You don't have to get married," said Roger, " necessarily."

" Then why go down — at all? "

" Why — just to have her know you're there."

" But if I don't stay. If I don't marry her. What good
will it do? "

" I don't know," said Roger, " I suppose it would
help her now."

" She's all right now," said Sandy, " or anyway I
can't do her any good."

" Then you're not going? "

" I don't know," said Sandy, " I'm asking you? Would
you go? "

" I don't know, I can't tell."

" Well, try and think. You concentrate so well — you think. It's not very hard. Would you go or would you not? "

" But," said Roger, wisely, " it's not quite as simple as that."

" I found that out."

Wisely? Roger said, " Gee, Sandy, I wouldn't go. What good would it do? "

" A second ago you said I should — what harm would it do? "

" You'd get her all excited about your coming down. Then you'd feel you'd have to marry her."

" You're not much of a help," said Sandy. " I thought I could count on you." He turned to the counter and ordered another bottle of milk.

Roger was at a complete loss. He couldn't think of anything to say, to tell, or advise. No suggestions. He tried to imagine himself as Sandy and failed. He tried to project himself out of his own personality, to be like Sandy, to look and talk like Sandy. He could do everything but feel like Sandy, and that was all that would be of any help. Sandy was looking at him.

" But, Sandy," Roger stalled for time, " would you like to marry her? "

" You know how it is," said Sandy. " I told you all about it. You see what it is. It's just do I go down or not."

" Flip for it," said Roger weakly.

" I have — four or five times."

" Flip again," losing ground.

" No," said Sandy, " you tell me."

" But, Christ, boy, I can't — how can I? "

" I'll do anything you say. Just say it — Yes or no? "

Roger couldn't open his mouth. He suddenly felt cold, unable to feel any pity, any affection for Sandy. He wanted to very much. His whole mind was concentrated on breaking through to the place where he could feel for him, for only then could he feel competent to advise. His strain only packed the forces tighter. He felt nothing. Sandy relaxed on the bench.

" Did I ever tell you," he said, " that the goddamned fit I threw at club last spring, was a real epileptic fit, epilepsy? "

" Why, no," said Roger, striving to shift his mind to react suitably to this new shock.

" We Pinckneys, sir, have been old epileptics for generations."

6

Sandy Pinckney didn't go down to New York — and Marjory died as everyone had feared. The next fall Sandy was reinstated in the college and stopped drinking and really worked as hard as he possibly could. He got passing grades at least. Every so often he would go off in a terrific drunk, but he decided this was really a good thing since he always worked the harder as soon as he recuperated. He saw little of Roger. They were perfectly friendly whenever they chanced to meet, but Roger had discovered a whole gang of new friends who were wholly uncongenial to Sandy, and he really preferred their company in the long run. But towards spring Roger would get him, maybe once every two or three weeks, and they would go for rides in the woods, or shoot at sandpipers at a nearby beach with Sandy's revolver or go to the movies together. They were still

good friends, but no longer essential to each other.
Sandy never once spoke of Marjory and Roger supposed
he was appeasing his bad conscience by strenuous forgetfulness. He surely looked a lot better now that he
wasn't drinking so much. But the odd, half-detached,
simple, ironic humor persisted, coupled with the curious
incapacity for action, the threads of inertia that had
infected every vein in his body, working with hardly
any interruption, he scarcely accomplished more now
than formerly.

Towards the middle of May Roger suggested to
Sandy that they have a party again. There was to be
a crew race one Saturday afternoon. They'd get a hold
of Corey Lawson and Peet Sanford and some girls.
They'd go to the races, come back to the room for
cocktails and go to a show. It was a fine idea. Sandy
agreed and sir, he could stand a little wholesome relaxation. Roger got a hold of a very nice girl whom he'd
met at some amateur theatricals. Her name was Grace
Pierce and she had come out the year before. She was
tall and lithe, but not too athletic, although her tennis
was excellent. She really liked games, football, the boat-
races as spectacles and she never made any pointless
conversation about the boys she knew, or had met on
the teams. Sandy brought Florence Creighton, a cousin
of Peet Sanford's, and the other two had perfectly
pleasant girls whose names Roger never got. They all
had lunch at the club and motored over to the start of
the races — a wide green area, an embankment running
along the riverway. Sandy was extremely gay and happy.
At the slightest request he would burst into song,
" From this valley they say you are going. We shall miss
your sweet face, your bright smile," or the song from
Patience, " Silvered now the raven hair." Sandy knew

hundreds of Gilbert and Sullivan, but perhaps his best
song was Beneath the Barren Rafters. He visualized
himself so completely as the Colonel Gordon who had
been in Karachi during the mutiny, a kind of cross
between Hamlet and Hotspur in kilts. They leaned over
the rails, the girls in light spring frocks blowing on
to the air above the water, watching the shells line up.
All the boys had put on their white flannels for the first
time that year. When the shells were well off, the idea
was to get in their cars and follow them down the embankment. It wasn't a very big race so the traffic would
be slight. Sandy was extremely gallant and kept asking
the girls if there was anything their little hearts
desired.

Roger had petitioned the proctor of his hall if he
could have girls in his room for tea and it was O. K.
They brought down a lot of rum and orange juice and
had the cocktails on ice in the bathtub. The girls sat
around the room smoking and talking quietly. The late
afternoon light of spring came in through the open windows and no one troubled to put on the lights. Peet and
Corey passed around the drinks and sat on the arm of
their girls' chairs. Sandy absently stroked Florence
Crieghton's hair, standing behind her. She leaned back
her head and smiled up at him. Roger and Grace looked
out the window at a sky which was slowly assuming its
sunset glory, the illicit glory, they were sorry to admit
to each other, of a calendar cover. But why not calendar
cover, thought Roger. Grace said she loved sunsets, but
she really must wash her hands and face. Roger showed
her where and came back to do a little cleaning up of
empty glasses. Florence Creighton and the two other
girls were looking at the books in the cases and the
pictures on the walls. One of the boys left to get some

more liquor. Sandy was sitting at Roger's desk fooling
with a revolver which he'd taken out of the middle
drawer.

" That's where I parked my gat," he said to Roger.

" You left it here last week," said Roger, " but it's
not customary for gentlemen to ransack their friends
drawers." He smiled.

" I've got the jitters," said Sandy. " I was just nervous.
I pulled it open, you know, just for fun."

" Well, then," said Roger, " see that it doesn't happen again."

" Yes, sir," said Sandy, shoving the gun on to the
back of the desk. He went over to join the girls who
kept pulling books out of the shelves and not putting
them back.

" Ladies," said Sandy, " we always replace the divots."
He stooped to fit in a book. Roger went over to the
desk and picked up the revolver. He twirled the barrel
and uncocked it. He took all the bullets out of it and
piled them up in a heap. No use taking any chances.
He looked around for some more empty glasses. The
girls insisted that they would clean up. Grace came in
with wet fingers and asked for a towel. The girls went
out to wash the glasses up and Roger went off to find a
face towel. Peet Sanford slumped down in a chair in
the study. It was getting darker outside and they'd soon
be thinking about supper.

Suddenly they were startled by a loud report. Sanford
sat up straight in his chair. One of the girls dropped a
cocktail glass into the washbasin. It broke. Roger walked
into the study. Sandy was smiling and lay the pistol
down.

" What the hell did you do? " asked Roger quickly.

" Nothing at all," said Sandy. " Did I scare you? "

"Well," said Roger, "it's no joke fooling around with these damn guns."

Sandy smiled sheepishly and clenched his fist slowly. Then he pressed his right hand on the desk. He looked at Roger.

"God, you're funny looking." Sandy looked up at Roger and snickered.

"You're not looking so damn good yourself." Roger was irritated.

"Count on me," said Sandy. He fell on the desk.

Peet Sanford jumped up and rushed over to Roger.

"We'd better get these girls out of here quick. Take my car. I'll get a doctor." He dashed out of the room slamming the door. The door slam made Sandy raise his head. The girls came into the room.

"Sandy was fooling with the gun," said Roger. "It went off by mistake." He cursed himself for not having thrown the bullets away but after he'd so carefully taken them out he'd merely left them in a heap on the desk top.

"We'd better go. . . . I mean if he's all right." Grace looked pale.

"Yes, you'd better go. I'll take you," said Roger. They looked frightened. There was Sandy on the desk.

"Will he be all right?" said Florence. "He will be?"

"Of course," said Roger. "He's not hurt. Come on." Roger bent over Sandy. He was afraid to look to see where he was shot. He said, "Are you all right?"

"Sure," said Sandy in a low voice, "take these girls home."

"We can go home by ourselves," said one of them whose name Roger never knew.

"No," said Sandy into Roger's bent over ear. "You take them."

" I'll take you," said Roger. " He says to."

The girls looked at one another. Then they looked
for their coats, their pocketbooks. They seemed to move
like people in a slow motion film. Only their white
hands fluttered. Hurry, said Roger, ever so slowly to
himself — slowly.

" Sandy," said Roger, " are you really all right? Tell
me if you're not."

" Sir, a Gordon . . ."

Roger said, " Don't kid — tell me."

" I'm O. K." Sandy remained immobile. His voice
was low but steady.

" I guess I'd really better take you." Roger appealed
to the girls. The four of them seemed to infect each
other with a slow speechless fright. This fright was what
finally decided Roger to move. They wouldn't seem to
budge unless Roger made them. Only Grace looked at
Sandy.

" I'll be right back," said Roger. " Peet will be right
back, too."

The girls left, passing before Roger, without a glance
back. The room was considerably darker. The wind
slightly ruffled the curtains. Outside like a water-color,
the calendar sky. Roger shut the door softly and went
to drive the girls home. It was a wonderful dusk. The
girls didn't speak at all. Roger bolstered up their fears
as best he could. It helped himself to do so. Besides
Sandy was a goddamned fool and he hoped this at least
would teach him a lesson. He wished he hadn't driven
the girls home.

Roger left the girls and promised he would phone
them at once. He drove back to college as fast as he
dared, but he found that he could not go very fast since
something made him take the most complete cautionary

measures. He scarcely dared to pass another car on the broad roadway. He suddenly felt terribly hungry. He decided he was quite sure Sandy was all right. When he got back to the room Peet Sanford and Corey Lawson were there. Corey had brought back a jug of pure alcohol. It stood on the middle of the table. They had taken Sandy's shirt off and laid him on the couch. Roger squinted his eyes but he saw no wound. No one spoke when he came in. He couldn't see Sandy's face. He felt wild and more than drunk, crazy, eager to help — but he couldn't move. Fright and impotence like ghosts whispered before his eyes the scene of the initiation. He could feel himself scratching the back of his head.

But Sandy Pinckney was not dead. The doctor turned him over and touched his head with his fingers and Roger realized he wasn't dead. That somehow absolved him from fear. He no longer dreaded to see the wound. When Sandy was lying on his back, straight out, Roger looked over. There was no wound at all anywhere. Then Roger thought he had shot himself in his belly. His pants were still on. The doctor, however, stood up and put the boy's shirt over the exposed part of his body. He turned and faced the boys. " Heart failure," he said, " the bullet grazed the side of his ear. His ear drum's broken." He looked at the thin red smear on his finger. " The bullet never touched him."

" Gee," said Corey Lawson, " wasn't that lucky."

7

Sandy left college for good. Roger had no idea where he was, where he could be reached. He did actually write him once but the letter came back and Roger

couldn't tell why as he had sent it to a bank who could
forward it. Sandy's friends seemed to have less idea or
interest in his surroundings than Roger. " Oh, Sandy,"
thought Roger, " In a year's time — I'll never know I
knew him."

The college year ended and Roger had to move all
his belongings from his old dormitory rooms to his next
year's lodgings in the Yard. He left a few boxes of
books and a couch with his old janitor and said he'd
call for them when he came back from vacation. He
tipped the janitor and felt vaguely that it was a weak,
flat, lousy ending for a year.

Sometime in the late summer he called back again
for his books. The town was deserted. The town boys
lounged on the street corners and pretended they belonged to the Harvard Summer School. The janitor
was not there but his wife made Roger comfortable
in their parlor, smelling of rubber plants and restricted cooking. Roger sat uneasily in a wicker arm
chair, fumbling absently at a dusty pile of old magazines while she went off to see what could be done
about the boxes he had left. Suddenly she turned
back.

" Oh, Mr. Baum," she had almost forgotten it —
" There's a letter here for you — "

" A letter? " asked Roger — a bill, an advertise-
ment —

" I thought you'd be coming back or I'd have sent it
to you." She handed him a thin envelope. It was square
and the blue stamp was surcharged " Maroc."

" I'll go look for your books " she said.

" Oh, thanks," said Roger tearing at the envelope.
Hotel de l'Univers et de France he read.

Meknes

Dear Roger

    *I've gotten as far as Morocco and it's all very fine.
Aside from a kind of dysentry affecting such leather
linings as my own I feel O.K. The weather is a good
deal like football weather, believe it or not. The houses
are not made of wood but the streets are as wide and
shady, palms not elms, as Brattle Street. Did you get
through your exams? How are Lawson and Sanford?
From here my plans are uncertain. Some caravan talk
of crossing the Sahara. Or maybe I don't like Africa.
Do I like Africa — you tell me — No. — Well . . .
Maybe we'll go on to Spain — or I've never been to
Egypt — Where else haven't I been? You tell me. If you
want to write me you'll have a hell of a time finding me.
I just can't tell — maybe you can. Yours — how do I
sign myself —*

                Alexander Gordon Pinckney.

    The janitor's wife came back. She looked sheepishly
at Roger, holding the blue letter vaguely in his hand.

    "I'm sorry about that letter," she really looked con-
fused. " I guess I should have forwarded it anyway."

    "Never mind," said Roger. "It doesn't make any
difference." Before he left he made sure, and gave her
his new forwarding address.

Flesh was Fair

. . . Their thrilling dances then gave me a sharp pang of yearning to get a closer view of things immeasurable and unattainable, such as no poem of Heine's, no prose of Poe's, no fever dream has ever given me, and, since, I have had the same sensation, at once sub-conscious and acute, which I attribute to the silent and nebulous precision of all they do.

1929

1

Roger had been in London again for almost a week. He'd not been here for two years and his excitement was enormous. The amazing change of atmosphere between his own land and England seemed like a veil between himself and whatever he saw. Everything seemed " so English," " so English " not insomuch as it was not American, but mainly in the scale, the rhythm and the breadth of happenings whether in the streets or in the square. He had forgotten it was so much like itself. The people he knew of course, were human beings, but somehow the buildings, the galleries, their physical geography had a curious quintessential quality that had reference only to the defining exterior shell of each one. Roger was standing in front of a tobacconist's shop on Haymarket. He was looking into the eighteenth century shop front on a pile of curious smokeables, cheroots, Australian segars and snuff. He thought what a pretty affectation it would be to use snuff again. He considered going inside to get a package.

" Well, if it isn't Roger Baum," girl's voice behind him.

He turned to find Christine Forrester, whom he knew quite well in America. She had been the best friend of another friend of his. She was tall with curly, blonde hair, a delightful frank open sweet face, boyish perhaps, but rather more the face of an adolescent girl on the body of a perfectly mature woman.

"Christine!" cried Roger; he was really delighted, "I'd no idea you were here!"

"Well," she said, "here I am for a fortnight."

"What are you doing?" said Roger. "Are you very busy?"

"Busy? Busy? Good lord, no. I never have anything to do."

"Well, then have lunch with me."

"I can't," she laughed, "as it happens I'm tied up for lunch."

"Well, tea then," said Roger. He decided she was one of the few people from home he was really glad to be with abroad.

"I've got to go into the country for the week-end at four."

"But I thought you weren't busy." Roger began to feel he was too pressing.

"It doesn't sound like it, does it?" she said quickly. "But look, next week."

"All right," said Roger, "Tuesday night; I'll take you to the ballet."

"The ballet," echoed Christine dubiously, "is that opera?"

"No, it has nothing to do with opera. Haven't you been to the ballet?"

"Never heard of it. Is it nice?"

"Nice," said Roger. "It's the most marvelous thing in the world."

"Then I am very excited," Christine remarked, "and I will see you Tuesday night." She dismissed him with her address and he was left with a curious equivocal feeling, that perhaps she had not really meant to get tied up with him, that she was putting him

off, that — Oh, come, said Roger to himself — you're
always getting up these little futilities to tease yourself
with.

2

He called for her on Tuesday night a little early. He
wore a white tie and the lowest button of his stiff shirt
kept sticking out above his vest and catching on the rim.
He couldn't seem to fix it. She had just finished dressing. She looked well in a long white dress with a large
white satin collar all across her breast, high and somehow in a ridiculous sense, he felt, modest. She saw him
and jumped up.

" My, how nice you look," she said, " all white and
pink."

" This damn vest won't stay put," he smiled.

" What's the matter, too small? " Her genuine interest in detail.

" No, you see this button here keeps sticking." He
showed her.

" Well, let's have a look at it." He presented his
belly.

" I see what it needs," she said. " Take your coat off."

He looked at her a moment, smiled and peeled off
his coat.

" Now your vest." He stood before her in his shirtsleeves.

" I feel, Miss Forrester," he said with gallantry, " this
is not a becoming garb for a lady to see a gentleman in."

She fiddled with his vest and took up a scissors. " It's
quite all right," she laughed. " It would be different if
it were I."

" But why? " said Roger, " except that I wouldn't
know what to do."

"I mean it's all very well for you to gape there in your shirtsleeves."

"Well, it would be all very well if you gaped there in your chemise."

"It would not," she said sharply.

"Of course it would," said Roger, "don't be silly."

"Of course it would not, and it isn't silly." Roger was surprised to feel that she meant what she said. She handed him the vest. It was all right now, and he thanked her and slowly put on his coat again.

At dinner the conversation was mainly about friends at home. Suddenly she asked, "What shall we do after dinner?"

"Why," said Roger, "I'm taking you to the ballet."

"The ballet, I forgot all about it. Will that be fun?"

"Why it's the most wonderful thing you've ever seen," said Roger.

"Well, tell me about it. Where have I been that I haven't heard?"

"The ballet," said Roger. "The Russian Ballet. You've heard of Nijinsky."

"Oh yes," said Christine. "Of course; are we going to see him?"

"No," said Roger, "we're not. He started it though. The ballet that was before the war."

"Well now what about Nijinsky," said Christine fiddling with her celery.

"He lost his mind," said Roger. "He danced too hard."

"How horrible," said Christine. "Is dancing such hard work?"

"You'll see," said Roger. "But there are lots of new dancers."

"Well, who puts this all on?" she asked. Roger was

not going to allow her to take the attitude of the indulgent pupil. He was determined to interest her.

" A Russian," said Roger, " called Diaghilev."

" Is he nice? " asked Christine.

" Nice," said Roger. " Nice. I don't know him. I wish I did. Some people call him the wickedest man in Europe."

" Well what on earth do you want to know him for? " went on Christine.

" Because, don't you see, he had the imagination to put the ballet across. You wait and see — "

" I'm sorry to be so stupid," she said. " I'm really interested."

" Of course," said Roger, " Only it's quite simple. He's taken all the best painters and musicians and dancers. The very best and put them all together and it makes the most perfect thing an artist can do."

" Better than painting a picture or writing a poem or discovering the cure for cancer," asked Christine. Roger could see she was trying.

" I don't know about the cure for cancer," he answered. " It's surely better than painting most pictures or writing most poems. But you wait."

Covent Garden was pretty well filled when they found their seats. To Roger it seemed an audience set apart from all other audiences in the world. They had not come to be merely surprised by novelty. In fact most of them had seen the evening's productions time and again. Their quiet anticipation, the general familiarity in their expectancy somehow turned them into a community, a society, not drawn here by the arbitrary circumstance of chance or hearsay, but by a complete comprehension and love for a traditional form.

" Who is that man with a beard? " asked Christine.

" That is the Poet Laureate," said Roger.

" Who is that tall woman with the gold turban," asked Christine.

" Where? " Roger craned his neck.

" Right ahead, but to the left — "

" Oh I see," said Roger. " I don't know who she is."

" Who are those Indian women? " asked Christine. " It must hurt to wear jewels in your nose. Are they princesses? "

" I guess they must be," said Roger. " There is my cousin."

" Which one," asked Christine. Roger pointed. " Oh. What does he do? "

" He is Mason Browne," said Roger. " He is a sculptor."

" Well," said Christine. " I'm really glad I came."

And the lights dimmed out and the conductor got into his stand and there was a shuffle of applause, taps on his music stand and the overture started.

The curtains parted. There was an orange sky, smoky and russet towards the top. There was a rounded tent of skins and a subdued and general movement of circling women in red baggy trousers and chiffon veils. They raised their arms and the veils fluttered and dipped like trains, small dusky clouds. The women formed into lines and commenced a strongly cadenced dance with a knee-bent gesture to mark the phrase ends. Roger had seen Prince Igor so often that he knew it by heart and could afford to watch Christine's face; the low orange light from the footlights faintly outlined the girl's profile so that it seemed half-glowing from within, and almost beatifically amused. She looked like a very happy child.

On the stage the Tartars hopped and leaped and

twirled like tops. They were fierce and passionate and
their mongolian savagery was inherent in the curves of
their painted moustaches, their eyelids and their legs
kick out and replace, their hands thrust forward and
swept back in the most perfect precision and gracious
order. The figures revolved round and round, the
women in their veils swaying and passing the stamping
men, then stooping to let the archers form a ring around
them. Sometimes there was a pause in the music and the
dancers paused, but the audience never rested for a
second, for the gaps in the action were as rich in texture,
in feeling as the highest leaps or most sinuous glides —
and always the beat, the breathless easy precision, the
rightness as if every possibility of visual and active
development had been exhausted. The mould filled
perfectly with the most molten and yet immutable
bronze.

The archers leaped high and pulled their bows and
all the thousand invisible arrows flew into the sunset of
the Tartar plain. The women ranged on the edges of
the encampment shifted their trousered legs and swayed
softly in perfect counterpoint to the strenuous vaultings
of the cone-capped hunters, and suddenly the ballet
gathered itself into a maelstrom, and all of them —
hunters, archers, concubines and warriors swirled about
the stage, opposing the rhythm of each group as strenu-
ously as in a physical combat and the curtain fell on a
mounting fort of men, their bows taut to the sky, mounting up in a shifting din of gongs and clangor and
bronze fire.

And applause, and applause and the chief dancers
came out in front of the curtain and bowed and the
buzz of resumed remarks filled the dome of the theatre.

Roger turned his head expectantly to Christine.

"Oh, but wonderful," she said. "It's too marvelous. You were quite right."

"Wasn't I?" Roger was pleased that she was so excited. "Isn't it extraordinary? Why, there's nothing else in the world, you know."

"But tell me about it," she begged. "Tell me all about it. Who is this Russian, are the dances his?"

"Diaghilev?" asked Roger. She nodded. "Why I don't know much about him. Of course he has a curious reputation."

"So you said." She looked at him. "What sort of a reputation?"

"Well, he never has any money and yet from year to year he goes on and gives the ballet and commissions painters and musicians and they seem to work for him."

"Well, that seems very shrewd," said Christine. "Don't they ever get paid?"

"Why, sometimes they do I guess, but not very much. But often if you have a ballet done by Diaghilev it makes your name."

"Well, I think that's fine," said Christine, "what's the matter with that?"

"Nothing," said Roger. "He's got very strong personal connections with everybody that works for him. I mean they work well because they like him."

"I see," she said, "one of those men who devours people's talent."

"Not at all," said Roger, "he makes them use it in the best way. Or at least he can get them to work better for him than for anyone else."

"Just because they like him," asked Christine.

"I guess that's as good reason as any," said Roger. "Sometimes they happen to be used up. They go out like a light. But it was marvelous while it lasted."

" And he has power to destroy people? " asked Christine.

" More than that. He creates them." Roger was determined to overcome her resistance. He could see she was unconvinced, holding off.

" What difference in the long run," he continued, " whether or not Nijinsky went mad from dancing or a religious mania? "

" I think it makes a great deal of difference," she said.

" Of course — to him — and it must have been terrible for Diaghilev. But all of his marvelous force and spirit that makes him a myth still; it was all concentrated and it burned ten times as bright as anyone we see dance tonight."

" There's no excuse to make people go out of their heads," said Christine. " I see what you mean. He just preys off other people — like a parasite, only it's their talent — and that's so much worse."

" No," said Roger. " He really loves them." He wasn't going to argue much longer.

" Loves them," echoed Christine, " well that makes it all the worse." But fortunately the lights turned down again and the music started.

The curtain rose on an enormous water-color background, a landscape with a cylindrical tower. Vaguely, the sea, a dark cloudy sky. It had been painted very freely so that one was conscious all the time of the great richness in the breadth of the brushstrokes. All the modulation of water in paint, fusing into layers of transparent color, shining through one another and overlaid with heavy outlines in black had been preserved from the small sketch in transference on to the gigantic canvas backdrop. It was Rouault's set for the Prodigal Son.

And it was the Bible story they gravely danced. In
the gravity of the free action of the dancers the parable
took on the overtones almost of an ecclesiastical panto-
mime. It was not Oriental, that is from the Muscovite
iconography, not Byzantine. Rather in the painted velvet tunics on the dancers, with the anatomy boldly described in heavy brushstrokes, under the breasts, over
the buttocks — it seemed as if the characters stepped
from a stained glass window — only their articulation
was never stiff. The gestures flowed smoothly and richly
into one another like honey into a jar. The velvet whites
and black in combination, bottle-green and glass-blue
clothed the Prodigal Son and his young friends. He
bade his father farewell, he knelt to receive his father's
blessing, his great yellow straw hat hung on his back.
His two black-haired sisters in purple and green with
wide sweeping gestures of their arms and legs begged
him to stay. His temptress floated in on her extended
toe points with one outstretched arm and a half-averted
head. Her crimson cape floated behind across the whole
length of the stage. His companions became a boat to
take him to further excesses. The temptress leant forward and formed the ship's figurehead and the great red
cape flew back and became the ship's velvet sail, and
so on through a hundred adventures described in the
most perfect geometry of gesture, a kind of Hebraic
recital of a continuous lyric narrative. The men had
shaven heads and a curious inhuman, almost eunuch
quality clung to them; some overtones of the Thebiad.
The Prodigal Son rushed up on the peak of a platform
that his companions held and half knelt with one arm
flung out, the other clutching at his throat. From then
his descent into poverty, his degradation, his return.

The father stood at his house door with his two daughters, awaiting but not expecting the son's return. The
boy crawls in, in the dust, on his hands and knees and
gradually gains the gate of his old home. His back is
to the audience, his arms are raised, his head falls back,
and with a gesture of exquisite tenderness the bearded
father places his own arms under his son and draws
him up to the support of his own body and his great
cloak falls to cover both of them.

And there was applause, again and again the dancers
tiptoed out and bowed, maintaining even in their ac-
ceptance of the appreciation of the audience, of flowers
and wreaths, a precision and formality in the expression
of their gratitude.

" Why it was like Parsifal," said Christine, " only
much shorter."

" Shall we go out into the lobby? " said Roger, and
put his folded coat under his chair. He stepped out into
the aisle and Christine followed to precede him into
the hall.

" Nevertheless," she said, " I think there's something
decadent about it."

" About the Prodigal Son? " said Roger. She nodded.
" That's not decadence, that's not what you mean by
decadence — that's Jewish. It's cruel perhaps — relent-
less."

" No," said Christine. " I mean it's horrid, now I
think of it. All those shaved heads on those men
dancers."

" But you enjoyed it? " asked Roger.

" Oh, to be sure! " said Christine. " I think it's delightful." They walked into the great hall filled with
all sorts of groups of people all of whom seemed to

know each other intimately. A great deal of gushing
and too-polite talk in too-loud voices. Roger and Christine stood by a pillar and watched the people.

" There is your sculptor friend," said Christine.

" Where? " asked Roger. He looked for Mason
Browne.

" I wonder who's that he's with," said Christine.

" I don't see him," said Roger.

" Over there with that greasy looking man."

Roger looked. Mason was talking to a largish man
with a broad rather loose handsome face. He was to be
sure inclined to stoutness. His brow was high and his
eyes roved around, away from his interlocutor in an
easy, familiar distinction. His full mouth was fringed
with a longish, very soft, or so it seemed, black moustache. Roger suddenly caught Mason's eye, who nodded,
as if to say, " Later."

" Isn't that man repulsive looking? " said Christine.

" Mason's friend? " asked Roger. " Oh, I don't think
he's so bad."

" But horrible — that mouth." Christine wrinkled up
her young face.

Presently Mason came up and Roger introduced him
to Christine Forrester. Mason was breathless. He gripped
Roger's arm impulsively. " Oh," he said, " it's really too
exciting. I've just been talking to Diaghilev. Come —
you must meet him."

" So that's Diaghilev," said Christine. " I might have
known it."

" He's the most amusing man in the world," said
Mason, " come over and I'll introduce you."

" Not me," said Christine, and looked at Roger.

" Oh, come on," said Roger.

" No, sir," said Christine, " not me."

"Come on, do come," pursued Mason. "Now you'd like him very much."

"I've nothing to say to him," said Christine.

"But Christine, really he's wonderful," said Roger.

"Don't be frightened. He'll do the talking," said Mason.

"No, really," said Christine. "I'd rather not meet him." A silence. Then she went on as if suddenly remembering. "But Roger, you go ahead and meet him if you want. I'd just as leave stay here."

Roger looked at Mason appealingly.

"Really, Roger — go ahead now. I'll wait here."

"No," said Roger, "of course not. It's all right. I mean —"

"Of course," said Mason, "of course. Well some other time then — I only thought — I mean he's very good fun. I must go."

"Mason," Roger began. He was going to say — You see how it is. But he knew Mason could see perfectly well.

"Goodbye, Mr. Browne," said Christine helpfully, to relieve the tension.

"Oh, goodbye, so nice to have seen you. Call me up, Roger . . . er . . . goodbye."

He smiled, went off and was lost in the crowd. A few moments later Roger could see him with Diaghilev. And though he could not hear the laugh that must have greeted Mason's return, on account of the noise in the room, he saw it light up all the faces that were talking around the great man.

"I suppose you think I'm just silly," said Christine.

"No," said Roger, "only why couldn't you meet Diaghilev?"

" I hope you don't think I stopped you from meeting him."

" Of course not — but why wouldn't you? "

" I may be old-fashioned," said Christine, " but there are some things — "

Roger knew what was coming and it was too much for him. He spluttered incoherently trying to formulate a sufficient anathema.

" Well," he said. " Well, er — I suppose you know you've lost a chance to meet one of the greatest — the greatest men in our century." He heard himself sounding ridiculous, but he was too irritated to care.

" What good would it have done, if I had met him? " asked Christine.

3

Two months later Roger was in Venice. He had never before been there and it seemed to him curiously unreal. It was almost as if Venice existed purely as a justification for all the pictures and photographs he had all his life seen of it; that it was merely a neat approximation of all these pictures, photographs and talk and in itself it had little real existence. All of its color for example seemed to have been burned or washed out of it. The long façade of the Library of St. Mark's seemed to have the most one-dimensional painted-in-perspective look. He looked about and saw a crowd collecting under the great red flagpoles. He sauntered over and was amused to find a boy of about his own age in Dutch costume and with wooden sandals leading a large horse. The crowd of Venetians were very excited. This must be an advertising stunt thought Roger. I wonder if any of these people have ever seen a live horse before.

Don't be silly, he went on with his interior soliloquy, Venice after all is not the end of the world. But, nevertheless, the people were interested, and as the horse became more and more impatient and more and more like a horse. The pigeons swooped down in a terrifying cloud in appreciation of an unsuspected and novel bounty. Roger looked into the face of a nearby person and laughed. The person happened to be a girl and the girl happened to be Christine Forrester.

" Picture finding you here," she said — very pleased to see him.

" Why," Roger was at a partial loss — " I haven't seen you for a long time."

" Not since that night at the Ballet," she laughed.

" I left London soon after," said Roger. " I've been all over the continent."

" Picture horses in Venice," said Christine, " isn't it awful."

" Awful? " said Roger. " I think it's awfully funny."

" Funny," Christine was very sure of herself. " Why the next thing they'll be having here are automobiles. I, for one," she continued, " like old things."

" Well," laughed Roger, " the horse is hardly a modern invention."

" I don't think it's a bit funny," said Christine, " and all these pigeons."

" How long are you staying? " said Roger.

" Oh, I've just come."

" Are you alone? " Roger felt she was, very alone.

" Yes, but I don't mind it a bit." Christine was so sweet looking. Her face and her merriment and her easy humor.

" Oh, come on. We'll go for a walk," said Roger.

" But where to? " asked Christine definitely.

" Let's just walk." Roger paused. " Well if you want
an objective, I've got one. I want to find a Greek church
here."

" A Greek church? " asked Christine. " Greeks in
Venice? When? "

" El Greco, the painter, you know. He lived here."

" I thought he was a Greek," said Christine and
changed her step so that she would be keeping proper
pace with him.

They walked down an alley behind St. Mark's into
passages and over bridges and canals. It was all very picturesque and every corner, every turn of path had its
own personal smell. One could plot a map of Venice,
thought Roger, by the smell.

" Do you know where you're going? " asked Christine.

" Vaguely," said Roger. " I have my guide book."

" Because there's no use going out of the way," and
she gingerly pushed aside a baby with a filthy face, so as
not to knock her over.

They finally crossed a bridge and after a quick glance
at the guide book map turned down a paved pathway,
directly next to the canal, that was bordered by a solid
stone balustrade and came into a little courtyard. There
was a gateway with a rounded and broken pediment. In
the center was a stone ball. Roger and Christine passed
through.

" That is the Church of St. George of the Greeks,"
said Roger. He pointed to a palladian front above which
rose a dome with an umbrella cup and bulbous swell,
not unlike the one on St. Mark's.

" St. George-and-the-Dragon St. George? " asked
Christine.

" I guess it must be the same one," said Roger.

Then they noticed a considerable activity in front of

the church. There were men in black uniforms and cocked hats, trimmed with gold braid, walking up and down in front of the area before the church. Roger went over and looked out a stone window pierced in the wall looking onto the canal. Moored there was a large shiny black gondola or barge. From it the beadles were taking wreaths and sheaves of funeral flowers and carried them into the church. Roger looked at Christine and silently followed a woman with a heavy veil into the open portals. Christine followed.

Though it was hot and noon outside, within it was cool and dusky. Great Byzantine paintings of The Last Supper and the Crucifixion seemed to hang from the walls, their gildings tarnished and the gesso cracking. In the center of the floor was a bier guarded by four large wooden gilt candles. The coffin was banked with flowers of all kinds. Roger and Christine stepped to one side of the door, under the shadow of a balcony to watch. There seemed to be a great many people in the church, their silent shadowy forms displacing some part of the sweet scented atmosphere in the half light. The gloom hid every definition but a feeling of pronounced, suppressed grief, and somehow anticipation. Aside from the scuffling of feet the place was silent. As eyes grew used to the lack of light Roger looked around. Everyone was waiting for something to happen. These people, thought Roger, these people, where have I seen them before? These people do not seem to be Italians, not poor Italians. Maybe it is a prince (the wealth of flowers) who has such a funeral — a Greek prince — perhaps. But what were they all waiting for?

" Come along," said Christine, " we'd better get out of here."

" Why? " whispered Roger, " nobody's asked us to."

"I know," she said under her voice, "but this is all private. We have no right . . ."

"We're not hurting anybody," said Roger, enchanted by the feeling of mysterious anticipation.

"Well, I'm going anyway," said Christine, "I don't like to butt in."

She turned and made her way to the door. Roger followed her out into the sunlight. As they were passing under the very arch of the door, a choir of unaccompanied voices commenced the Greek orthodox service for the dead. Roger replaced his hat, squinted his eyes from the hard sunlight and looked at Christine.

"You know," she said, "it's not very nice crashing someone's funeral."

"I suppose not," said Roger. "What shall we do now?"

"Well, don't you want to find El Greco's church?" said Christine.

"But that was El Greco's church," said Roger.

"Oh, was it?" said Christine, surprised. "What a pity you couldn't look around."

4

That night Christine decided she just couldn't stay in Venice another second. It was too constricting. No matter where you walked you always landed upon some little place where there was a canal and it smelled and there weren't any trees. Roger suggested Padua.

"Well, why not go to Padua? That's part of the mainland," he explained.

"Is it very far?" asked Christine.

"It will take us all day, that is if we want to spend any time looking around."

" Is there a lot to see? Pictures and things? "

" Yes," said Roger. " Giotto's — you know."

" Oh, Giotto's," said Christine. " Why I'd really love to go."

The next morning was Saturday and they took the steam launch up to the station and found out they had half an hour to spare. Roger wanted to walk around.

" We'd better sit down and wait," said Christine, " I hate to miss trains."

" Good lord," said Roger, " don't be ridiculous. We have plenty of time to go out for twenty minutes. There are several good places around here to be seen."

" Well, I'd rather wait here," said Christine, " you go on. I'll get a paper."

" All right," said Roger — for once, he thought, I will go ahead. " Here's your ticket, I'll be back in time. Don't worry."

" Oh, I guess I'd better come along," Christine decided. " You never can tell." She followed him down the white station steps. " Where are we going — we'd better hurry."

" There's a wonderful palace around here with a ball-room," said Roger, and tried to orient himself by his guide book to put him in the proper position for finding the Palazzo Labia.

They banged at a large door, ornamented with the grim stencil of Mussolini's frown. They banged the knocker until the door seemed to jar. Just when they were about to turn back to the station, the door swung open and an old woman came out.

" Ask her," said Roger, for he spoke little Italian, " if we can see the grand ballroom." Christine asked. The old woman shook her head and Roger reached in his pocket. " Give her this," said Roger.

They followed through a vaulted stone hall and up
a broad flight of dirty stone steps. Over every door, upon
the distempered walls was the stencil of Mussolini's
frown or a fascist bundle of rods and the axe. There was
a good deal of unlocking of tall varnished doors, with
the paint recently freshened up to simulate a coarse-
grained yellow oak. Electric light bulbs hung naked
from the white plaster ceilings and the wires were led
on the face of the wall in ugly uncompromising lines.
They were taken through a series of chambers into a
courtyard and they came out on a balcony. Hundreds
of pigeons had frosted the old stone walls. The woman
pointed in through some shut windows and turned to go.

" Here it is," said Christine.

" Well," said Roger, " ask her to let us in."

" She won't," said Christine. " She says it belongs to
the government."

Roger pressed his nose to the window. Inside was a
large hall heavily decorated with an architectural treatment. Series of arches, pediments, columns, balconies,
all in a miracle of graceful order and lightness seemed to
exist behind the surface of the walls. Perched on the
pediments were bronzed figures of seated satyrs, allegori-
cal women and cupids. Under the two main arches were
two large scenes from the lives of Caesar and Cleopatra.

" But," cried Christine, " all that stone work is only
painted." She seemed outraged.

" Yes," said Roger. " Tiepolo. Isn't it marvelous? "

Cleopatra in one panel sits back proudly in her chair.
Caesar is at the other end of the table; around them
are their blackamoors and buffoons. On the steps leading
up to the table is a dwarf with a toy terrier. Cleopatra
is a beautiful Venetian lady, one of Veronese's women
with a small head and noble neck. She holds the pearl

that she is about to dissolve into the golden beaker. Everyone in the fresco is vaunting the parody of interest. They are preoccupied, not with the pearl about to be thrust in the wine, but how each exists in space, within their armor and brocades, in relation to each other, the epitome of a formal self-consciousness. Above them on a baroque balcony a band of musicians look down on them. It is all sunny and somehow faded by the sun.

In the other panel Caesar is helping his Venetian princess down from the gangplank; the galley has just arrived from Egypt. High in the background the gilded shell shelters a bronze Neptune on the ship's high prow. With a gesture of delicious courtesy and royal animation Caesar, with the slightest deprecatory gesture, takes her arm in his. Behind them their servants and the fine arched head of a white horse; to one side a little negro in slashed sleeves and ruff, leashes in a sleek greyhound. The dog's legs are bent in a soft resistance against the servant's arms. The moment was of anticipation, something was about to happen.

Christine and Roger were silent. He looked from Christine to the wall and back at Christine.

" Why," said Christine, " you'll probably think me silly — but you know, it reminds me of the ballet."

" The Ballet," said Roger, " that's just what it's like. It's a ballet all by itself — " and for the first time that day he was glad that Chrisitne was along.

Suddenly she said, " Good Lord, we've forgotten all about the train. We'll miss it if we don't hurry back, and I want a paper. Come along."

Roger followed. As he walked down the steps he said to her, " You know it's dreadful the way these things are allowed to go to pieces. That room was just ridden with cracks."

" That's funny," said Christine, " because this is the Fascist headquarters — all these pictures of Mussolini — "

But they did get the train in time. Christine was reading the London Times on the seat opposite Roger. They were passing Mestre. Roger was trying to think of something he could do about the preservation of the Tiepolo frescoes.

Suddenly Christine said, " Look here, Roger, here's something for you." She read, " Death of Serge Diaghilev. We are advised that Serge Diaghilev died at the Lido, August 19th from bloodpoisoning. Services will be held at the Greek church on Friday, August 23rd. Memoir on page 15."

Roger took the paper from her and turned to page 15. He read the long memoir with interest of course and with a curious feeling that he was somehow in the flow and passage of events, that however small a part — he was also nevertheless a particle in the flux of history.

" Does that depress you? " asked Christine.

" Depress me? Why no. I'm sorry of course — I suppose that means the end of the ballet."

" I shouldn't think necessarily," said Christine.

" It will be the end all right," said Roger definitely.

" Is there no one to take his place? " she asked.

" No one I know of," said Roger. " No, I can't think of a soul."

" I don't suppose anybody has the money or time," she said.

" No one has the ideas — the interest," said Roger. " He never had much money."

" You never met him? " said Christine, " did you? "

" No," said Roger, " I never did; almost once, Oh

but . . ." and he broke off and smiled and started reading the memoir over again — the list of activities of
connections — all the great names in continental art,
in letters, in music, that make the first quarter of the
twentieth century most worth remembering.

At Padua they went to the Arena Chapel and saw the
Giottos. Roger was surprised they were so blue.

" Now," said Christine triumphantly in her ridiculous
naive way that was almost lovable, " here's something
you can look at."

" What do you mean? " asked Roger.

" Oh, there's no fuss to these. They stay where they're
put. They're wholesome."

" Wholesome," he echoed, " wholesome? " The Giottos as illustrations to a Presbyterian text?

They took the land route back; the tram that went
along the Brenta. Roger was determined to do as much
as possible that day. He knew there was a lost Tiepolo
ceiling somewhere near Stra and he was determined to
find it. There was a name in his mind that he would ask
someone about, only he couldn't remember it — some
Italian name ending in a ta or a or za — that Tiepolo
decorated the ceilings — only he couldn't remember it.
Christine was beginning to be tired of all this vague
sightseeing. She wanted to get home and lie down, but
as long as Roger was actually on the road he decided
to be firm and persistent. He was going to find his
ceiling.

And though Christine would have very much liked
to have gone back to her hotel room in Venice across
the bay, Roger some miles down the road got down from
the tram, bent on finding the lost Tiepolos. She followed. They went up to a place which was plastered
with more stencils of scowling Mussolinis and looked

for information. A man had a bicycle upside down in the grass beside a road and he was spinning the wheels around, tinkering with it.

" Please ask him," said Roger to Christine, " if he knows of any paintings in this neighborhood — it would probably be in a palace, by Giovanni Battista Tiepolo."

Christine did so in her excellent Italian.

The man with the bicycle shook his head and twirled his wheels for a moment. Then he said, " Ecco," and dashed off to a garage. Presently he came back with someone who seemed to be a mechanic. There was some talk of " Amigi."

" Ecco," said the man, " Giambattista Tiepolo."

" He says that's Giambattista Tiepolo," said Christine.

" It can't be," said Roger, " he's dead." (More conversation.)

" Well, that's his name," said Christine. " He's a chauffeur."

They hired the Tiepolo car and went off looking for Tiepolo frescoes. The new Giambattista was hideously effusive, helpful, informative. He was much interested in art. He had wished to be a painter himself, but the war, sir, and you know how it is and he turned down a bad road. At the end of the road were two large low lying pavilions. Roger recognized them as two wings of a Palladian country house.

" Ask him," he turned to Christine, " when the middle part was burnt down? "

A great deal of information at this point, and gesticulation.

" The middle part was burned before his father was born, he says. He also asks how on earth you knew it was burnt? "

" I've seen plans of such places," said Roger. " I think this might be the place."

They got out of the car and walked through a high arch. In the inside was a floor of earth and some men and girls in shirtsleeves bending over great tubs of water. It was cool in here and one could see the sun shining greenly through vine leaves hanging outside over the broken window frames. It was a laundry and steam from the washing rose up to the roof. The laundresses stood up, bent their backs, wiped their hands on their thick aprons and smiled.

Giambattista Tiepolo explained why they had come, and as he said it Ecco, Roger looked up at the ceiling. There was a huge, undiscovered Tiepolo fresco. It was very exciting. He could hardly see it in the half-light and soon all the men and women were routing about, opening doors and windows and letting in as much light as possible. But he could ultimately see nothing but the fact that the ceiling was in very bad condition, that the steam of the laundry was loosening the plaster from the walls. He told this to Christine, who indignantly transmitted the technical information to Tiepolo — who, in turn told the boss and owner of the place. Many smiles and much Italian conversation.

Then said Christine to Roger, " He says he will sell you the ceiling for about fifty dollars."

" But," cried Roger in amazement, " it would take fifty thousand to take it off the roof. How dreadful! "

" Can't the government do something about it? " said Christine. " Haven't they funds for such things? "

But Roger was pleased that he had found the fresco at all. The scholar's, the adventurer's and the discoverer's pride. He was quite ready to go back to Venice content, tip Tiepolo well and even admit Christine was fun

to travel with. She spoke Italian so very well. As Tiepolo
slammed the rusty door of the car, he spoke a few words
to her. Roger could make out, " Pintura " and " Inglese."

" He says," she interpreted, " that there's an Englishman who has a house with a lot of pictures in it nearby.
Shall we go over there? "

" Do you mind? " said Roger, " aren't you tired? "

" I just as soon go," said Christine. " It won't take us
very long."

Giambattista Tiepolo was very pleased with his
double fare. He whirled his ratty car past the pillared
laundry leaving the men and women turning to watch
them go past before they took up their work again. One
of the laundress's children waved to them impulsively
and quickly put his hand down.

They went on down the Brenta following the tram
rails until they passed by, standing directly above the
muddy stream — a large palladian country house. A colonnade of six brick columns, from which the plaster had
fallen off, except around the ionic capitals, held up a
heavy cornice and pediment. Along the cornice was an
inscription but they passed it too fast to read. A flight of
steps came down one side. The chauffeur made a great
curve; they passed from the front to the side of the house
and saw how stone work had been indicated on the plaster facing and drove around and up to the back. The
car stopped.

" Ecco," said Tiepolo, " casa Inglese."

" Here," said Christine, " is the house of the Englishman."

5

They all got out and went through a broad low-arched
open doorway let into the basement. It was a heavily

vaulted brick crypt, supporting the top stories. The brick floor had been scrubbed a bright pink and indeed everything was spotlessly clean. The English of it, thought Roger. No one seemed to be around. A huge bin of apples rested under a kitchen table. The chauffeur strode interestedly over to it, looking carefully at the architecture all along the way. Then he faced around and winked in the direction of Roger and Christine and reached for an apple. Munching sounds, and his insolence.

"Tell him he ought not to do that," said Roger.

"How can I tell him?" said Christine, "after all, he brought us here."

"It would be awful if someone found us here with him." Roger looked at Tiepolo with as much of a frown of indignation as he could muster. The only effect was that the man put two more apples in his pockets. Roger shifted uneasily. This was obviously a very grand house they were breaking into this way. He nervously looked about for someone to ask. Christine was busy investigating various half-open doorways. "Here," she called, "is the stair."

"Ecco," cried Tiepolo and quickly followed after her.

Roger was not at all sure they should be so forthcoming but reluctantly went up the stone steps after them. They emerged into a large cross-shaped hall, covered with a high double barrel vault. The floor was paved with large square red tiles. Through an open door one saw the colonnade they had seen from the river bank. The three strangers huddled together in the center of the room. Roger for one felt very intrusive and tentative. Then he noticed the walls. The walls had sometime been whitewashed. But under the white wash there were frescoes. Over the doors and windows some of the distemper had been removed and great solid figures in armor were appearing like gods through a mist.

Suddenly a door slammed and a man came out of one of the corner rooms. He was slightly bald, dark, and was wearing a black velvet jacket. He came up to them quickly with his hand outstretched.

"I'm so glad you have come," he said, "I'd no idea you'd be so soon."

Roger was confused and not knowing what else to do said, "This is Miss Forrester." The man bowed to Christine's laughing smile.

"Pintura e bella," said Giambattista Tiepolo appreciatively to bring himself into the conversation. Roger looked desperately at his host. There was more than an apology in his eye.

"E questo vino la basso," said the man kindly to the chauffeur. That was enough. He was off downstairs like a shot. Roger considered how wonderful the tact of some people, the power of relief in such a contingency.

"Well," said the man with a crooked smile, "I've worked hard, have I not?"

Roger looked at the wall, at the reappearing paintings. "Yes," he said and went on precariously, "Do you call them Veronese?"

"No, his master Zelotti. Veronese may have helped."

"Is it hard work?" said Roger. "It must be."

"I get little time for it," the man answered vaguely. "It's just all chip — chipping."

"It will be wonderful some day," said Christine enthusiastically.

"Yes," said the man and abruptly turned. "The drawings are in here."

Roger looked at Christine in amazement, but she passed before him and they followed into a corner room.

" I'm sorry my wife is not here to greet you," said the man undoing a large folio of drawings. " She has gone to Venice." He drew out a large sheet of old paper. On it in faded brown ink was the architectural ground plan of some sort of house. There was a central block and two semi-circular pavilions.

" The wings were destroyed in the eighteenth century," said the man. Then Roger saw it must be the original plans for this house itself.

The man held the sheet of paper to the light and stared at it. Suddenly he dropped it and stared hard at Roger.

" Why," he said and wrinkled up his brows, " you're not Markham at all? "

" No," said Roger quickly. " I'm Roger Baum. I came quite by mistake."

" It's all right," said the man. " It's quite all right. Only I was expecting someone else."

" I think we had better go," said Roger, " I was just looking for frescoes."

" Oh," said the man, " an art student."

" I've discovered the most marvelous Tiepolo ceiling," said Roger eagerly. " Down the Brenta in a laundry."

" It's by his son," said the man. Then, " Do you want to see more drawings? "

" Surely," said Roger carefully, " if it's no trouble."

" No trouble," the man answered slowly. " You must forgive me. My best friend has just died. It's very upsetting. Forgive me."

Roger made some sort of deprecatory noise and looked for the first opportunity to go.

" But," the man looked at Christine and smiled, " first we must have some tea. You must be famished with your explorations."

He led the way into the loggia of the colonnade. It was fair and cool and across the little strip of water the breeze shuffled the poplars. A voice came up from below the balcony. The man in the velvet jacket leaned over the baluster and cried, " Oh," it's you — To-To. Then come up."

A lady walked up the steps slowly. She was dressed in summer chiffon and carried an umbrella which also seemed to be made of chiffon. She looked as if she had stepped out of the most elegant and chic fashion photograph. She seemed to carry the labels of her dress makers, floating on her chiffons behind her. She came up the stairs and slightly elevated her chin. Her whole face was tan and firm as peach-down.

" My friends," said the man vaguely, " Princess Trenti-Malarni." She smiled. " This is Paul Markham — and Miss — " he paused.

" Forrester. Christine Forrester," said Roger quickly and ineptly.

" We will have tea, To-To," said the man and turned to talk to her.

Roger went over to Christine and said, " We ought to go."

" It would be rude now," she answered, " wait a moment."

The tea was brought in by a maid with a bright yellow apron. The man served the Princess and looked at Roger.

" What will you have? " he held the sugar tongs poised.

" Two lumps and lemon, please," said Roger.

The man dropped two lumps of sugar into the cup. He poured some tea. He took up the cream pitcher and let too much fall into the cup. He looked at Roger gravely and bit his lip. He put down the tea cup on the ledge too hard and broke the handle. It tinkled on to the floor. Then he walked quickly out of the door and Roger never saw him again. The princess turned away. Christine raised her hand as if to pat her hair. Roger seemed poised, his hand in the air as if to take something that was not there. It was a crisis of suspended action. There was no thought there, only control on the verge of action, and then the ballet arrived.

As Roger and Christine turned to go through the arch that led into the great vaulted and frescoed room there was a commotion at the far end, and they were halted by it. A group of people, a great many people were advancing across from the stair end of the room. It seemed as if they were a grave and solid company marching curiously subdued, to a situation of anticipation. They were marching towards the commencement of something. Roger watched them closely and he knew that these were the people he had seen in the church of San Giorgio dei Greci. They wore dark clothes although some of the women had white summer frocks. They came slowly across the room like a wave of dancers. Roger recognized a few of the faces. There was the prodigal son with his animal eyes. There were some Tartar girls in muslin dresses. There were musicians and painters, the devoted cabinet of Diaghilev. They flowed through the arched door into the loggia. The princess was there to meet them, to prepare them for whatever was about to begin. Roger, without a glance back, strode across the hall and down the stairs. There was the maid with the yellow apron who had brought them tea. He wrote his thanks on his card and told her to give it to her master. Christine was waiting in the car. Tiepolo smiled. What was happening upstairs? What was starting? What were the dancers doing? The

car drove slowly around the driveway, out onto the
road beside the Brenta. As it passed the house he
could clearly see them all ranged under the columns
of the portico. The slim figure of the prodigal son sat
against the base of one of the pillars, his arm dropped
over the ledge of the balcony, the men and women
were ranged in composed groups along the whole row
of columns. They were silent and their eyes seemed
to be unfocused. They were waiting for something to
happen.

Was it a guest they were expecting, thought Roger,
or a ghost? All of his friends gathered to console themselves in their grief, would not Diaghilev come through
the archway himself, and his gracious presence call them
to a magic attention? Were they waiting him? And suddenly it seemed to Roger, as the car bore his eyes away
from the house and from the picture of the quiet throng
of dancers, as if a ballet was about to begin. The dancers
were waiting for the conductor's rap on his music stand.
They were all waiting, with their initial positions and
attitudes soberly assumed, waiting for the curtain to
go up.

And then Roger realized, and the realization clouded
his eyes, that they were waiting only an end; this gathering was the end, the last noble congress that was to sit
a period at the end of an epoch. A dynasty had ended,
the king was interred on the Island of Saint Michael
among the marble headstones and the cypresses. The
court in mourning met for a final few words before their
ultimate and immediate dispersal. It was the end indeed, the end of youth for a distinguished company of
human beings, the end of power and endeavor, the end
perhaps of the first quarter of the twentieth century.
Century, thought Roger, centuries, centuries. This must

have been the immemorial atmosphere that hovered
above the death beds of all kings from Egypt to Ver-
sailles when there was no heir and blackness faced the
succession. And yet how nobly, with what precise dignity, what consciousness of each separate personal role
had these dancers performed the commencement, or the
denouement of the last ballet. " Fin du siècle," remembered Roger with a smile. " Fin d'un epoque? Non,
m'sieu — Fin du monde."

6

They disembarked at the Piazza San Marco. There
was half an hour before supper. Christine had been
quiet a long time. She really must be tired, thought
Roger. They went over to Florian's for an aperitif.
Roger felt he must do something, say something — in
some way define all the company of feelings that
crowded him out of relaxation. He turned to the waiter
and asked for some pen and ink and paper.

" What do you want to write a letter for now? " asked
Christine.

" I've got to do something," said Roger, " you help
me."

" Why don't you wait until after dinner? " said
Christine.

" I've got to do it now." The waiter brought some
pens and ink and paper.

" But who are you going to write to? " asked Christine, sipping her pernod.

" I'm going to write to Mussolini," said Roger, sucking his pen.

" To Mussolini," said Christine, " don't be ridiculous."

"It's not ridiculous," said Roger. "It's about those frescoes. They ought to be preserved."

"What do you mean," said Christine, "are you crazy?"

"The frescoes of Antony and Cleopatra — the Tiepolo's — they're falling to pieces."

"Why the letter won't ever get him," said Christine.

"Ask the waiter where he lives," said Roger. Christine slowly did so.

"Well, where does he live?" asked Roger.

"In the Palazzo Chigi, Roma," she said. "You better say ' Your Excellency.' "

"You will translate it for me into Italian when I have finished," said Roger.

"Why he gets thousands of letters every day he never sees," said Christine. "It's the craziest thing I've heard."

"He may see it," said Roger.

"I can't see what possible use," said Christine, and looked over his shoulder. "You know perfectly well he won't ever answer."

"His Excellency, the Duke Signor Benito Mussolini — is that right?"

"That'll do in English," said Christine.

"Your gracious excellency doubtless knows," wrote Roger, "of his glorious fascist headquarters in Venice in the old Labia palace. It is a very beautiful building decorated by Giovanni Battista Tiepolo."

"Don't say that," said Christine, "that's not the point."

"But it is a beautiful building and that is the point."

"But he knows that," said Christine, "tell him in what rundown condition it is."

"The ballroom in particular is fine," wrote Roger, "having scenes from the lives of Caesar and Cleopatra."

" Tell him they're falling to pieces," said Christine,
" that's the point."

" I will in a second," said Roger, " give me time."

" Not that he'll read it at all," said Christine, " but
he'd be more liable to if it's shorter."

" The frescoes in that room from the lives of Caesar
and Cleopatra," he continued.

" You've said that once before," said Christine.

Roger put down his pen and folded the unfinished
letter in two. He put it in his pocket and paid for the
drinks. Then he got up and walked across the piazza.
The pigeons wheeled and fluttered and they were taking
the flags down from the great red masts. The sky was
overcast. People walked in front of him and behind him.
When he got home to the pension he found he couldn't
finish his letter.

Flesh is Wrath

Set me as a seal upon thine heart, as a seal upon thine arm: for love is strong as death; jealousy is cruel as the grave: the coals thereof are coals of fire, which hath a most vehement flame.

1930

1

Roger was spending the summer with his sister at her place in the country. It was a farm insomuch as they supported themselves with things to eat except for meat which they brought from town about fifteen miles away. There was nothing much to do but swim in a pool fed by cold hill streams, ride the horses and read and loaf. Guests were coming up all the time to stay for a weekend or a week or ten days. Mostly his sister's friends but sometimes Roger would have a girl he knew from home or one of the boys from college. When Daphne and Roger got sick of the peace and silence they'd go to New York for a little while, to return quickly to the peace and silence. There were a lot of dogs and cats. Some one of them was sure to be in heat at one time or another during the summer, and they had to be exercised safe from the others. Then there was always some turf to clip, some garden bed to weed, some ramblers to tie up. When it was very hot the days melted and one could do nothing but sit under a grape arbor and be plied with cooling drinks. They lived like vegetables and expected shortly to have green tendrils sprout from their feet and fingernails and leaves unfold from their ears. In the middle of the summer a plague of green-backed saddle worms marched across the countryside attacking all the trees but the conifers. When you walked through the woods you heard a ghastly ticking noise, like thousands of muffled clocks

ticking in staccato whispers. It was the worms eating.
They stripped the trees before August and by September new leaves were coming out like spring in midsum-
mer. The worms were very large and fat, with little
green scales all over them. They had red humps on their
backs and their young were a ghastly flesh-pink. Daphne
would rather have died than touch one. Roger kept two
in a pierced candy box for a week to see what would
happen. They only grew fatter and whiter.

After lunch Roger was to go over to town to get
Jimmy Foster, a friend of his sister's who was coming
for the weekend. He also had to call for Master, a sealyham who had been having a mange cure at the vets.
He went alone in his own car so that Daphne could ride
over in hers to get some laurel in a deserted pasture
some six miles away, so that she could decorate the house
for Jimmy's arrival.

Roger set off for town. The day was extremely warm,
but with a heavy dry wind which rustled the leaves and
blew the dust up from the country road. He went down
over the bridge, passed their farmer's house and waved
to the baby who was cooped up in a large packing case
on the front lawn. He remembered to avoid all the
stones that would hit the car from underneath if one
weren't careful. He stuck out his hand and caught some
hay from a passing wagon and sucked the dry straw all
the way to town. He called for the sealyham who barely
recognized him. He'd been away for almost a month
and looked thin. Roger put him on the front seat with
him until he should get Jimmy Foster. He wiped out
the corners of the dog's eyes and looked at the mange
scars. He felt the damp nose. It was cold enough.

Jimmy Foster was a mining engineer of about forty.
He looked like an Indian and from city dwelling lately

he seemed pale. His hair was very black and his eyes had
bony frames like the cheek-bones on a mummified skull.
He was extremely easy going and pleasant and full of
various information, not alone about mining but about
Indian reservation life. He would tell how badly the
government had done by the Indians, how the women
sometimes would squat in the roads and fill themselves
with sand at the sight of drunken government inspectors,
how there was definitely not any human sacrifice but
various curious customs prevailed still. He also had a
certain bluntness, an inability to perceive situations,
almost an emotional innocence, which was somehow irritating in its bland, stubborn inappreciation. But
Roger really liked him a lot and gladly stuck Master in
the rumble seat with Jimmy Foster's bag, to talk for half
an hour alone before he would be more or less monopo-
lized by his real friend, Daphne.

"And how is Daphne?" asked Jimmy Foster when
they were settled and rolling along back to the farm.

"She's simply fine," said Roger, "better than she's
ever been since Clay died."

"It must be great for her that she has you up here
now."

"I love to be here," said Roger. "I'd rather be here
than anywhere else."

"How does the place look?" Jimmy Foster had only
been coming up for two or three years, yet he took a
courteous, proprietary interest in the farm.

"Extremely well," said Roger, "except for the
drought. I've never seen it look as well even when Clay
ran it."

"Does she find it hard to run?" Jimmy Foster took
his pipe out.

"Well she did at first. It was really hard as hell for

her. She kept trying to think what Clay would have done."

"I know," said Jimmy.

"She'd always try to think what would Clay want — what would Clay have done. Then she'd do what she thought he'd do."

"But not so much now?" Jimmy Foster bent his head under the windshield to get a light.

"Oh no. She's much better now," said Roger. "It was hard though at first. You know the farmers around are hard as hell. They'd come around and pretend that Clay had told them things to do before he died. Then they'd ask to go on with the jobs."

"Did she let them?"

"Of course she did. At first. Pesty Fazon, up the road said Clay wanted a bridle path cut from the house, way around through his property down to the north clearing. It took him the whole spring and summer to do and it's an ugly path. Clay would never have done it."

"Must be a smart farmer." Jimmy Foster puffed on his pipe.

"He's crooked as hell. Oh, then they'd come up here, farmers who worked for Clay, and sniff around and tell her she'd never be half the man Clay Cooper was."

"She must have guts to stay up here, you know."

"Well," said Roger, "it's all right now. She does what she knows best. She's fired Pesty Fazon and she knows all about the best way to get rid of the cream — all that sort of thing. It just took time. You know she never did a thing like that before Clay died. He did everything."

"Then it's damn lucky she had the place really."

"You're right it is. She'd gone crazy if she hadn't had something to work on. Then there was so much of Clay

around. She discovered trunks full of his college pictures, diaries; books he'd marked. She looked up all the
bills and records of things he'd bought to see where
they came from and she has all his old friends come up
here. His secretary was here last Sunday."

"Then Daphne is not really lonely," Jimmy Foster
paused.

"Why, no," said Roger, "she's not lonely much.
Sometime she gets low and depressed. But much less
now than before. Something always happens up here
and time flies past like nothing."

"Do you suppose she'll ever marry again?" asked
Jimmy Foster.

"I certainly hope so," said Roger. "She ought to. I
think she wants to."

"Maybe she doesn't."

"No. I know she does. She really needs a man around
her. I know she'd like to get married. The day Clay
died, I remember I took her out for a bus ride
and she couldn't think of hardly anything to say.
When we turned around up at Grant's Tomb she
said, almost apologetically, that she'd have to get
married."

"And Clay would have wanted her to, wouldn't he?"

"Of course he would," Roger was certain. "If he
could have picked out the man."

Jimmy Foster laughed. "Why, wouldn't he have
trusted her?"

"Oh, I guess so," said Roger. "But he would have
liked to have known all about him."

"You know, I never knew Clay," said Jimmy. "What
was he like?"

"Oh, I thought you'd known him."

"I saw him once at a football game, only for a sec-

ond, after they were just married. But I never saw him
again."

" I thought you knew him," said Roger thinking.
" It's hard to describe him. He wasn't in any way re-
markable except in ways I couldn't express. He was like
hundreds of other nice people, only nicer, with no re-
strictions. To look at him you'd think he was the most
conventional man in the world."

" Yes," said Jimmy, " he looked to me like any num-
ber of clubmen I know: good fellows, too."

" Except that Clay was really profoundly unconven-
tional. That is he always did what he wanted. He always
said balls when he wanted to. He wore what he liked
and saw whom he liked."

" He was very much in love with your sister though."

" Yes, he was," said Roger, " and that's funny, too. He
was crazy about her and the more excited she got, the
more nervous and hysterical, as she sometimes does, the
better he liked it. He was wonderful that way. It never
phased him. He even taught her not to be afraid of boats
and horses."

" Well," said Jimmy Foster with a puff of finality on
his pipe, " she'll marry again all right."

" She ought to," agreed Roger. " I've talked about
it to her a lot."

2

When they got to the farm Daphne had not yet returned. Roger put Jimmy in his wing of the house, on
a porch overlooking a small garden. There were two
large beds there and Roger put the weekend case on
one. He usually slept in the other. He took off his
clothes and drew on a pair of swimming trunks. He
advised Jimmy Foster to do the same.

"I don't ever swim you know," said Jimmy. "I haven't swum in years."

"Well, take off your clothes anyway," said Roger, "and get a little sun on your back."

"I don't want to get burnt," said Jimmy. "I burn like hell."

"You'd better," said Roger, "you look like a plant that's been too long under a board."

"No," said Jimmy Foster definitely, "I'll watch you and Daphne."

They went down to the big hall of the farm. It had once been a barn and Clay Cooper had turned it into a music room. There was a balcony at one end and heavy rafters held up the roof, plastered smooth on the inside. One window had shelves across filled with blue and green glass. Light fell in pools from the high triangular gable windows and defined little groups of brass candle-sticks, snuff boxes and bowls of iris.

Daphne came into the hall from the stable, her arms full of flowering laurel. Her face was tanned and her black hair was disordered all over her head, showing one ear. She looked no older than twenty. Roger stopped to look at her, was about to say "Here's Jimmy" — but Foster stepped down the hall before.

"Hello, Jimmy," cried Daphne, "I'd kiss you if my arms weren't full."

She looked beautiful, of course, thought Roger, too beautiful and then was ashamed of himself for the thought.

"Let me take the laurel," said Jimmy, "I want the kiss."

"Take both," said Daphne and kissed him on the cheek. "Well," she continued, "did Roger get you over here safely?"

"Yes, indeed," said Jimmy, "in fine shape."

"His driving has improved considerably," she said, looking around for something to put the laurel into. Roger searched vaguely and lit on a biggish terra cotta pot.

"You're so efficient," laughed Daphne, "why not bring me a finger bowl."

Roger set the pot down.

"There, Jimmy darling, bring me that copper kettle." Foster went over and dragged a big orange metal bowl from under the piano. When Daphne went to change into her bathing suit, Jimmy Foster turned to her brother and said enthusiastically, "She does look marvelous — doesn't she though?"

"Why not?" said Roger. "She has nothing to do but sit in the sun all day." He paused and troubled to survey Jimmy. "That's what you should do." He stooped down, stuck the laurel in the pot and dragged it back to its place in the curve of the piano.

3

Daphne led the way down to the pool. Jimmy followed. Roger brought up the rear with the fresh-washed Master.

"And did Master miss us?" cried Daphne. "Did Master miss his mistress? Come, Master, come."

He doesn't know her, thought Roger, any more than he knew me.

Daphne ran on down the wood path to the pool and stopped to pick some red berries off a high bush.

"I'm such a pig," she laughed back to Jimmy Foster, "and I know this will spoil my tea." Master sniffed at the branches and lifted his leg.

Daphne parted the birch boughs that marked the entrance to the pool and they all swept through. Green lawn went down on both sides of the water to border a natural hollow that Clay Cooper and his farmers had dammed up ten years before. A family of ducks fluttered off the grass and paraded in grave tandem up the stream. Daphne went out onto a projecting rock and dipped her toe in the water.

" Do change your mind, Jimmy," she said, " It's so very cold."

" No, thanks," he answered. " I'd so much rather watch you."

She stuck her other foot in and took it out and shook it. It usually takes her hours to get herself wet, thought Roger, what with all this dipping in and out and getting one shoulder watered. Suddenly Daphne stood on the lower side of the projecting rock, poised for a second and sprang into the water. A good dive, thought Roger. He hoped Jimmy Foster would appreciate it. He ran down to the rock and jumped in too quickly. As he sprang off the rock he didn't leap quite clear and so cracked the big toe on his right foot a nasty clip. He tried to dive all the deeper to make the pain more quickly cold and intense and so stop it. When he came up to the surface with his nose full of water, Daphne was smiling a few feet off. She started splashing him with her legs up in front of her. He didn't feel like fooling by this time so he turned and deliberately swam to the other side. He pulled himself up on the bank, his feet sinking into the mucky bed of drowned leaves by the bankside. He looked over at Jimmy Foster who was trying to make Master swim. The dog wouldn't budge. He would merely lay limply, or wiggle off. Roger called, " Here Master, Master. Come boy."

Daphne in the water turned around and cried, " Here, come Master — come swim, boy, swim."

The dog looked vaguely at the water and started running up and down the bank.

" Here, Master," called Roger, standing up and clapping his hands.

" Here, Master, Master," cried Daphne from the pool, " here, Master."

" Come, Master," called Roger from across the pool — " Come, boy, come."

" Come here, sir," said Daphne sternly, turning towards him.

The dog stopped running up and down and looked into the pool. Jimmy Foster laughed and came down on the rock.

" Come now, Master, here," shouted Roger. With that the dog lopped heavily into the water and swam over to Daphne, his body turning sideways in the water, showing its one back and one front leg, milling in a silly way — but making some progress.

" There's a bright dog," said Daphne, " there's a clever Master."

4

Roger went up to put some pants on for tea and dinner. Presently Jimmy came in and looked for a pair of white duck trousers in his bag. He took off his city pants and coat and stood in his shirt tails, his hairy legs bound about with black socks and white brass garters. Roger thought how ridiculous he looked and drew on his own flannels. Jimmy drew off his socks and articulated his toes. The big toe on his left foot was splayed. The nail seemed to have been split and grown together again. Roger suddenly remembered his own hurt toe.

He felt of it. It did not, he was forced to admit, hurt very much.

"I have everything, Roger," said Jimmy Foster suddenly, "but a belt. Have you got an extra one."

Roger stood up and buttoned his pants. He was thinking. He went over to his bureau drawers and opened the top one. He drew out a coiled white calf belt with a gold buckle. He uncoiled it and gave it to Jimmy.

"You're sure you don't need it?" asked Jimmy, slipping it through the loops of his trousers. He bent his head and twisted his shoulders slightly to do so. Funny looking, thought Roger. "This is a damn nice belt," said Jimmy. "Where'd you get it?" He looked at Roger.

"It belonged to Clay," said Roger significantly, but somehow faster than he had intended.

They went down to find Daphne in a pair of light green chiffon pajamas. She had paraphernalia for making iced tea spread out on an iron table under the grape arbor. Roger and Jimmy Foster sat on an iron bench opposite, like schoolboys about to be given a treat.

"You know, Jimmy," said Daphne, "I've not seen you for so long that I completely forgot how you take your tea."

Roger wondered what would be the effect if she simply said, "How'll you have your tea?"

"It is lemon and two sugars, isn't it?" continued Daphne.

"It's lemon and no sugar," said Jimmy laughing.

Right again, thought Roger.

She turned to her brother with the same hostess manner, "And now, how will you have your tea?"

"Four lumps of sugar and cream and lemon, thank you." Roger added, "As usual."

Daphne dropped four lumps of sugar onto the ice, put in a slice of lemon, and poured cream in. " Is that all? " She looked at him and poured in the tea.

" Thanks," said Roger, taking the potion.

" Oh, you're welcome, I'm sure." Jimmy Foster and Daphne Cooper laughed.

At dinner Roger was even worse. He made a fuss about not having Master in the dining room on his first night home in so long, although he knew perfectly well Master never stayed still for a second and merely tripped up the maids. But Daphne humored him.

" What," cried Daphne, looking at his plate, " you didn't take any chicken? "

" No," said Roger shortly, " it's too much trouble to cut off the bone."

" Well then, baby, let me do it for you? "

" No," said Roger, " I'm not really hungry at all; too much tea."

" Did your cream and sugar and lemon make you sick? " asked Jimmy in fun.

" Not at all, really. You ought to try it sometime." Roger picked at his vegetables. He drank a great deal of water and snapped his fingers under the table to attract Master. Since he had no meat on his plate, Master however refused to stay very long when he wasn't fed.

" Oh, do take that dog out of here," said Daphne to the maid, who was changing the salad plates.

" I'll take him out," said Roger, jumping up from the table. " Here Master."

" Let Nelly take him," said Daphne. " You stay here and finish your dinner."

" I'm all through," said Roger. " Here, Master."

" Very well," said Daphne. " You're missing a lovely dessert."

" Come along, Master," said Roger. The dog wouldn't move. He seemed to have sensed the dessert.

" Now go along, Master," said Daphne sharply. The dog followed Roger out of the room.

Roger went out and put Master in the barn. He didn't want to arouse the other dogs who were already quiet in the kennel. He didn't care what Jimmy and Daphne were talking about. He could guess anyway. He knew he'd behaved like a perfect fool, but it was too tiresome of Daphne to act so unnaturally, to play up to Jimmy Foster so. It would be different if she cared anything about him. Roger wouldn't have minded so much then. But just someone in trousers, thought Roger bitterly. So goddamned undignified. He looked up at the clear ultramarine dusk. There would be plenty of stars. He couldn't face going back into the big room for coffee, and listen to all those polite reminiscences about things he'd never had any part in anyway. He could just hear them laughing over some inane incident which could have no possible point except as some private little co- quetry. He decided to go for a walk. His feet crunched in the gravel of the stable courtyard. The back of his car was still open from having taken Jimmy Foster's bags home. He pushed the rumble down and passed by the white mounting blocks that Clay Cooper had sent down from Vermont so that Daphne could dispense with a soap box she had formerly used. He walked out into the road and looked back at the long group of whitely glowing buildings, submerged in the expanding night. He felt hungry and cursed himself for being a fool. There was no reason to sweat but he felt sweaty. He decided not to go for a walk but went to his room to make up his diary. He kept a diary, a record of events. It was much better than a journal because when you

looked back on a journal you were always embarrassed
at the way things struck you — while a diary could give
just the bare facts and your memory could reclothe them
however it cared to at the moment. It was hard to keep
a diary up in the country because one day usually stood
for another. It wasn't particularly interesting to note
that after six weeks with mange, Master had come back
from the vets. And it was hard not to turn it into a journal when one mentioned Daphne and Jimmy Foster. He
turned back the leaves of the full diary and saw nothing
to hold him, to read over. He put the present volume
away and looked at last year. He saw what he was doing
a year ago today. He was in London. The day started on
the motor trip through Cornwall. He remembered even
the faces of the people in his train compartment. He
flipped the pages back. No good. Then he looked for the
blank book he used to keep three years back. It wasn't
really a diary at all, just the documentary record of
things that happened to him, the few things that he felt
bound to record against the frailty of memory. The
pages were partly yellow and orange, partly white, two
or three were grey. Some were lined. Some had pieces
torn out of them or places scratched away, where the
ideas or the incidents had served him again in some other
function, in a story perhaps or in a poem. He turned to
five or six creased yellow-green pages, closely written
over in blue ink, there was a forgotten quotation at the
top of the first page.

> Et que faut-il que je dise
> Chante. Explique
> Ce qu'au fond de mon coeur je comprends déjà
> Obscurement, comment — à moment digne —
> Supreme et le plus aigu,
> Pour un moment est déjà là qui ne passera plus —

5

Only his own handwriting convinced him he had
actually copied it. Who its author was he had no recol-
lection, no, nor why he had seen fit to place it here.
He read on. . . .

*In the morning Daphne had to go out to have a
dentist appointment. I didn't see her but Mary Carr
said to me — that she hadn't bathed yet. We were having breakfast together and she suggested we should
have lunch together and not come back till late. So I
thought that was a good idea and we dressed and
started up Madison Avenue looking at all the interior decorating shop windows. At the corner of Fif-
tieth Street a sidewalk elevator carrying a tremendous
Jacobean table was being lowered into the cellar.
Suddenly there was a rasping noise and the whole elevator plunged down a storey with two men and the table
on it. The thing broke into a thousand pieces (it was obviously no antique as it was only tacked together). The
men were very frightened. We passed on. Mary Carr
remarking such small realities were commonplace in
New York. She said, noticing a lovely pine settle in an
antique shop window, that a year ago she hated all old
furniture but that Clay had made her love it. We both
found something nice and spontaneous to say about
Clay. The day was fair. Calm was the day and bright.
We were feeling very merry. We had lunch at a place
called the Lobster. Talk all around from the butter and
eggmen and their secretaries. I had bought Mary the
London Graphic so she could see the General Strike
pictures. We ate a large, slow fish lunch. Mary said, " I
want to send Daphne some flowers." As we were going
out the door of the florist shop, who should walk in but
Clay with a friend of his called Murray Stout, a stock*

*broker. Well, said he, looking very doggy and sprightly
(gardenia in his buttonhole). What are you doing here?
Getting flowers for your girl friend, said we. Well, said
he, the worst has happened. Joe Peyton has come all
the way from New Orleans to see us. He thought we
were going to be married at five o'clock in the afternoon
instead of one in the morning. I forgot to let him know
about the legal complications. Now he's gone to the Ritz
and taken a suite and had it all decorated and he has
to go back to New Orleans at six. He's in a perfect state
and I don't know what to do. We left Clay to get the
champagne, and went back to the hotel. Daphne was
dressing. She had a green satin dress cut low with bows
on the hips and a tremendous black leghorn hat. She
wore her jade and diamond earrings and looked wholly
desirable. I am, said she, going over to see if I can calm
down Joe Peyton. He was a fool to get everything ready
although Clay should have let him know. I'm going to
make a tremendous fuss over him and see if I can't make
him stay over. She went out and Mary Carr and I put
on the gramaphone and danced to Valencia. The telephone rang. Daphne said for us to come right over to
the Ritz. Joe Peyton has a tremendous party and as
many as can must come. We washed up and went over.
Joe Peyton is one of Clay's college friends; he got badly
wounded in the war and has only one eye. He is about
forty, very attractive with a black moustache. The room
was full of white peonies, tea roses, lilies of the valley
and orchids. On a large white clothed table stood twelve
goblets, a huge wedding cake, sandwiches, etc. In a tub
champagne floating on ice. I was conscious of much
gallantry. Bantering. High courtesy. I couldn't keep
up with it. Joe Peyton was reconciled. He had to do
everything. This is my party — don't you move, let*

*me give you something. Clay's father came in. A fine
bluff tall old gentleman looking very sweet. He proposed a toast immediately. Indeed it was a succession
of toasts. Clay sat on a sofa with Murray Stout, talking
about one of his old loves, a woman called Josephine
Crane. Daphne with Clay's father. Mary and I lay
back on a couch flushed — eating. Joe Peyton, slapping
me on the back — Roger, you and I are going to be
great friends. Take a little caviar, and you won't feel
dizzy. Gaps in the conversation, not painful, but gaps.
Charlie Morris, Clay's architect. Greetings. By-play with
Joe Peyton and old Mr. Cooper. " I really must go
back to N'Orleans as much as I'd like to stand up with
you! I've put this meeting off for three days now." I
paced about the floor talking rapidly — green-panelled
room upon the tenth floor. I kept looking out the window. I started the rudimentary Charleston step. Ah,
Murray Stout said, do you know any new ones? I
haven't learned a new step in a week. It's terrible.
More champagne. More and more joie-de-vivre. Pranks.
Daphne teasing Clay for being so silent. I don't believe
I'll marry you after all. He says, unfortunately there's
nothing you can do about it now. She says to Clay's
father — Really, Mr. Cooper, you know how hard I've
tried. Mr. Cooper leaves to get the train back for the
country so as to prepare Mrs. Cooper for all the guests.
One last toast. He kisses Joe Peyton playfully, Daphne
gallantly. Clay and I leave to dress. Back at the hotel
we put on Valencia. Everyone so gay and worked up
to such a pitch of excitement. Judge Behn calls up.
He had said before if Daphne wanted some older person to take father's place he would be glad to come.*
(The family happened to be abroad.) *Steve David the
lawyer. We talk about exams. I ask after his wife and*

kids. I excuse myself rather in a daze — bathe — cold
water and felt better. Cocktails — Cable received from
Paris. You know what is in our hearts today — much
love, Mother. Dad. We leave with the gin on the table.
I put it into the umbrella stand. Why, Roger is getting
smart, says Clay. The victrola goes too. There are two
cars. Daphne, Clay, Judge Behn and Steve David's wife
and who lives out towards the Coopers, but who can't
stay to dinner as her kids have just been moved to the
country and whom she must see. Thomas the chauffeur
with the Pierce. In the other car Steve David, Mrs.
Schreyer, Mary Carr and myself. Mrs. Schreyer takes
off her hat and smooths her hair. The night was lowering and through the darkening twilight we passed up
the Grand Concourse. Through Harlem streets nigger
children rushing about. Street cars. Shrill cries. Headlights ahead. Then lamp against lamp. Across the sky
bursts a sudden gleaming eye.

We drove up a short carriageway gravelled. The car
swished on the stones. There was a brightly lit up doorway with stone steps. It had begun to rain. Everyone
got out. The house door opened and two butlers came
out to take the ladies' bags. We went into a big hallway,
short flight of steps into a panelled room. A semi-circle
of people in evening dress standing quietly to greet us.
I dash in and out getting things. Someone says to me, Oh,
you're the brother. Daphne and Mary Carr and Mrs.
Schreyer go up to dress. Clay kisses his mother and two
sisters and his young niece, a fair girl called Ruth or
Helen. She wore a chiffon dress of red and orange very
soft. She is very tall and well-developed, finely made —
sweetness and light, sensitive mouth like a thorough-
bred racing horse — After the first tumult and the
shouting we retire into a small room hung with brown

*photographs and lined with red striped antique Ameri-
can furniture. Mary Carr comes down from dressing and
laughs in her high voice. Much conversation about the
drive up. It transpires that Thomas our old family
chauffeur who drove them drove wretchedly and almost
crashed three cars on the slippery pavements. Daphne
was terribly nervous all the way as she was supersti-
tious, etc. Then Steve David's wife was about to have
a baby and that made Daphne more worried about the
car. Old Mr. Cooper talks to Judge Behn. Mrs. Cooper
about seventy-two very sprightly, lively, nervous with
white hair, very much the grande dame — whispers in
my ear — But you are just like Daphne, my dear. Her
very image.*

*Daphne came down with the white gardenias in
her hair, a white Greek evening dress with silver bands
under the breasts, and a white cape like a chiton
bound in silver with a silver ornament falling down
her back. She wore no jewelry at all which Mary Carr
said was very smart of her. She was very pale which
became her. Mr. and Mrs. Cooper kissed her. After
which cocktails and sandwiches were brought in. Clay
said I should not drink gin and champagne so I didn't.
A toast to Daphne and Clay. It was now about quarter
to nine. The butlers took away the cocktails and dinner
was served. Daphne and Mr. Cooper sat at one end
with Clay at her side — and Mrs. Cooper and I sat
facing them with the young girl at my side. Mrs. Cooper
told me very emotionally she had never seen Clay so
happy, that the reason Mr. Cooper and she had gotten
on so well for so long was that she just went her way
and he went his. That is why they have always been in
perfect harmony. She knows Clay and Daphne are just
the people for each other. Why, she said, when Daphne*

was here last, Ruth (and the girl next to me blushed)
said to me almost with tears in her eyes — Grandma,
Miss Baum didn't kiss her goodbye — Yes, she con-
tinued, we have an extraordinarily interesting set up
here. They all write or act in our Barnstormers or paint
or do something distinguished — and all so delight-
fully informal. No fuss and feathers with us — pop-
ping in on one another the whole time. I have some
talk with Ruth, the girl whom Clay calls Peaches, be-
cause that's her favorite adjective — i.e., Uncle Clay
gave me the peachiest tennis racket. We had the peachi-
est times at school — isn't Daphne — I mean your sister
too peachy? Yes, said Mrs. Cooper, I'm so glad Ruth
will have someone to look up to now. Judge Behn pro-
poses a toast to Mr. and Mrs. Cooper. Mrs. Cooper
lowers her eyes and says well I'm sure it's all very kind
of you. Presently the dessert comes. Peaches, as it is ten
o'clock, retires. She kissed her family goodnight very
prettily — ending up with Daphne — standing behind
her chair, which was tight up against the others — so
many were at table, and bending down to Daphne's up-
turned face. Daphne puts her arms up and around her.
I get up and shake hands with her and she goes to her
bed. The whole party reminds me rather of a Sargent,
not the style or the surface but the whiteness and fresh-
ness and flair, roses and white candles and silver, New-
port in 1901.

6

Roger stopped reading his old diary. He looked
around the room. The pictures that Clay had put on
the walls. The print of Daniel Webster which no one
liked much but which Daphne had saved because he'd

once said it was the first antique he'd ever bought.
There was a low double seat, with a straw back that
he'd found in New Hampshire, once used as an extra
bench in a sleigh. Roger looked out the window. The
stars as usual over the barn and the beasts inside shifting and thudding, turning in their rest. On the other
bed were Jimmy Foster's pajamas spread out, the covers
drawn neatly down and his slippers at the foot of the
bed. Suddenly Roger felt hideously ashamed of himself for the way he had behaved all afternoon and at
dinner. It was the worst possible thing he could have
done. He had behaved like a two-year-old. He almost
felt so sick about it that he thought he'd better go to
bed and sleep it off. But he knew Jimmy Foster and
Daphne would not really hold it against him and it
would be a little more decent to have the courage to go
downstairs and talk for a while. Just as if nothing had
happened. He went over to the mirror and looked at
himself. He tried to look natural, pretending he was
someone looking at him in a crowd of people. He
changed his expression. He flexed his mouth. He needed
a haircut. His image·didn't afford him much confidence
or satisfaction. He turned out the light and went downstairs into the big hall to find Jimmy Foster and Daphne,
and talk for a while before going to bed.

The big hall was dark. Not a single light was lit. All
the windows had also been closed as for the night.
Roger bumped against a table. Had they all gone to
bed? But impossible. It was not later than ten o'clock.
Perhaps they had gone walking, but that was unlikely.
Daphne had been in pajamas and she wouldn't have
changed again. Perhaps they'd gone out for a ride.
Roger stopped still and listened. No sound. Also he
would have heard the auto in the courtyard if they'd

gone for a ride. He looked into the darkness of the hall.
The blackness collected, packed itself blackest toward
the ridge pole and in the corners. It was a living blackness. It swarmed with the negation of color, the absence
of brightness and textures on the brass and furniture
and curtains that were so familiar from the daylight.
Roger stopped himself from thinking. He walked
cautiously through the darkness over to the bookcase
that walled the far end of the room. There was a side
light, he would turn on. He would get a book and go
up and read for a while and wait. Wait for Jimmy
Foster. Who had been, where on earth, where? He
stumbled over a light cord and switched on the lamp.
Its brightness pooled over the corner of the bookcase.
The rest of the room went blacker. It was the section
of biography, and letters, history, lives of Mary Wortley
Montagu, Carlyle, Byron. He didn't want that section. He turned the light out and moved across the
wall to the poetry section. Halfway across he stopped
and listened again, no sound. Surely, with impalpable
steadiness and strength a wave of cold, uncoagulated
choking jealousy took possession of his body and like
poison made his limbs stone, and caught the heart of
blood in a vice of granite. He could not move. The
quality of hate was fanning itself in his brain. He wanted
to hate more. The hate he was feeling would be only
the beginning of a consuming directed passion, a
withering black light of destruction which he could
send out of his eyes to crisp the traitors. He pressed the
valves of his hate. There must be more hate. I hate.
And yet it was a failure. The hate was only a sickness,
it had only a lurid brilliance in his mind. It flickered.
It was only the sick fever of jealousy that paralyzed him,
that made him unable to consider, that rendered him

incapable of wishing to consider, that made him know and wish to know that Clay Cooper was betrayed. That he himself was betrayed. He stayed rooted in the black room, swinging in the blackness. He had failed to evoke a hatred which could release him out of himself. He must evoke the dead. He must call up the corruptible to be his genie. He thought of Clay dead, Clay buried, Clay sick and dying. It was as useless as his hatred. Clay dying, on a cold January day, far from the farm. Not that he had been there. He had only arrived to see them taking the steel tanks of oxygen away and all the other ghastly machinery of death. But this failed. Clay dead was no Clay, no part of Clay, only the dead part of Roger, the dead part left over from his infancy, the self-torture, the amorphous illness of a willful insecurity. He must evoke Clay alive, the living Clay to dispel the murky fetor of this swamp. Clay alive, Clay playing with the new litter of pups, Clay in London, Clay at Maidenhead on the river after they had been too late for the Regatta insisting on seeing the proprietor of the inn who had not been there in a hundred years.

7

After dinner they had sat in the front room and talked for an hour or more. They brought the gramaphone in and started to dance. Roger asked Mrs. Cooper and they sailed about the room, slowly on the heavy carpet. The brothers-in-law and the sisters filled in the conversation. Daphne talked about practical details of honeymoon, the trip — getting the bags to the boat — coming back to find the farm settled. They must surely come up for long visits. Judge Behn looked over the legal documents attendant to the unusual occasion and asked Mr. Cooper's unprofessional but desirable advice. Mary Carr sat on the sofa talking to Mrs. Schreyer; a butler brought in more champagne and the slight lull that had fallen over their gaiety after dinner, not through anything but physical lassitude reasserted itself. Roger had danced with everybody and sat wiping his forehead with a handkerchief borrowed from Steve David. Would he never learn to dress himself completely, with everything he needed?

They said goodnight to the elder Coopers and goodbye. It was too late for them to stay up and Clay and Daphne sailed at noon the next day. Mrs. Cooper was inclined to cry a little and Clay went upstairs to say goodnight to her alone. Roger began to see about getting the bags back into the cars. The goodnights and thanks were said all around again and again and the cars finally shoved off from the doorsteps, followed by the flutter of hands and handkerchiefs.

It was half an hour's ride to the nearby city. As they passed some sleeping village, the bells of midnight tumbled across the elm-girdled green. The streets were slick from the rain, but in patches only. The clouds were blowing over and it turned cold. There was more or less silence in the cars, not much to say, and no longer the necessity to speak from spontaneous gaiety. The two cars drove close together into the small suburbs and main street of the city. The walks were void, the brightness from the lamps fell on the plate glass shop fronts, on a solitary hydrant and at the end of the row a yawning policeman. They drew up by the curb, in front of a massive granite fronted bank building, pierced like a bastille, and with small plate glass windows. It was very tall, ending in a tower, lowering and ugly. It had been the biggest building in the city before 1910. The wed-

ding party got out and looked up at it. Clay was the only
one to laugh. He said he supposed a jail was as good as
anywhere to get married in at one o'clock in the morning. Roger took Mrs. Schreyer's and Mary Carr's arms.
Daphne hung back to speak to Clay for a second. Should
they ask Thomas the family chauffeur up for the legal
ceremony? Clay decided it wasn't necessary. They all
agreed it wasn't necessary. Mrs. Schreyer had taken off
her hat and the night wind troubled her hair ever so
slightly. There was light burning at the far end of the
hall behind the small plate glass window in the side door
of the bank. Judge Behn knocked and rang the bell. The
rest stood uneasily on the cement pavement and looked
up and down the empty street canyoned with layers of
blank glass darkened windows. The door opened and
they broke into action.

They walked down a long dirty hall to a steel cage
where an elevator was waiting. The negro elevator man
had let them in. He was very sleepy and old. White
bristles came out of his black skull. Was it only a caprice
on their part, or did he look really evil, like a witch
doctor's skull on a burnt stick. He hobbled into the
elevator without speaking or smiling and half of them
walked into the cage. They had all unconsciously lowered their voices as if not to disturb the absence of any
life in this grim quiet bank. There was only room for
half at a time in the elevator. Roger and Mrs. Schreyer,
Steve David and Mary Carr stayed below. Roger watched
the elevator clank slowly up out of sight. He almost felt
like calling it back. If it should go on up, straight
through the roof piloted by that black devil. Mrs.
Schreyer held his arm. She seemed upset. Presently the
elevator came down again. The door opened and the elevator man indicated with a single gesture that they

should enter. Charon's gesture before he unbinds his barque. Roger was the last one in the elevator. He felt queerly. He recalled once when he had his appendix out in a hospital he was taken to the anesthizing room in an elevator. He was careful to let the nurse out before him. He almost felt that the gesture, at the time, deserved comment. The elevator door shut with a series of clanks and the elevator shook and lifted up. It rose uncertainly two or three stories. Then it stopped. The elevator man bowed his head curiously but made no move. Mrs. Schreyer held Roger's arm and said she was frightened, in a low voice. Roger said quickly it was all right. Then the elevator started again, rising through empty layers of the darkened office building.

The Justice of the Peace's office was high up; on the fourteenth floor. It was brightly lighted from round globes in the ceiling. Papers in neat piles on many desks awaited the now sleeping secretaries, for the morning. The justice was introduced all around. Roger was nervous and shook hands with him as if he had been a long lost friend. Strangely enough a huge square clock three stories high shone in the windows from another municipal building across the street. Its black arms across the blazing transparent face said ten to one. Clay got out the marriage certificates. He laughed uproariously. They were decorated like cheap valentines. He complimented the notary on their gaiety. The J. P. wrote things on filled out blanks with a steel pen in a steel Spencerian hand. They were waiting for the clock to strike one before they began. Judge Behn stood at a desk with a little unbound copy of the civil marriage service. Mrs. Schreyer stood next to Roger holding his hand. Steve David leaned against a green metal filing cabinet. Clay, smiling and extremely animated, had his arm on

Daphne. They stood to the right of Judge Behn. The
notary to the left. Mary Carr whistled a bar of something
in a low clear sweet voice. She stopped suddenly, seeing
everyone else was quiet. Steve David looked at his wrist
watch. A clock ticked in the room. Then from across
the street the great hands of the transparent Big Ben
arranged themselves in their logic, the wheels and
ratchets and cogs swung into one another and their har-
monic chord was one.

Judge Behn read the marriage service very simply in
a steady voice. At the part of " sickness and health, weal
and woe," Mary Carr whispered, " They're surely getting themselves in for a lot." Roger said, " They know
it." Mrs. Schreyer's eyes were liquid. Roger listened very
hard. It was the first time he had heard the service and
he found he could understand it. Daphne and Clay made
their responses seem lighthearted. But no one else in the
room felt lighthearted. This is not sad, thought Roger.
Perhaps if there were music it would be gayer. After the
formal service Judge Behn said a few words about happi-
ness, and duty and the possibility of undying love, words
that Roger's parents would have wanted said if they had
been there. Then they all signed their names in the
Record and Roger included his middle name Isaac for
the first time since he had been at school. Clay was amusing and executive. He told Daphne in the car that she
would have to wait for her wedding night till they got
on the boat. As for him, he was perfectly exhausted.
Roger slept on the front seat of the Pierce all the way
home, nor did Thomas the chauffeur ask any questions.

Roger had gone down to their stateroom, inspected
their big cabin and seen all the telegrams and letters and
flowers. Daphne had been sent a single gift of elaborate
caprice — a pair of black silk sheets. The stewardess

was embarrassed to make up the bed with these objects
of decadence, so Roger undid the package and helped
Daphne wrap the bunk in the wicked bedclothes. Clay
had given him his own personal flask of whiskey and a
large extra box of candy. The other people who had
come to see them off had gone off the ship and the steward was banging the gong and shouting, "*All ashore,
going ashore, ashore please.*" Roger had given a few last
messages to his parents, taken the last addresses, made
the last promises to write often. Clay was as easy as if it
had all been an everyday occurrence with him. He
winked at Roger on opening undesirable gifts and read
off the names of the shops as if he were announcing guests
at a ball. Roger shook his hand warmly and Clay slapped
him on the back and said he was a good boy, a bright
boy. He kissed Daphne and said he hoped she wouldn't
be seasick. He stepped out of the cabin and walked up
the companionway. A steward passed him carrying more
baskets of fruit and flowers. The passengers were milling
around the purser's desk in a wild scramble. Everyone
seemed excited and nervous. Roger was very glad he
wasn't sailing. Two sailors helped him onto the gang-
way, their arms like levers. They barely touched him.
They did seem to help an old lady in front of him
though. He passed down the gangplank — making the
heels in his shoes fall against the wooden strips nailed
across the rubber matting. He went down and sent a
cable telling his parents: Clay and Daphne safely off.
Then he went out on the dock and stood as near the
edge as he could. Hundreds of people shoved around him
waving. The Yale crew was on the boat going to compete
at Henley. The band struck up Boola Boola. There were
cheers. An Italian official was being sent back to Rome.
Perhaps the same band boomed out the Giovanezza.

Three loud Eja, Eja, Eja peeled out. Very marked
Italian faces waved American and Italian flags. People
started throwing long streamers and confetti. Someone
dashed up the single connected gangplank with a little
bag, like a surgeon's instrument case. The gangplank
was taken down. A big rope splashed into the water.
A man beside him lifted a little girl upon his shoulder
and made her hand wave a dirty handkerchief. Roger
looked for Clay and Daphne. They quickly appeared
where they said they would, on the boat deck. Daphne
blew kisses. A fog horn and a whistle. Boom and screech.
Cheers and confetti and the band plays the Star Spangled
Banner. Roger seems to feel the dock move slowly away
from the boat. Daphne waves. She is smiling. The boat
is definitely slipping away like a great piece of the earth
detached. The boat slips away and its grave progress, its
bells, its streamers seem like a salute to the land. Roger
takes off his hat and holds it high over his head. Sunlight
breaks through the end of the pier and gilds the tops of
the smoke stacks, the flags. There is a loud roar, a sus-
tained organ note of cheering. All the people on the
dock and on the boat fuse into two separating entities.
Farewell. Daphne turns and says something to Clay.
They are on the water. Roger moves his hat. Clay suddenly stands more erect. He raises his right hand almost
in a gesture of welcome, his hat is off. His hand stays
erect. Roger can no longer distinguish his smile. A great
coil of flying streamers pink and green and yellow whirl
down and catch around his welcoming arm. Clay waves
the banner up and down. The cheering swells to a louder
roar and the ship's whistle blows one piercing and tri-
umphant blast.

8

Roger was still in the darkened hall. He listened to the
steps on the hall outside, on the lawn, on the roof, in
the room. It was his own heart. It was his own spongy,
pumping heart. He still listened. There was nothing, not
even a lively silence. Not even yet had Daphne and
Jimmy Foster returned. No lights, no voices, not a step
on the corridor nor on the gravel path. He relaxed his
stance. His step sounded only like his step upon the
oaken floor. He was afraid that those ghouls of jealousy
and malevolence would overwhelm again and he consciously braced himself for their assault. But nothing
came, nothing assailed him. Clay, himself, had never
seemed such a thin and disappointed ghost. The house
was like a deserted tomb tonight, a canopy of threadbare
rafters over an untenanted bridal bed.

Roger felt his throat. It was dry. His eyes were dry.
He had a feeling in the corners of his mouth as if he had
been crying too long. He detached himself from immo-
bility and walked stealthily across the hall. Some light
fell in from the windows, on a pewter ash tray, on a glass
bottle — dark pooling at the bottom with its brandy. He
walked across the lawn, patting the prickly hedge of
evergreens. Under his heel, the gravel rattled in the
courtyard. All the cars were in their little booths. None
had been taken out. If they had been he would surely
have known it.

He clicked the latch on the barn door and walked
into the warm and living odorous darkness. Master, the
Sealyham, crushed against his legs. One of the horses
was unaccountably staling, at this hour, smiled Roger
to himself.

He picked up Master and stuck him on the seat of

his car. He slammed the door and listened, no sound. He started the car, switched on his lights and backed through the courtyard onto the road that passed in front of the house. He passed the white long range of buildings and out buildings, as quietly as he could; he went cautiously over the road and let the shadow of the rocks cast by his headlights guide his course along the bumpy road.

Fifteen miles farther on they came to a college town. All the boys were at vacation, so it was more deserted than ever it would have been on any other late night. The buildings on the campus cast darker shadows at their feet onto the darkness of the ground. Roger got out of the car to take Master for a little run. They met no one. Roger felt like a thief pursued, and a fugitive somehow about to give himself up, after years of hiding, of disguise, of starving. He was bound no place. He was just driving but when Master started rutting about under some vines and barking Roger decided it was time they all should be in bed.

Master liked to ride. He stood with his paws on the window ledge of the car looking out, the night wind in his walrus, tobacco-stained whiskers. Every so often Roger would slip his hand into his collar when he seemed to be projecting himself too far out of the car.

When he had been driving for some two hours since his start, he pulled into the courtyard of the farm again. He noticed a light in one of the maids' rooms. As he watched it put itself out. He replaced Master in the barn. He didn't put on the light for fear of involuntarily arousing the horses. They seemed to be sleeping lying down or folded up. He clicked the latch of the stable and walked halfway across the courtyard. A neighbor's dog tethered half a mile away was barking at nothing

at all. Roger crossed over in front of the lawn. There
was no light anywhere around. He let the wet lilac bush
leaves freshen his face and went into the garden. He
slipped quietly under Daphne's window. He listened. No
sound. No breath. Maybe she wasn't there? He considered calling her to find out, but why? He went back
through the brushing lilac leaves, damp and fresh on his
face, across the damp lawn, indoors, upstairs. A light
had been left on in his bathroom for him. He undressed
there and went into the bedroom. The door was open.
Jimmy Foster lay sleeping quietly. Roger took good
care not to wake him.

Flesh is Heir

Il Commendatore: Don Giovanni, a cenar teco
                 M'invitasi, — è son venuto.
Giovanni: Non l'avrei giammai creduto
          Ma farò quel che potró,
          Leporello, un' altra cena
          Fa che subito si porti.

expression to give the words color. "He was a fine old fellow, with a white beard. A Norwegian or Finn or some Scandinavian and he had sailed for forty years in the Gustavus Adolphus. There he was in Vancouver with one of the last honest to god wooden ships, the kind that can sail properly around both Capes." Tom paused and scratched his neck.

"Alex wants to see you very much," interposed Larry Reynolds. "He's been asking all day for you — when we thought you'd get here. I don't know where he's gone now." Then he stopped to listen further to his brother. Roger would have said, "Well, I want to see Alex a lot, too," but he could only listen to Tom.

"There she was — in Vancouver — at anchor. They'd offered the skipper to buy her for the movies but he wouldn't even listen and the crew all deserted."

"Well, what did you expect Father to do about it?" asked Larry.

"I told the skipper I thought I might get Dad to charter it. If he could get a skeleton crew I'd get you and Georgie and Nelson and Pete and Sheldon and we'd learn the ropes and we could sail her to China."

"You'd better speak to Dad about it some more," said Larry. "You never can tell what he means when he's so uncertain at first."

"Would you really like to sail that schooner?" asked Roger. "Just to sail it?"

"Just to sail it," echoed Tom, laughing, "Just to sail it. You ought to come along. You'd see what just sailing is." And Roger kept still and tried to think of this argosy manned by a crew of young Reynolds — all carefully schooled in a forgotten craft — set in the rigging of a flying Dutchman like wayward stars from the land on a vast night of sea.

1930

1

In the cool gabled room, under the eaves upon which the sun poured outside, were two iron beds, set lengthwise from opposite walls. On tables and bureaus lay piles of yachting magazines, neckties and jack-knives, the beginning of whittled ship-models and clothes slung about the floor. On one bed, with his arms underneath his head, lay Lawrence Reynolds, a boy of twenty-seven or eight, with the characteristic cast of his family face; large eyes framed by a generous bony cheek and broad forehead, the eyes themselves hazel and liquid, the mouth thin but never pinched; the chin firm, the ears delicately attached beneath the cap of fine dark brown-black hair. On the other bed, opposite his brother and with his arms lying at his side, yet with his legs off center to destroy any semblance of sleep, was Thomas Reynolds, some years younger than the other, but only his more youthful image. His eyes, too, held the family attribute of waking sleep, the contentment of an half-domesticated animal, with the animal's physicality, the animal's lurking nostalgia for complete wildness.

When Roger came into the room the two recumbent Reynolds looked sidewise at him and greeted him warmly with their voices, without changing their position.

"So I went down to the hotel and asked for the skipper," Tom Reynolds spoke almost as if he were reading a story out of a book, with the slightest dramatic

Then from the bottom of the house it seemed, and it must have come from a voice four flights below, using the whole entrance hall as its amplifier, and increasing in clarity and volume as the voice shifted from step to step until it paused on the landing of Roger's floor, came a voice of resonance and musicality calling, " Ruggiero, Ruggiero, Ruggiero," like a voice off-stage in an opera, if there had been no stage, no scenery, no audience and no lights and the only aria and action that single phrase.

Larry and Tom Reynolds rested on their cots and even their conversation slept but Roger was drawn to his feet by the magnet of energy approaching their threshold and he could brace himself consciously against the arrival of Alexander Coronado, whose groomsman he had come to be.

Coronado flowed into the room like a wave of sound. He no longer called Ruggiero. He said it in his natural voice as a greeting and as, almost, a simple explanation in its intimate and affectionate intonation of why he had not been here before to greet his friend.

" Ruggiero," he said, " why have you been so long? I've waited all morning. Where on God's earth have you been? "

" I'm sorry," said Roger. " I thought I was supposed to get here around now. You didn't tell me how to get over — I didn't know what — "

" Well, come now," said Coronado, " I've two horses below. Get into your boots and we'll go for a ride." He looked over the reclining figures of Tom and Larry Reynolds stretched out as if to receive his equivocal presence. They smiled amiably at him. Roger wondered how soon Tom would continue his conversation about the four-master. Coronado turned to him, " Come along now. Get your clothes off. I'll take you where I'll

become the brother of these men." He indicated the
Reynolds demesne with a rapid gesture, and passed into
the hall, to take Roger's bag into an empty bedroom.

2

Coronado held Roger's pony because it was curveting
around at a great rate. The Reynolds' horses were strong
enough but since they were ridden only in spasms of
hard riding with long rests between, they quickly forgot
the rudiments of manners that were impressed on them
as colts. The two boys rode along a roadway down from
the house, and through a gate, to pass into a path that
led straight into the heart of the woodlands.

" I've so much longed for you," said Coronado. " Ever
since I've seen you I've been among lions and lovers and
I must keep my mouth shut or . . ." Coronado rode up
to and a little ahead of Roger. He did not turn his
head, so that the last words were lost.

" You know," said Roger, almost apologetically, " I
wondered if I'd ever really come here or not. I never
heard from you — not that I minded — but you know
how you are."

" Yes," said Coronado. " I'm not surprised to find you
here, but that I'm set on this prancing donkey," he
shoved his heels into his horse, " and with you beside me,
one day before my wedding — Oh, surprise! Pandora's
box holds nothing now but time."

Roger laughed, " Well, how is Sylvia? I've got something for her. I didn't see her anywhere around."

" Where is that little lady and my wife, indeed? Off
with her Dad, I daresay, saying goodbye to her herds and
valleys, or sailing with her sisters on their private ocean."
His horse missed a step or two and Roger's right stirrup

iron clinked against Coronado's left. They linked and parted.

"Is she well?" asked Roger. "Does she still love you?"

"She loves me right enough," he answered. "I'd wish I could doubt that."

"Doubt that," said Roger, "what do you mean?"

"Mean — mean," said Coronado. "I mean I've lost my mind. It's gone like the wind. How could I write you all summer if I'd no word to say?"

"I don't mean I was worried you didn't write," broke in Roger, "I only meant."

"Don't mind," said Coronado. "I only know I've been overtaken in my silly flight. Everything's gone so blooming and so well and yet I've always known that at some wall or other my devil would step out and call the proper names to fit my crimes," he laughed at Roger.

"But you are going to be married," asked Roger, "tomorrow, aren't you?"

"Who knows," asked Coronado, "how many of us die in our sleep?"

"Not at our age," said Roger. "You're too healthy for that."

"What of health?" he asked. "I've never been so sick; my head's full of gangrene. It comes like tears through my eyes and furrows these old cheeks."

They rode along through the afternoon woods. Every so often a partridge drummed and flicked its feathers away from the green mosaic of light through the oak leaves. "No, Ruggiero," and he caught his reins in his other hand. "I'm in love. Crazy in love and that's my sickness. Where's my cure?"

"What more could you want," asked Roger, "your wedding's cure enough."

" No cure at all," he answered. " Love won't stop at
the parson's book."

" Well, let it start there. As long as you love her and
you don't doubt her loving you — what more possible? "

" Why ask me? " he whipped at the passing branches.
" Why ask me? Tell me. Tell me Sylvia loves me. To be
sure. Tell me I love her — Well, I do. But my love is
more than heartache at her absence, or a pain when she's
here."

Roger looked at him and considered the possibility
that he was improvising on a vague theme, and that only
because they had not seen each other for so long did
his language seem outlandish. They rode along in the
woods.

" When I was a boy," said Coronado, " about thirteen
or so, I'd been put to bed early, for no reason, I couldn't
sleep but tossed and undid all the bedding from my mattress. I couldn't sleep but presently heard loud voices
from the floor below. I listened. It wasn't nurse or the
cook or the kitchen maid in the small house. It was my
mother and my father screaming at each other and I
was so frightened I had to go down to see. My father saw
me in the door. He made my bones go icy. He spoke to
me as if I were his own age and had never been a child.
' Child,' said he, and yet he meant me man, ' your
mother and myself can no longer live together. I'll go
find somewhere else to stay.' My mother cried and I
couldn't put my arms around her. I saw wholly now
what I had seen piecemeal before. Then I told Father
he couldn't go. He must stay and look after us. And
since he did me the honor of addressing me as a man,
I spoke to him as if he were four years old. My mother
seemed to die from then on. I went upstairs to bed worn
out from crying and sure I'd saved them both. There I

found in my bed a girl much like my mother, with her
same bright hair. But she thanked me for nothing. She
knew who I was and what I'd done. I never slept so
deep but when I woke I knew I'd never sleep again away
from her and so I looked for her all day."

The gates of Dagotan were all high, and divided the
island into pastures and large areas which segregated
the sheep and the deer so that there would be natural
fodder for all, without any one pasture being completely
consumed. There was no need to dismount to open or
close the wooden barriers and now Coronado cantered
ahead of Roger to unlatch a red bar of boards and
waited till he had passed before wheeling around to
shut it. Roger said nothing. He only tried to keep
his imagination as clear as he could for Coronado's
benefit.

They passed the clicking and settling noise of the
swung gate and trotted on down into a hollow.

" I know very well what the world is," said Coronado
laughing. " It is a very hot tray of baking earth and like
hot clay it cracks into all directions until there's a net of
dry breaks, all over the gigantic plane. And smoke issues
from the cracks and smoke springs from the sighs of the
particular damnations of all our friends." Roger grinned
in a deprecatory way as he continued, " The sun is a
black sun, you know very well, and it casts no light but
night. My sun and my shadow are a girl. Her eyes are
the spots on the sun, and if her hair were not so much
like mine . . . there! Oh look there! "

A red doe sprang up from the side of the road, disturbed by the dull hoofs of the trotting horses. It stared
for a second, ducked its head and turned like a leaf in
a stream. Here only the stream was full of sunlight and
green haloed leaves and as the red deer frisked away,

its white tail flashed in the underbrush like a brandished feather.

"This girl . . . this girl," Coronado's laughter was pitched so evenly to the tune of his voice that he laughed and spoke in the same resonance. "This girl I met again at a ball — or after a ball. I'd been dancing all evening with a hundred pretty people. I saw only one and her brightness consumed us both. Both knew where we had seen each other before, but neither of us danced, approached or spoke. And yet I knew which way she'd pass and I took her hand, and took her home. And we sat all night before her fire and she told me and I knew all the rest about her that before I only guessed. I looked into my mirror and saw my own laugh only it was her laughing. Though now I wished to God I'd asked her name so I could have sent her flowers next day."

"And you never saw her ever again?" asked Roger. "Never . . . ?"

"I never ever saw her again at all," laughed Coronado. "Never again. And I never missed her either, and whenever I come home she's always there. It's she alone I love above myself. She can no more let me go than I can shoo her away. More of my flesh than fingernails." The peals of laughter uncoiled themselves behind the horses and reverberated against the leaves already trembling with sunlight and against the ground echoing with hoof-beats.

"This golden lady is my shadow now. She gets me up each morning and soothes my head each night. Her shadow is always about me like a bird's. She obsesses my sleep. She is my counterpart. My wife. I cannot be more unfaithful to her than to my name." He paused. "Alexander," he spoke his name and laughed again. "Alexander, an explorer, crowned, a conqueror. Her name must be Alexandra." Roger laughed too but without an excess of gaiety. For he was cursing himself, now as always, when in the presence of Coronado, like a paid spy he was trying to prick holes in his friend's defences, trying to discover a specious action or an elaboration of conceit that would tumble the edifice of Coronado's metallic activity. But now as before he failed and the insistent failure made him feel as usual, a cheat. So Roger laughed and heard the ring of his laugh against Coronado's, and its emptiness did not for an instance dull the sterling clangor of the other's.

" Alexander," continued Coronado, " with his Alexandra constant beside him. I seek my face and friend. Papageno encounters Papagena." He started whistling and it was like his speech and laughter.

" And Sylvia," said Roger. " What about her? What is her name? "

" Her name is Sylvia Reynolds, the first daughter of Sylvia Starr and Lawrence Reynolds. The Reynolds have been sons and daughters of their own name before the notion of Coronado was prophesied by Mother Shipton or Daniel, or Joseph the dream peddler before him. Sylvia Reynolds; how I love her. Her demureness casts about her like a pilgrim's cape and I catch some saintliness from its holy contagion. Reynolds is compact of an ancestry of spectres and Sylvia smells of the garden but neither name rhymes with Coronado and I'm punctilio for proper rhymes."

He started to laugh again. His laughter laughed and laughed. People who knew Coronado slightly never referred to him as the boy with the hair or the Reynolds' visitor — or anything but, Oh you mean that boy with the laugh. When you first heard it you laughed too. But Coronado laughed incessantly with no strain or forcing.

After the first peal you stopped laughing, but his laughter rang on. Was he laughing at something we do not
see? But there's no guile in the laugh. Is he laughing at
us, ourselves? Does he think we're comic — to be laughed
at? But there's no malice, no brittleness in the laugh.
And yet it laughs on in a monotonous good humor —
pitched to the tone of his conversation itself so that often
his words were but the bass accompaniment, the counterpoint to the melody of laughter that even when one
attributed it to a most irritating, sardonic profundity
it was simply the laughter of a care-free man.

" But you do like Sylvia? " asked Roger, beginning to
be uneasy.

" Like her? I love her. I love her to distraction. I must
marry her quickly or I'm undone. Alexandra undoes
me."

" But then you can't marry her. Good God," said
Roger, " you can't marry her at all. You don't love her
at all."

" I tell you I love her." He laughed at Roger's un-
easiness. " How could anyone help loving her? So sweet
and kind and so demure. I'm her perfect husband except
for the ghost I'm host to."

" But seriously, what will you do? " Roger shifted his
reins and wiped his mouth with a handkerchief. He
continued weakly, " You must be terribly careful."

" Careful no — what's to be careful of? Careful of my
wedding? Why that's all cared for. It's almost over. It's
practically passed."

" That's exactly it," said Roger. " That's why you
must be so careful. There's still time."

" Still time for what? " snapped Coronado.

" Still time to consider," said Roger, " whom you
really love."

" I spend all my time considering," he said. " I consider I've asked Sylvia Reynolds to marry me. She says
she will. She told her people so and they consented
to it."

" But still there's time," said Roger.

" Too much time," he said, " if it were over now, I'd
know what to do."

" What's that? "

" I'd take her to the shore's edge and leave her and
she could swim for land, or I'd shove her off a cliff and
she'd fall into her father's lap."

" But do it now."

" And then I'd turn to bed and find Alexandra warm-
ing my sheets — perhaps."

" Only perhaps? " Roger smiled.

" On such occasions she never fails me. I'm not always
sure of her presence. She may for all of me be riding
postillion on my saddle now. But she's timid and you
might have frightened her away."

" But be serious. Be practical. I don't know anything
but that you can't go on this way: you can't marry
Sylvia."

" What will I do then? " Coronado and Roger walked
their horses out into a sandy area, covered with large
stones and patches of sundried grass.

" You must leave Dagotan. I don't know how, but I
guess I can help you. My car's across the bay. I'll take
you wherever you want to go, in no time."

" And I suppose I'm to leave the customary notes of
regret? " he laughed.

" You know what you want to do, then? " Roger
looked at him and couldn't tell whether he did or not.

" I shall leave word for Sylvia expressing my pain at
this hideous mistake — which she wouldn't believe be-

cause she thinks I never could make a mistake in my life. That's why she marries me."

" Say whatever you want. But if you marry her, you'll ruin her, too."

" And if I don't — tomorrow at this time she'll be dead of grief and all the Reynolds will swear on her death bed to have the heart out of this rascal." He thumped his chest.

" Oh, no, Coronado. It will be hard for her at first, but after —."

" I know her so very well. I swear it would kill her."

" She'd have her family — Tom and Larry and all the rest."

" She marries me to lose them."

" Is that her only reason? " Roger looked around — almost for fear someone might overhear them.

" No — she loves me, too."

" But you do see it's impossible, don't you? You can't marry her? "

" You don't think I'm mad, Ruggiero, do you? " Roger shook his head and laughed. " You think I talk too fast and my tongue gives more color to the crisis than you'd care for yourself. But you know I'm not crazy."

" I know you're not crazy," said Roger. " But what then? "

" Then don't think I'm —," he mocked Roger's " crazy " — " crazy when I ask you why not better kill myself now."

" But what good would that do — Sylvia would still — "

" Yes — but if I were dead — Alexandra would be dead with me and no cause for jealousy." He laughed and leaned forward to pat the horse's neck.

" I think you're crazy," said Roger shortly.

"No — if I were dead — it would be quite simple.
I could fall from my horse on the cliffs into the sea and
let the water take me, and you could lose your horse as
well and run home and be my witness."

"But do you think I'd sit quietly by and let you
drown?" asked Roger.

"You would if I wanted you to," he smiled. "No,
but I mean what I say. I would be perfectly easy in my
mind to drop dead now."

"You'd better get married," said Roger quickly, "and
settle down."

"Or if I married too — tomorrow — as I will — I
could quite as easily kill Sylvia as myself."

"That," said Roger, "seems to me a much better
idea."

"Why should she care whether she dies or not, if I
don't. She'll be married then. She'll have what she
wanted."

"And I suppose," laughed Roger uneasily, "you'll
come back from slitting her throat and find that girl
waiting to wipe your knife."

"I live like a Christian," said Coronado. "There is no
time in my day when I should not be ready to die. Each
night I sleep expands the unity of life. Its apex shifts
nightly so whenever I'm dead the pattern is complete,
the end would be a logical easy end."

"Nevertheless, I think you'd better marry Sylvia. You
can do what you want with her after you're married."
Roger was disturbed, a little scared. He caught up his
reins and broke into a trot, to avoid the necessity of continuing this particular conversation. He had come down
to Dagotan to see Coronado's wedding, not to act as his
accomplice in a murder.

3

They rode along the shore back home in time for supper. Roger was silent, completely at a loss to know what to do or say. He felt his presence had been demanded and in a way, his advice requested. Since he was devoted to Coronado he felt he must make some answer and yet he could not see how, in any way, he could help his friend, not even by speech or silence. They rode past a little sandy knoll — on whose top was driven a ring of stakes. The sea licked a beach of stones on the other side and Roger asked what was this marked spot.

"A mariner's grave," said Coronado, "His body washed up on the stony beach there fifty years ago. They buried him under the bank and set the stakes for a gravestone. No one knew who he was."

"You know the history of Dagotan pretty well," said Roger smiling. "You learned quickly."

"I embraced its catechism like a convert the church," he said. "Its history'll be my litany." He rode on ahead and left Roger to come after, relieved somewhat at the distance between them where no words could easily pass.

And yet the lapse in the conversation was worse than talking. Roger felt spurred to talk, to say something. The tension of silence demanded the increased tension of a direct intercourse. When he saw Coronado, Roger felt he must be in as close connection with him as possible, even to the extent of risking inane remarks, or of being ignored.

"Sing me again," said Roger, conscious of the lameness of his conviction, "sing me again that war song you sang the night the storm, . . ."

"I'm no mummer to use my masks again," snapped

Coronado. " See how the gulls scoop the air. Did I never
tell you the story of Myles Bennett and myself? "

But while Coronado rode along by Roger's side and
started to tell the story of Myles Bennett and himself,
Roger stayed tense on his horse and in his mind. A tide
of resentment welled up in him and he knew he hated
Coronado. He was no mummer to use his mask again,
and he could afford to ignore Roger's petition without
a word of explanation. The request was stupid but Coronado could have submitted, thought Roger, bitterly, to
the claims of human error. Once Roger and he were
walking in a cemetery. It was at the end of April and
the wind was like a fresh tide among the tombs. Coronado had been rehearsing all the mythologies of death,
in his most vivid and lively manner. He had invented all
the existences of the ghosts who lived in these white
marble houses. He had named each angel and bleated at
each of God's granite lambs. He had tried to lift each
cross that settled heavily on the dates and births and
breasts of all those interred there with a gaiety and flow
of good humor that was like a melody. And Roger had
been listening to the fine tune of his fantastic narration,
the declaiming of epitaphs and the joyful recitation of
their resignment and holy ends and he had never looked
at Coronado's face. Suddenly when, after they had both
stopped to read a verse of prayer, they stood up, faced
each other and Coronado burst into peals of laughter.
Roger stood stock still, the chill of the white marble slabs
all about him, entering his spine and like hemlock, making his each separate limb, bone, vein and marrow turn
to icy rock. And as Roger was thinking these thoughts in
the light of his memories, the story of Myles Bennett
went parallel to the battles in his mind.

" Since my parents were often unhappy," continued

Coronado with no look at Roger to see if his face betrayed any lack of interest, "I was put to live with
friends. These people rather than my own family reared
me. From them I gained whatever reading I call my
education. Myles Bennett was a lawyer and he taught
me Latin and French and I wanted to be a lawyer like
him. His wife was much more than my mother to me
because she served me for mother the first time I needed
one since I was suckled. I lived with them for nearly
seven years until I went to college. I cannot describe to
you how close we three were. I was son to Myles and
Helen and brother as well. I knew Helen to be the one
angel in the world and Myles was the absolute portrait of
Roman justice. Then I went away for a while and I came
back some years later to my friends, I found them —
at first — so I thought, changed. Helen indeed was the
same as she had always been. When I saw her I only
marvelled that I'd not missed her more. Myles had made
a name for himself. He'd become well known. Then he
was called to another city on a difficult case. The case
of a man whose guilt was in some question, but to all
of us there was no doubt of his innocence. The case
bred a lot of bad feeling, particularly in the papers.
It was the start of a feud perhaps, of a dangerous injus-
tice that Myles could have stopped. We knew he'd go,
of course. Did he go? He did not. He stayed pat. He
stayed home and didn't risk a night's rest. I told him
what kind of a traitor I thought he was. He was still fond
of me and it hurt. He hates me now. He's the only man
I've ever known and it cost a lot to let him go."

"Good God," said Roger, "why did you have to hurt
him? He did what he could for you."

"For me, to be sure," said Coronado, "he did nothing for himself. He was a devil and I had to tell him."

" It must have hurt his wife a good deal," said Roger.

" Surely," said Coronado, " but she's safe enough. She still trusts him."

" But good God, what do you want from people? "

" Only their best," said Coronado, " it's little enough to ask."

" Do you ever see them now? " asked Roger.

" Helen died last March. I've not spoken to Myles for three years. I couldn't write when she died. But I knew she'd have wanted him to be at my wedding."

" Did you ask him? "

" Yes, I asked him to marry me." Coronado laughed.

" But why, if you think he's such a bastard? "

" If he had read that service over me," said Coronado, " he could not have helped but see where lay the strength."

" Well," Roger looked at him inquisitively, " will he? "

" No," said Coronado. " He'd have no hand in marrying me." Coronado tossed his head, as if to rid himself from the duplicity of Myles Bennett. And they galloped on through the wood with the long shadows of horse and cavalier in front of them.

4

After they had put their horses in the stable and set the blankets on a rack outside the barn door to dry, they came back to the big house and found Mr. Reynolds, Coronado's father-in-law with a notebook in his hand. He looked like his sons, with the same hazel eyes, the vagueness and the eloquent bony structure of his face. His flesh was pink against the short-cropped grey-white hair, and he was abstractedly regarding a notebook.

" Oh, hello there, Alexander," he said stumbling a
bit, as from unfamiliarity over the name, " I am having
some difficulty with these lists."

" Let them go as they want," said Coronado. " They'll
get there right enough."

" They would if the wedding were within a decent
distance." Mr. Reynolds looked up without rancor.
" Five miles is not easy for the whole family to manage."

" Let those come who can," said Coronado. " Don't
worry about it."

" I know, I know," said Mr. Reynolds, " but we want
this to run smoothly, now don't we? "

Coronado brightened into a laugh, " Of course we do.
Here let me help you." He took the list of guests and
carriages and started to figure out who would walk and
who would ride.

" You will ride in the surrey with Sylvia and your
mother-in-law," said Mr. Reynolds sucking his pencil.

" Yes," said Coronado, and then abruptly to Roger,
" and you can ride with Larry and Tom and the rest can
follow at dog's trot behind."

He thrust the notebook back into Mr. Reynolds'
hands and darted across the lawn to the house. The
older man scarcely looked up. Roger hesitated a second
as if to make an explanation for Coronado's brusqueness,
but seeing none was expected, he followed his friend into
the house.

" If it rains," said Coronado, " the service will be indoors." His head sank back on his shoulders and he
laughed. " Don't you know they're praying for rain."

Roger went upstairs to change his sweaty riding
clothes and bathe. The bathroom was big and full of
large toy sailboats, — relics from generations of Reynolds childhoods. A window beside the wash basin

looked out on the open sea and across the bay of Dagotan where the lights in other Reynolds' houses were
winking on to bid the late sun a good evening. Roger
soaped himself more methodically than usual. Dressing,
he felt his shirt take the roundness of his body with a cool
caress and he tightened his belt so that the white linen
stretched suavely across the buttons of his breasts. He
combed his hair with a deliberate raking and set his
tie in the propriety of the central line of his collar. All
of this almost to convince himself that there still remained an order in circumstance, that he must never lose
a hold on logic and though Dagotan, Coronado and the
race of Reynolds were a fantasy, he must honor that
dream by the flattery of an attention to detail, and by
his own punctilious behavior, to fool this dream into
thinking he believed in it.

5

The whole younger generation of Reynolds were giving Coronado and Sylvia a party that night. All the first
and second and third cousins were to dine in a new house
across the bay of Dagotan and then dance afterwards.
There was a great feeling that it must be a fine party —
that it could be a fine party, even if no one else was coming, really, except members of the family. But since many
of the cousins saw each other seldom and many of
them had married strangers, there was novelty in the
faces.

Roger rowed over in a boat with Sylvia and Coronado
and Larry and Tom. Their oars troubled the tranquil
waters of the bay, spilling the slight reflection of sun
still left, under the waters. The air was clear but not too
cool — and the sky was strained of every ruffle but its

most crystalline and darkening luminosity. They rowed
past the large black hulls of the yachts and the small
flotilla of resting sailboats. No one spoke. Coronado
whistled a tune every so often, a single phrase over and
over, with no variation but in an agreeable pitch. Roger
looked at Sylvia but not too hard. He did not expect to
find much to disturb his ideas of Coronado in her, and
yet he did not care at this precarious time to risk too
long a look.

The Reynolds cousins had made sure there would be
plenty to eat and to drink and to insure a good start
they had made the cocktails pretty strong. Coronado
went about among the youngest girls, scarcely more than
children, and lifted them off the floor in his arms, or
played around with them in the hallways. The introduc-
tions were superfluous. Roger already knew that practically everybody's last name was Reynolds and he could
not possibly remember all of their first names. He
stopped to think how extraordinary it was he did not
feel more out of place. None of the Reynolds took much
trouble about him. That was the best thing about it.
They gave him the credit for being as responsible as
any cousin. He spoke casually to anybody who happened
to offer him some food. He looked at those who didn't
seem to have any and went off to get them fed.

But, in spite of the strong cocktails and the general
amicability, the party seemed to go flat. Tommy Reynolds and Larry talked together in a corner as usual,
probably, thought Roger, about boats. A girl felt moved
to inject some spirit into the occasion so she volunteered
a solo dance in the middle of the floor. Someone saw to
it that she had a phonograph accompaniment. The rest
sat about paying little attention to her. The dance started
with some gusto but it ended in a low monotone of gen-

eral conversation. No one noticed exactly when the
dance did end. Someone put on the " Beautiful Blue
Danube " and Roger started waltzing with Sylvia. He
was dizzy to begin with but he danced more elaborately
than necessary into wide-reaching circles. He brushed
up against other people yet he couldn't seem to scale his
waltzing down to the size of the room. Sylvia tried hard
to keep up with him. They stopped before the record
was finished. Roger leaned up against the wall and wiped
his forehead. Someone suggested that they play charades
but there seemed no concerted determination to do so.
One of the small Reynolds girls, very fair-haired and
lacking the obvious strength of bone in her face that
most of the rest displayed, sat at the piano and sang jazz
songs very well indeed. She imitated professional music
hall technique. It was a neat approximation, scaled
down to this living room and yet somehow it seemed
pitiful. The main charm in her singing lay in her inability to overcome her innate good-mannered reserve to
reach the necessary vulgarity the songs demanded. Only
Coronado seemed to be at all alive. Not that the others
were moribund, but they seemed veiled, or rather they
were behaving as they would have behaved together on
horseback — or in their boats or on walks in the country
or on any other night in front of their respective family
fires. The presence of one Reynolds seemed to affect another only by the medium of repose. Their eyes were
open but their legs and arms and bodies slept. Smiles
slept sweetly on their faces and vaguely dreamed Coronado's progress around the room. Perhaps it was only in
contrast to their somnolence, but Roger had never seen
him burn so bright. At one moment he stood by the
black piano and injected some bars of frenzy into the
blonde girl's voice. Then he was away to animate a cor-

ner of quiet talk. He stood there for a second and the
area detonated with laughter, as if they had been waiting all evening for him to set their crackers off.

Roger went over to the punch bowl to fill his cup. He
felt restless and talkative. Yet there was no one whom
he might address. As he held his glass over the bowl and
brought the large silver ladle to its lip, his fingers suddenly became wax and the ladle and cup splashed into
the ice and fruit rinds. Roger looked sheepishly around.
There was Nelson Reynolds whom he scarcely knew.
The boy smiled and handed him a new glassful. Roger
almost snatched at it. The only thing Roger saw
was Coronado buzzing about, stinging some other
sleepy flower with the juice of his inexhaustible
gaiety.

" Coronado there," said Roger mouthily to Nelson
Reynolds, " look at him."

" Yes," said Nelson, " he seems to be having a good
time tonight."

" He always has a good time when there's enough for
him to lay his hands on."

" Well, there's enough here to eat and drink, too."
Nelson was turning away.

" I didn't mean that either," said Roger intent on
holding him.

" What did you mean? " Nevertheless, thought Roger,
I'll tell you anyway.

" I mean," he said, " he's eating you all up. He's exhausting you. He's devouring you — "

" He's a very nice kid," said Nelson Reynolds.

" You know nothing about him," railed Roger, " he's
an absolute devil."

" Not at all," said Nelson, " he's just got a good imagination."

" I tell you solemnly," Roger smiled in spite of himself, but he meant what he said, " that he's the most dangerous man I've ever known. He'd like to kill you all."

" He's always been more than friendly to me," said Nelson.

" Only to gain your confidence." Roger pointed at Coronado's back, across the room where he bent to whisper a word to Sylvia. " Can't you see all evening he's been insulting all of you? "

" Nonsense," said Nelson, " I've never seen him more charming."

" That's just it," said Roger, " he's got you all where he wants you. What difference whether he marries Sylvia or Norah or Faith or you or any of you? He's got you where he wants you." Roger was actually buttonholing Nelson Reynolds, who nevertheless seemed to suffer him goodnaturedly.

" Well, what does he want of us? " smiled Nelson, " Does he want to eat us? "

" I don't know," said Roger. " I don't know at all. Maybe he wants to kill you. Maybe he wants to make you alive."

" I'd rather let him kill us," Nelson smiled.

" That's just it," Roger knew he was talking too loud. " He thinks — I guess he thinks he can make you alive. The crazy fool. You're dead. You want to be dead. I never knew anyone like you — "

" Not at all," said Nelson, " we get along."

" You're all sleep-walkers. You all look as if you'd been kept in a cellar all winter. Or under a board — like dead grass, like — "

" Oh come on," said Nelson, " you ought to have some more to drink."

"I do not need another drink," said Roger. "You just don't dare listen to me. You'd better before you're all really dead."

"I thought you said we were dead already." Nelson was being patient.

"Oh, stand there," cried Roger, "be good-mannered, be gentle. Why don't you get sore. You've got a whole family to fight for. It's worth it. It's wonderful. Coronado's a thief. He'll steal it." Roger put his hands on Nelson's shoulders. He tried to make the conscious intensity of his eyes say everything that couldn't be crowded into the will of his voice. "Oh, but please, please, please listen, you goddamn fool."

"What's all this?" said Coronado, coming up suddenly. "Why all so serious?"

"They won't believe me," said Roger — his voice higher. "You tell them."

"He says you want to kill us all, Coronado," said Nelson.

"What else does he say?" asked Coronado. "What else did you say?"

"I'm telling them to wake up," said Roger boldly, "before you get 'em."

"Is that all?" laughed Coronado. "But why so serious?"

"I tell them you're crazy wild," said Roger. "You don't give a damn for the whole tribe. You'd chuck the whole lot — you'll —."

"The punishment of Cassandra," laughed Coronado. "What an agony for us to see the truth and these blind sheep here never to know —"

"He admits it," cried Roger. Nelson bleated obediently.

Coronado looked at Roger. "You couldn't betray me

even if you wanted to, Ruggiero." He smiled and walked away.

Roger felt dizzier and more tired. He saw Sylvia across the room. He had hardly spoken to her since he had come to Dagotan. She preferred not to dance so they sat in a corner of a built-in couch.

" It was terribly nice of you to come," she said, " Coronado was counting on you a great deal."

" I'm very glad he wanted me here. I was delighted to come." He felt at a loss. " I was delighted."

" I wish you could have come down earlier," she said, " we had another party last night, too."

" Was it as good as this? " asked Roger blankly.

" Well, it wasn't so noisy. Lots of the older people came," she laughed. " It was rather a Reynolds party you know." She stressed her own name, intimating the cadence as an explanation. Roger said nothing. He tried hard to overcome his drowsiness, to look interested.

" Isn't Coronado beautiful? " she said suddenly. He was back in the room again.

" Why yes," said Roger, " I think he is. He is."

" I'm frightfully lucky, aren't I? " she looked at him.

" You bet you are," said Roger easily. " You bet you are."

" I think I'm going to be terribly happy." Roger said nothing. Sylvia continued, " Don't you think I'll be happy? "

" Of course you will be. How could anyone not be with Coronado. Why happy, huh! "

" That's what I think," said Sylvia. " Sometimes I'm scared of him."

" What's to be scared of? " asked Roger. He must maintain his interest here. " Scared, why scared? "

" I love him so much." She says all her responses,

thought Roger, as if she had known them from birth
and now was talking in her sleep. " I love him so
much. Sometimes he's so wild that I don't know what
I'll do."

" I wouldn't worry about that," said Roger primly,
" that's his great charm."

" I know — but suppose, some day," she laughed,
" he'd just pick up and leave me? It's hard to be sure
of him."

" Nonsense," said Roger. " Why, the most he can do
would be to kill you."

" Kill me? " Sylvia smiled. " Why would he want to
do that? "

" I don't say he wants to," said Roger. " I said it's
the most he can do."

" Oh," said Sylvia, as if to ask him to continue.

" I only mean you wouldn't care if he did — would
you? It would make no difference to you if he did, would
it? You wouldn't care if he did would you — Can't you
see? "

" I don't know," said Sylvia. " I can't tell. I don't think
he'll kill me."

" You can't tell," said Roger doggedly. " You can't
tell."

" No," said Sylvia, " I can't tell, at all."

" What difference would it make? " said Roger with a
gesture of generosity. " What real difference? You'd have
with him at least the illusion of excitement. You'd think
you knew *something?* "

Coronado came up to them and looked at them. Roger
got up — and Coronado took his seat.

" He says you might kill me, darling," said Sylvia.
Roger braced himself against the wall, the liquor was
even in his feet.

"And so I might," laughed Coronado, "and so I might."

"No, darling," said Sylvia, "not before tomorrow night."

"Tomorrow," he said. "O no, I'll be busy tonight killing Roger, my traitor. If he wasn't so drunk someone might believe him."

"It's true," said Roger lamely. Sylvia appealed to Coronado.

"But if I wasn't so drunk," said Roger, "I'd never say a thing. Coronado likes me to talk; he thinks it's funny."

"Well," said Sylvia looking up at him, "don't you?"

Then the little girl who sang the jazz songs rushed up to Coronado and dropped into his lap with her bare arms around his neck. Their heads were both bright yellow under the light and when they kissed each other there was a single head of hair.

"Dear Coronado," she said, "I wish you were going to marry me."

Sylvia put her hand on the girl's lap and laughed.

"I don't care," she went on, "I wish you were marrying me." Coronado kissed her again and said, "What difference whether it's you or Sylvia? You know I'm always here."

Roger walked across the room very steadily, as he put his hand on the knob of a door leading out onto the piazza he felt Coronado behind him.

"Where are you going?" he asked.

"Outside to get a breath of air."

"Is it too hot here for you?" And this was not the first time Coronado's laugh seemed to mean nothing but laughter.

"It's as hot as hell in here."

" Stay one second," said Coronado, " aren't you enjoying yourself? "

" No," said Roger, " are you? "

" Yes," said he. " I love to hear you warn my friends
against me. That has the most delicate sound in the
world."

" You know what you're like," said Roger, " you're
no fool."

" Why, what do you mean? "

" You know damn well — either. Either I'm wrong
about you or they won't listen to me. What's the difference? "

" No difference at all. Come back and dance." Coronado held his arm. " I want to introduce you to my
friend."

" Who's that? " said Roger. " I've danced with everybody."

" Not with her," said Coronado, " she hasn't come in
yet."

" Have you been expecting her? " asked Roger, somehow sobered.

" I've been expecting her all night. She knows I
wanted her here."

" Why doesn't she come then? " Roger was talking
more seriously than he expected.

" Perhaps Sylvia scares her away? Do you think so? "
Roger was remembering hard. He spoke slowly.
" Well," said he — the data in its correct order in his
head, " your mother didn't scare her away. That girl at
the ball didn't scare her away. Where's your pipe —
Papageno? — "

" Maybe you with your warnings have only warned
her," Coronado looked kindly at him, and let his hand
drop from Roger's sleeve.

" I couldn't scare anybody," said Roger. " I was only telling Sylvia . . ."

" She's not anybody," said Coronado. " Nobody — or somebody. I wish she'd come now quickly. If she does not soon — I'll be bound to look for her."

" No you've got to stay here," said Roger. " You look after Sylvia."

" She can look after herself," said Coronado.

" She can't if you go off looking for somebody else." Roger straightened his tie and rubbed his fingers in his eyes to clear his head

" She'll come all right," said Coronado. " She'll come and tell me which ship I'll take to shore." He turned quickly and went to find whomever.

6

Roger stepped out on the piazza. Voices and quiet music followed the bang of the shut screen door. Lights from the wide windows fell in square pools from the house walls. Pine needles under his feet, the sound of water somewhere below, Roger passed down the gravel path to find the boardwalk leading to the dock. The stars above were large and warm. He walked down the flight of wooden steps to the pier.

He sat on the dock and felt the water. It was deliciously warm. His fingers played about in the black wetness and stirred up the thousands of minute algae that made the phosphorescence. The more he rumpled the slick surface, the more luminously the clouding whiteness foamed up. Yet he could not forget Coronado at all.

Presently voices and scuffling above told him the party was over. Many had gone back to their houses behind

the hill. But George Reynolds and Faith, and Larry and
Tom and Sylvia and Coronado all appeared on the dock
and made ready to go back in the boat. George Reynolds
felt of the water and let the phosphorus drip from his
fingers. He announced he would swim back. Roger
jumped up, his hand already unloosening his tie. He
would be delighted to swim back, too. All of the rest
started taking off their clothes. Tom said he would row
the boat across, so they all tossed their shirts and pants
and skirts into it. He stood in the dory, picking up the
shirts as they were thrown in, arranging them on the
seat so they wouldn't get messed or wet at the bottom
of the boat. Faith Reynolds jumped in first and her
body was clothed with the clouding phosphorus, as she
struck out from the shore; her hands caught great chunks
of water, illuminated at the touch of her wrists. She
called back in ecstatic shrieks for the rest to follow.
The vague naked figures upon the blackness that hung
below the stars over the dock, exchanged the pale dull-
ness of their whiteness for the pale luminosity of the
water. Each figure slipped into the water with a little
splash and left the dock vacant and darker for the va-
cancy, and the bay was spotted with the splashing rings
of phosphorescence.

On the eye level, in the water Roger could not see
anyone around him. No one any longer called and only
the splashing, the faint halo of light around a black
head upon the black water told him that the rest had
not drowned. A few yards ahead was the looming black
hull of one of the yachts. Underneath he heard a loud
splashing. Roger, his head ever so much clearer from
the water, struck swiftly out to see who it was. At each
dip and contraction of his hand into the wetness, where
the impact was most concentrated, a white coagulation

of phosphorus formed below, and floated up to the surface and disappeared into the dark.

Coronado was trying to haul himself up onto the yacht. He had one hand on a rope dropped over the side of the boat. Roger approached under the swelling smooth blackness of the yacht's prow. Its profile cut upwards like an expanding blade, and the water lapped gently round about its curving length. Roger swam up over and next to Coronado. The two pools of phosphorus merged into a single large moony bubble. Coronado placed one wet hand and arm on Roger's shoulder and gripped the rope with the other. Roger treaded water vigorously to maintain his proper position and thereby drew up for himself a thick shroud of pearly phosphorescence. With a final effort Coronado put all his sluicing weight on Roger's shoulders and sprang to gain the side of the ship. Roger was pushed deep under the water. He tried to open his eyes but could see nothing, and for a second, thought someone could have drowned him. He floated to the surface, and with his feet against the side of the yacht pushed himself on his back as far away as he could. He floated watching Coronado who had stepped out on the bowsprit, a dark man against the darkness, supporting himself in the black lines of rigging. Roger saw him sit on the end of the pole and balance. Then he seemed to slip sidewise and his head hung down. He gripped the pole above with his knees for a few seconds and plunged head down below the surface. Roger heard the splash and saw the smoke of light below the water and waited for him to rise. He seemed to take the most extraordinarily long time about it. Roger wondered for a second if he might never come up. If he had gone to seek a proper home among the valleys of pearl and phosphorus.

7

Once on the dock the naked boys and girls reached for their clothes as Tom Reynolds handed them out of the rowboat. Roger saw George bend over his wife and ask her if she were cold. He slapped her thighs with his hands and dried her off with his shirt and he held his coat over her as she drew on her skirt. As Roger pulled on his own pants he thought how easily those two were married together. They all walked barefoot up the dark leafy path to the big house. Coronado was the last one upstairs and the lights were left for him to put out. He went to stay with Sylvia for a little while before she went to sleep.

Roger climbed upstairs and threw his clothes on the chair in his room. He went into the bathroom a moment to get a towel, for he was still damp from the swim and he stood in the doorway of Tom and Larry Reynolds' room as he finished drying. They were quietly pulling off their clothes and putting on their pajamas. Their conversation coincided with Roger's thoughts. They were speaking of early marriages, whether or not they were successful — how it was a pity not to be as young as possible to enjoy one's children, the risk of becoming tired of one's wife and so on. Roger stayed there listening to the conversation silently, and wondered why on earth they didn't say what they meant. They were brothers. They could tell the truth to each other. They could share their fears about their sister. He knew they were not shy about Sylvia and Coronado on account of his being there. Deliberately the two boys folded up their pants and laid them across the chairs, and drew their shoes together neatly — and sat again on the beds buttoning their pajamas up. Their courtesy, their innate and conscious deliberation extended even to themselves. Indeed, thought Roger, it is more intense with themselves — although they never notice it. Why not say, for God's sake, Tom aren't you scared what will happen to Sylvia, Larry? I am scared to death — what will he do to her? But — *one gains as much as one loses in a marriage before thirty. And a first attachment is probably just as satisfactory as one after several violent affairs — taken all in all. And also.*

Presently Coronado came upstairs and stuck his head into Roger's room.

" Can I come in for a second? " — his face, as usual, laughing.

" Of course," said Roger, sitting up in bed. " Do." He came over and sat facing him, tapping with his heel on the floor.

" Home from the ball," laughed Coronado, " Don Giovanni and his Leporello — and the valet for one," — he took Roger's foot under the covers, " I daresay, hopes that nothing will be met with till morning."

" It was a wonderful ball," said Roger.

" All were gentlemen and every lady was a princess," — Coronado didn't seem to be following his own rhetoric. His attention wandered from his words. " But as far as Don Giovanni went — every girl he knew was the same girl — what satisfaction seducing the same silly creature? "

" What do you mean? " said Roger, " each was the same? "

" Oh, every one he found offered the same tug, rich or poor."

" I don't see what you mean? "

" Every woman was safe in the same way, and sure to surrender when he turned on his taps."

"It's a funny thing," said Roger, "but you look a lot like that girl who sang those songs."

"Yes," said Coronado, "both capped by the same crown."

"She's extraordinary," said Roger helplessly, "who on earth is she?"

"She's awake," said Coronado, "she seems to be awake."

"Have you known her long; do you know her well?" — and Roger awaited the answer he himself had formulated at the party.

"Not well," said Coronado.

"But you seemed so very close tonight," Roger insisted.

"Yes," said Coronado, "but I seem close to you now."

Roger was silent for a second. Only their breathing spoke to each other in the flat clatter of an impasse.

"Who are her parents — where did she come from?"

"The West, I've been told. Is she an orphan?"

Roger laughed at him. "I'm asking you," he said.

"Oh, Don Giovanni," laughed Coronado, "The fool, the furious fool — caterwauling over the Spanish hills to find those girls and every one the same."

"But even still —," said Roger, trying to keep up with the conversation.

"But even still," mocked Coronado. "But, even still — if if every girl was the same, each was the mother in himself. You know that quack's trick?"

"No," said Roger, "what do you mean?"

"I mean — I mean —. It was his mirror that he always kissed." Coronado laughed again and slapped Roger's leg. "God, but you're an admirable actor. I'd swear you're the thickest bootlicking knave one could ask for; if I'd my stick now I'd thrash you soundly."

"But honestly," Roger boldly attacked, "tell me about that girl."

"Oh, basta, basta," Coronado grinned, "that shock-headed light of love. Why, I've got a fine plan for you, my boy. We'll serenade her now and I'll be your accompaniment." He plunked his guitar.

"No," said Roger.

"But fall in love with her yourself. You're half in the quicksand already. Goodnight. I'm bound to go." He waved his hand and started swiftly back up, and out of the room. Roger gaped after him, his hand unraised in an answering goodnight. "Myself," said Roger, "fall in love with her myself?"

8

The next day dawned foggy and mist chilled the inhabitants of Dagotan. At breakfast old Mr. Reynolds looked healthier than ever. Roger felt that his prayers had been answered and that he was pleased. It might rain and then there'd be no nonsense about Sylvia's wedding. Coronado caught Roger's eye at the table when they were all talking about the weather. The happy and comforting hostility of Mr. Reynolds struck them both as indescribably funny. If Coronado had laughed, Roger would have roared. But Coronado only winked at Roger and lamented the weather to those around him. He described the tenacity of such mists in perverse detail. He gauged the unlikelihood of sunshine — and yet Roger saw he was convinced all through this foolery that the sun would shine for him and burn the mists away.

After breakfast Larry and Tom took Roger on a long ride to the other end of the island. Larry carried a huge

machete knife by which, with a neat trick of his wrist
and arm he could lop off even quite big branches that
had been allowed to grow too low over the bridle paths.
The island was not very large, but it included in its ten
or twelve miles a great variety of scenery. Larry spoke
to Roger every so often, pointing out some point of
vantage for a view of the sea. Or noticing the rise of
some blue heron from a marsh or a large buck, body
high in the underbrush and by no means afraid of the
riders. Roger learned from the two boys something
about the history of the island — how it had been origi-
nally commandeered by a Reynolds privateer — How
Indians had once lived here and how when the waters
between Dagotan and the mainland froze, the deer and
foxes went back and forth for food. The family had been
dominated in the middle of the last century by a man
whose contributions to politics and engineering gave
the Reynolds a national importance. As Larry described
his great-grandfather Roger knew that he might have
been his own great-grandson, except now there seemed
to be little enough pioneering to do. The West was
civilized. No mainland held much interest. To be sure
Tom Reynolds had wanted his dad to get him one of
the last of the four-masters but even he admitted that
so few men knew how to handle her that the whole business was rather artificial. The Reynolds were pioneers,
and it was a misfortune that their sons had only their
island of Dagotan to rediscover. Every hollow and hillock, every turn in the road had some association, some
family meaning. Here one of them was thrown riding
home from a picnic and the horse leaped the high stone
wall. Here cousin Houston shot the biggest buck ever
seen on the island. There Auntie Parker always wanted
a lookout station built. Roger appreciated the whole

tapestry of Larry's and Tom's intimacy with the island.
The names of Plunder Bay, Baby's Lake, Handsome
Hill or Parker's Perch, were all eloquent and redolent
of close familiarity and a blooded affection. Here they
lived and brought forth more cousins, and when the
time came married their cousins and were buried by the
surviving nephews and nieces.

Roger galloped ahead with Larry who explained as
he went the catalogue of names and places and their
parallel events. And every so often with his accustomed
deliberation he would reach up with the great steel
blade and slice off a green branch, and duck away from
it and ride on, in no way interrupting his narration.

9

When Roger got back to the big house he found
Coronado and Sylvia sitting on the grass of the hill,
below the flagpole whose snapping shadow diminished
and fluttered on the ground as the fresh breeze from the
sea careened the flag. Coronado asked Roger to join
them and he sat next to Sylvia on the sun-warmed grass
and felt the wet horse-sweat on his boots. Coronado soon
jumped up and said they must all take a sunbath down
on the dock. Roger begged off as he thought Sylvia
might want to be alone with him, but he insisted so
earnestly that Roger could only follow. Sylvia had a
prayer book in her hand. When they got down to the
water the boys peeled off their shirts and lay face down
to the sun. Sylvia turned away from the glare and started
fluttering the leaves of her book.

" Dearly beloved," she began, " we are gathered here
in the sight of God and in the face of this company to
join together this man and this woman in holy matri-

mony: which is commended of St. Paul to be honorable among all men."

" Let's leave St. Paul out of it," said Coronado, speaking to the planks of the dock. " We can be well married without him."

" And therefore," continued Sylvia in her sweet firm voice, " is not by any to be entered into unadvisedly or lightly; but reverently, discreetly, advisedly, soberly, and in the fear of God."

" Look there," cried Coronado, and lifted himself up on hands and knees pointing out into the bay. Larry and Tom Reynolds, with Faith and George, had run up all the signal flags on the big yachts. They looked very gay, set for the regatta of Sylvia's wedding.

" But," said Sylvia shutting the prayer book, and keeping her finger in the place, " but they're all too big. Those flags aren't right there."

" But don't they look pretty? " said Coronado.

" Yes, but they're not right; they're too big. They put them up in the wrong order."

" They're not signalling anyone, darling," said Coronado. " They're just for looks."

" I know," Sylvia seemed worried, " but there's a right way and a wrong way." Sylvia waved at Larry and Tom over the water. They called back but those on the dock couldn't hear what was said. Sylvia opened up the prayers again.

" Into this holy estate, these two persons present come now to be joined. If any man can show just cause, why they may not lawfully be joined together, let him now speak — or else hereafter forever hold his peace."

Sylvia paused. Roger looked over at Coronado who was lying as before face down. Nothing that day had betrayed on his part the slightest discomposure.

" Go on," said Coronado to Sylvia, " read on."

" And also speaking unto the Persons who are to be married, he shall say, I require and charge you both, (as ye will answer at the dreadful day of judgment, when the secrets of all hearts shall be disclosed) that if either of you know any impediment — why ye may not be lawfully joined — ." Sylvia closed the book again and patted her hair with her hand. She put the flat of her head on Coronado's bronzing back. He looked up smiling — " Larry and Tom are having races there — look." The boys had set the sails of two knockabouts and were sailing around the bay. They did everything in the most perfect unison. They would sail up to some imaginary mark, jibe quickly and come about, all without a command from either. They never once exceeded the other in speed, and yet Roger felt there was some competition in it; they really were racing.

" How lucky for them," laughed Coronado, " never to beat the pattern of their brotherhood." He jumped up on his feet to see the motor launch chug into the bay. He took Sylvia's hands in his and got her up as well. A figure in the launch waved to them and they waved back. It was Mr. Gilroy, the minister, an old friend of Coronado's and of the Reynolds' too. As they walked up to the house they spoke about possible prayers to use, even before Mr. Gilroy had a chance to make the formal expressions of pleasure at being here. Mr. Reynolds was still busy with his lists. They seemed to have overflowed from his notebooks onto long white strips of pencilled paper. He kept abstractedly biting his lip and arranging old Grandma Parker in the surrey with him, and Nelson Reynolds could have the new colt Tinder and Mrs. Payson Reynolds could go with Jimmy. But if she went with Jimmy where could Payson ride?

There didn't seem to be any more carriages or horses
even. Dear, dear, Coronado do be a good fellow and see
if you can help me here. Coronado did some perfunc-
tory shifting and took Mr. Gilroy to his room.

10

At the last moment Coronado slightly upset the arrangement of Mr. Reynolds in regard to the transporta-
tion for the wedding. He suddenly decided he would
not go in the carriage at all. He would ride with his
groomsman. But all the horses had been previously ap-
portioned. There was not a single one left in the barns.
So he decided to walk along beside Roger's horse. As
they passed from the hallway, various ones of the young
Reynolds were sticking up big branches of green beech
leaves behind the mounted antlers and in the lighting
fixtures, for the reception afterwards. Roger let the
screen door swing back and stepped out onto the piazza
and thence to the lawn. He leaned up against the mast of
the flagpole for a second and shielded his eyes from the
glare of the sunny afternoon. There were vague move-
ments all over the island. The leaves rustled and the trees
swayed and the birds strung lines of flight between blue
sky and the bushes. From their separate houses the
Reynolds were moving away and over towards the place
of marriage. Coronado came up behind Roger leading
his horse and held it for him to mount. They walked
on down the hill and passed various carriages full of
Reynolds men and women who waved but did not speak.
Down past the barns and out of the pasture, they opened
and shut the high gates. The grooms had put on their
Sunday-meeting clothes and grinned awkwardly as they
passed the stable yard. When they were once into the

woodlands Coronado saw that Roger would walk his
horse all the way so as not to tire him, so he jabbed the
brute in the ribs and they trotted along, Coronado's
hand on Roger's stirrup. Roger tried to hold in his
horse. He was very conscious of Coronado wanting to
spend himself, to run himself out in this ride. But the
more they ran along the more strength seemed to flow
from the runner, and the rider let his horse take its own
pace. Under the oak and beech of Dagotan, traversing
a road that was upon the backbone of the island, the sun
poured through the interlacing boughs and dappled
the roan of the horse's neck and haunches, and fell in
shifting pools of sunny warmth upon Roger's tanned
arms and fingers on the reins. Running beside him,
Coronado's head on the level of his hands caught the
sun's reflection in a tangled mesh of thick uncorded
silk, silk like corn thread, tossed like a mane. After they
had run a little way, without checking his gait, Coronado snatched off his shirt, to save it from his sweat and
handed it to Roger who let it snap out behind him like
a flag. What did the deer see, quivering in the bushes
beside their route? Two fleeing figures running from
an enemy, two secret couriers racing to warn their
friends? What did the partridge and the seagull find
below their beaks and bellies; the lengthening redness
of a horse's body, set with a booted rider, and next to
him, a shifting ball of yellow light streaming along over
the leafy ground, losing themselves in the green boughs
and reappearing in the flow of the dusty road.

11

Roger tethered his horse, with a rope the groom had
tied about its neck, to a tree whose whitened branches

seemed stripped of bark; carefully so as to give the horse
some leeway if he became restive and yet strong enough
so he would not snap his reins. He followed Coronado
over some stones and brambles and found himself above
and to one side of a natural rocky bowl.

Many of the Reynolds were already there, grouped
in a semicircle below a great rock like a dolmen or an
altar. Coronado stepped out into the bowl and smiled
at them. Imperceptibly they recoiled; but made no motion of recognition or alliance. He walked quickly up
the steep grade to the dolmen and leaned against it for
a second, almost as if it were a goal he was touching to
tell himself he'd gained it. Roger was below him on the
slope. The smooth soles of his boots gave him no support and he had to stand sideways to stand straight.
They looked down the gully to the sea, and to the open
spaces at the north and south of the island. The sun
was over towards its home and it fell in flashing bars
on the whirling spokes of the Reynolds carriages as
Roger saw them come from over the plain, from out
the woods, behind a grove of pine towards this valley.
The plains below stretched flatly. Every declivity, every
hollow was filled with pooling shadow for the sun was
low. The valley itself was all in its shadow. Roger felt
the presence of Coronado drawing these folk up into
himself, absorbing them in his will and in the concentrated purity of his equivocal essence. The rest of the
guests arrived — Reynolds and Parkers. Roger recognized a face here and there among the older people but
men and women were all merged into the anonymous
distinction of the type Reynolds face. Louis Parker,
apologetically stroking his moustaches seemed just to
have heard of Cousin Sylvia's wedding. He was trying
to explain to Mr. Reynolds about it. He had only just

heard. He had come as quick as he could. No one said
much. Mr. Reynolds had made the last pitiful defense
against Coronado's determination although he was here
in the valley and in his riding clothes. He at least had
assumed a proper wing collar and a wedding tie. Roger
looked over the ranks of the quiet, placid unfulfilled
faces, a race of virgin princes, whom as the years greyed
them took on more of the untouched and dispassionate
blandness of sleep. Roger looked about in vain for any
of the young Reynolds. There was not a child in the
throng, except to the left of Roger and below him on
the slope were four of the youngest, two boys and two
girls looking exactly alike even to the crop of their short
hair. They stood in a group in blue overalls and laughed
a little. They tried to get a more solid footing. Then
they all composed themselves, presenting their faces to
their elders. Coronado put on his shirt again.

A man came up from the bottom of the gully and
spoke to Mrs. Reynolds a moment. Coronado suddenly
laughed in a low voice and slipped by Roger to greet
him. Roger saw a smile of great graciousness come over
the man's face as he took Coronado's hand, whose back
was to Roger so he could not see his face. When Coronado turned away to come back the grace fell from the
man's face and it looked as grey as the rest but there was
a smile also on Coronado's for Roger to see. " It was
Myles Bennett," said Coronado, " marry me or not, I
knew he'd come."

Mr. Gilroy, the minister, stepped up to the rock and
smiled at them both, and Roger felt, as he stepped up
a step and saw Coronado laughing assume the bride-
groom's place, that the two of them were impostors. He
was some crafty servant, following his master through
the suburbs of his evil intent, whistling inside to keep

his courage up; Coronado as Don Giovanni in the grave-
yard, — and Roger felt himself bound to fulfil the command of asking the man his master murdered to his
master's midnight board. Then as from some given
signal the four young Reynolds in the blue overalls
began to sing. At first their childish voices sounded thin
in the free wind of the valley, but they gained strength
and surety as they sang on. The song was a Capstan
chantey Coronado had chosen. The melody was mourn-
ful, but it had the insinuating simplicity of a familiar
hymn. The eldest girl lifted up her steady voice to sing
Oh Shenandoah, I love your daughter — and the rest
swelled the solemn refrain of Coronado's prothalamium
— *Away, my rolling river*. The sky, blue, unclouded,
vibrated with the dance of its reflected sun within the
great blue hemisphere. *It's full ten years since first I
sought her*. And the gull wheeled and flashed its shadow
on the space of ground below where no one touched.
Then the chorus of four in the resonance of their slight
slow harmony — *We're bound away across the wide
Missouri*. Coronado looked down the valley. His eyes
were bright as a mirror, his whole presence seemed di-
vested of dross, clothing and flesh were refined into the
complete simplicity of his expectant attitude. *Oh Shenandoah, I love your daughter* — *away, away, my rolling
river*. And all the bells rang under the roar of all the
oceans. *I'll take her across the stormy water*.

Down the valley, up the hill came Sylvia Reynolds in
a red skirt and a white blouse, with her sweet face open
to her lover's sun. Her elder sister held her left hand,
her older brother, her right. She advanced between
them, supported by them and followed by a train of
the cousins, a silent troop.

Sylvia was released by her family, and stepped up the

incline by Coronado's side. The cousins completed the
semi-circle by the side of the older Reynolds and stood
uncovered, quiescent — side by side.

The minister opened his book and started to read —
" Dearly beloved, we are gathered together here in the
sight of God, and in the face of this company . . ." He
read so low that Roger could barely hear him. Coronado
was bent almost over the book. Sylvia and he drew themselves together in the single closeness of their conversation.

Afterwards Roger could remember little of the ceremony. He knew he gave the ring to Coronado, that
Sylvia's father gave her to her husband, that the minister seemed to fade into the rock. It seemed unending
hours before they were pronounced man and wife.
Roger prepared himself to be released from the tense-
ness of his position and the closeness of his observation.
But Coronado was having prayers read for his soul and
Roger could only listen to the monotony of the minister's cadence.

" O most glorious and gracious Lord God, who dwell-
est in heaven, but beholdest all things below, look down
we beseech thee and hear us calling out of the depths of
misery and out of the jaws of this death, which is now
ready to swallow us up; save Lord, or else we perish.
The living, the living shall praise thee." Roger heard
no more. Who were these enemies that hovered about
him like disease to pack him off to hell? Who were these
shadows that were his counterpart? From whence came
the hideous protection of his own brightness to stop the
greater or lesser fiends of his disaster? White and black
flash like swords the pain and supplication of this servant of servants. Roger willed his ears shut. A cold had
possessed the separate vertebrae of his spine and

clutched each bony rung like a ladder of icicles. But still, still there seemed to be a voice from a rock, speaking with a rock's grey voice and praying.

"In particular, we beseech thee to continue thy gracious protection to us this night. Defend us from all dangers and mischiefs, and from the fear of them; that we may enjoy such refreshing sleep, as may fit us for the duties of the following day. Make us ever mindful of the time when we shall lie down in the dust; and grant us grace always to live in such a state that we may never be afraid to die: so that living and dying we may be thine, through the merits and satisfaction of thy son Christ Jesus in whose name we offer up these our imperfect prayers."

Creatures out of the old earth, grey men, sleepers, gathered here, ranged here before this rock, and sleeping under the open lids of sunlight and the shut eye of night, shout once out against this proud man who rapes your daughter in her father's breast. Halt his vain prayers and banish him into the realms of air and darkness from whence he came and to where he does return now with your Persephone.

"O Lord, our heavenly Father, by whose Almighty power we have been preserved this day: by Thy great mercy defend us from all perils and dangers of this night, for the love of Thy only son our Savior Jesus Christ —" and amen to that, Coronado placing his kiss upon his bride.

12

Roger stumbled when he went up to shake Coronado's hand. He hesitated to kiss Sylvia. Even now he did not feel he knew her well enough. He clasped her shoulders. He felt he must not be too brusque. He felt the smallness of her shoulders, her small smile. Coronado's face was no face. It was featureless like the bottom of a brass plate. Roger was relieved to lose himself in the crowd of Reynolds relations.

Coronado quickly threw off his congratulators and with Sylvia in one hand, mounted with long strides to the top of the hill behind the rock. The rest all followed to watch the sun go down. Roger lost track of Coronado. He was too blinded to know what to do but he felt the necessity at least of an automatic action. He went up to Mrs. Reynolds and very warmly congratulated her.

"I never saw you before, young man," she laughed goodnaturedly. " I'm not Fanny Reynolds. I'm her sister. O Fanny, Fanny — look here, this young man mistook . . ." Roger went off and let the passing figures stir up the air around him and cool him off. He stood at loss. "But the most amusing wedding I've ever been to —" more voicy chatter and: "I'd just as soon get married myself —" "Oh Harry here —" Then he felt an arm slip into his own. It was a Reynolds woman — not yet middle-aged who knew him slightly. She had felt he needed the contact of a gesture for support. She had seen him sicken at Coronado's flame in the rite at the rock. Her arm slipped into his, stayed with him as a benediction for the rest of the day, like the sun setting in the halo of her hair as she walked away.

And Coronado and Sylvia and George and Faith and Tom and Larry and Nelson and all the rest of the young caught at each other's hands and in a long whipping, grappling line tore down the hill, over the gorse and boulders to the road. They were all shouting and as the last one reached the bottom many of them fell on the ground and bounced up again from sheer excess of spirit.

Then they noticed that Roger had been left with the guests and the family at the top of the hill and Tom and Larry started shouting Roger, Roger, and at first Roger did not know whether or not to leave his fortress of Reynolds in the top of sunlight and go down to their sons and daughters but he heard the unceasing laughter of one voice above the others calling Ruggiero, Ruggiero — and he tore on down the hill, leaving the smiles behind him to settle on the tired, happy quiet countenance of the Reynolds line.

They hoisted Coronado and Sylvia on their shoulders and carried them up the road to the first gate. Roger brought up the rear of the dusty procession and watched the heads and shoulders of the other catch the sun's last rays before him. He went to untether his horse and rode down to the road looking for someone to escort him home.

13

But when they finally reached the big house, the reception was already under way. People swarmed in the hallway. Sylvia looked very fresh and happy in a pair of green lounging pajamas. Roger decided to leave at once. They were sending a launch with someone over to Cricket Bay. Roger got his clothes together and decided to take it — at once. He said goodbye to the Reynolds. Mr. Reynolds thanked him very much for helping out with the wedding. Roger suddenly realized he had done no helping at all. Sylvia was talking to some aunts and uncles under the flagpole. Tom and Larry were coming to haul down the drooping banner. She was about to run indoors before she caught cold. She saw Roger and came up to him. She was terribly sorry he had to go. It was wonderful of him to have come to the wedding.

Well, it was wonderful to come. He looked at her a
moment and kissed her on the cheek. Coronado came
up and gripped his arm. He said he wanted to take him
ashore himself. He would insist on it. Roger became
scared. No. You don't. You stay right here. All these
guests, they expect you. So they said goodbye. Larry and
Tom carried the folded flag into the house. The lights
were being turned on. As Roger went down the road
he saw Coronado and Sylvia arm in arm waving at him.
Then they too turned and passed into the house.

14

Roger drove on for about an hour. The headlights of
oncoming cars flashed in his eyes and tired him. He
usually hated the mechanics of driving along, waiting
for the proper moment to pass the next car, watching
that nobody else would swing out to hit him. He tried
to keep his eye on his mirror to look out for possible
motorcycle policemen with their single headlight. But
since so many of the motors had one eye out, he quickly
lapsed into concentration on keeping up the average
of his speed. Then he felt hungry and remembered he
had hardly eaten since breakfast. He looked out for a
possible combination lunch wagon and gasoline filling
station, to save time. But he found none and finally
drew up at a lunch wagon.

The man who was inside the counter read a folded
newspaper. He was loath to put the paper down to get
Roger some ham and eggs. The bacon fat grizzled and
steamed and smelled sweet.

" Dja hear about these carbarn murderers? " he asked.

" No, what's that? " said Roger — glad of the conversation.

" Oh, two fellows from Bedford got the paymaster of a bus company by the South Weston carbarns and beat him up bad. The guy died. They didn't get nothing."

" Were they caught? " asked Roger, looking around to see the range of the food.

" Yes," said the man. " They confessed. One of 'em's only a kid, too."

" What happened to them? "

" Oh," laughed the man, and flattened a newspaper on the counter for Roger to see. " That's just it. They're gonna get electrocuted tonight."

" Are they really? " The ham and eggs looked done to Roger.

" They're waiting right now to hear whether they get another reprieve." The man poked the cooking food. " They won't. They got two already."

" Too bad," said Roger.

" Yes," said the man, " I'd hate like hell to wait looking at the clock to have the goddamned juice turned into me."

" How about my eggs? " asked Roger.

" O. K." said the man. " But hell, it might happen to anybody."

" Sure," said Roger and smacked his lips.

Larry led Coronado's horse and Tom had the reins of Sylvia's in his hands. The beasts stood and rubbed noses just beyond the pool of light that spilled from the big house into the darkness. They were going to spend their honeymoon in a remote cabin at the far end of Dagotan. Coronado came out of the house, and with a gesture of vague dismissal let Larry know he could take care of his horse himself. Larry went to help his sister. Coronado jumped up on the saddle, his reins hanging loose. The horse started down the hill of its own accord.

Larry and Tom and Sylvia stayed silent together for a second, looking after the disappearing figure. Then they helped her up. She called him, and called him, and then urged her pony to a little trot, even if it was night and there was a downhill grade. The brothers turned and went towards the house. They paused, kicking the ground, then assuming she had overtaken her husband, passed into the house.

As Roger ate the man told him what it was to be condemned, to be reprieved, and then the date definitely set for execution. He pointed to the clock on the wall. He said when its hands lay on each other at five to eleven they'd start the death march. Here he'd be watching the clock and there they'd be scared green. It gives you a funny feeling, he said.

Afterword

By Lincoln Kirstein

Raised in Boston, I was named after Abraham Lincoln. My father was an idolator and owned a library of Lincolniana, among which, fifty years ago, Herndon's *Life* was something of a secret, subversive book. It showed some warts on Honest Abe; my father prized his hero's humanity, the man within a myth. This gave me some hint both of the immediacy and magic of history, as well as its written shirking of responsibility in the normal accumulation of received and accepted ideas. My father taught me that history should not be learned from textbooks, that it extended into daily newspapers, which were also corrupt; that while journalism was not properly history, our present was much a part of our past as it was of a future. I developed a passion for "historical" novels, possibly as an easy way to learn something of the picturesque. The Boston Public Library, of which my father was president, the Museum of Fine Arts, later the Fogg Museum at Harvard, displayed rooms and objects that, for me, upholstered Dumas, Victor Hugo, Dickens, Stevenson, Conan Doyle *(Brigadier Gerard)*, Mark Twain *(The Prince and the Pauper)*, Howard Pyle *(Men of Iron)*, and a quantity of colorful romances whose names and authors are long forgotten.

When I read F. Scott Fitzgerald's first novel, *This Side of Paradise*, on its publication in 1920 I was fourteen years old. His book chronicles the decade and a half during which I'd been born and, so far, grown up. Promptly, it appeared to me as an "historical" novel. Its period was the years before the first world war, during it and, briefly after. I could identify my own restricted experience with its nostalgic and glamorous stylization which I eagerly devoured as an ultimate amalgam of wit, wisdom, and sophistication. Ten years later I wrote my novel which I hoped might contain an equivalent interest. It was easy for me to equate Harvard of the late 1920s with Princeton of the late 1910s. Both colleges were luxurious playgrounds of a post-Hamiltonian plutocracy; players were the sons and grandsons of historic clans, "rich, well-born, and able." The Boston that more or less bred me, the boys I knew in college, their behavior outside classrooms, their ancestral attachments, seemed all of a piece, a mosaic of local and logical tradition which, alive in the present, gave a vivid immediacy to modern history.

Fitzgerald was a provincial from the Middle West, who when he wrote his first book had no experience of Europe and who saw the Atlantic seaboard as magical territory. Due to the permissive generosity of my parents, I was familiar with a fraction of literary London, the main European museums, plus Northern Italy, Spain, and North Africa, where I traveled on my own in successive summer vacations. "History" for me was first illustrated, then illuminated, by works of art which I had already seen reproduced as slides in art-history courses. In the nineteenth century, Charles Eliot Norton, a friend of John Ruskin, promulgated the taste which, commencing with classical Greece and Rome, culminated in Pater's Italian Renaissance, providing criteria for several generations of young gentlemen who would become amateurs and collectors of costly objects. When I arrived as a Freshman in 1926, Norton's canon had been largely absorbed, and aesthetic interest was transferred to the French and Spanish gothic and romanesque in painting and architecture. My years at the Fogg were a watershed during which medieval emphasis was succeeded by the Hispano-Italian baroque. I wrote a dissertation on El

Greco which involved my visiting every church in Spain where
he may have worked, in search of a "lost" picture of St. John
the Evangelist, once in Valladolid, but which at the moment,
had I only known it, was safe in a State Street bank vault,
waiting transfer to the Worcester Museum, an hour from
Cambridge. However, my quest was a fair education, for the
small towns of Ronda, Avila, Burgos, Segovia fifty years ago
seemed to have changed little from the days of Don Quixote
and Philip the Second.

My attitude toward "history," or rather historical fictions in
prose or relics in paint, was considerably altered through T. S.
Eliot who by the mid-twenties exercised a considerable influence over undergraduate cerebration, although little enough
among the faculty who two decades later came to canonize
him, when students of my generation became professors
themselves. In his preface to a drama in blank verse on the
subject of Savonarola (by his mother!), Eliot remarked that
works with an "historical" pretext or background usually told
more about the period in which they were written than the
epoch they aspired to bring to life. The cautious, conscientious
revivals of classical antiquity by Sienkiewicz, Alexei Tolstoi,
Bulwer-Lytton in prose, of Alma-Tadema and Gerome in
painting could now be viewed as habitat groups of Victorian
stagecraft, populated by passionate bourgeois ladies and gentlemen who had doffed waistcoats and corsets to star in
museum charades. This purview made me see my own time
also as an historic period; the styles of dress, manners, and
morality of girls and boys in Boston were costumed in the
epoch: 1919–29.

As for self-expression, apart from appreciatory, decorative,
or fanciful ratiocination, I also had a small talent for drawing
and thought I might as well become a portrait painter. I
admired (and increasingly admire) the grand pictorial biogra-
phies of John Singer Sargent, in whose finest work the style,

stance, and story of personages incarnate their era. While
Sargent had already long refused to accept portrait commissions, his final work included the completion of a huge series of
murals in the high stone vault atop the Boston Public Library.
With him, my father was involved in an arresting doctrinal
controversy which embodied metaphysic as much as color
schemes and tactile values. Sargent's over-all program encom-
passed nothing less than a conspectus of world religions,
comparatively presented. The last two panels depicted "The
Synagogue" and "The Church." At their unveiling, a storm
broke, from two sides. On the one hand, the Jewish community
of which my father was a pillar (as well as being president of
the Library) objected violently to an image which they read as
defamatory; on the other, the fraternity of Cardinal O'Con-
nell's archdiocese saw the imagery of an Anglo-Catholic artist
as heresy, or worse. Sargent was a scholar, familiar with his
friend Henry Adams' *Mont St. Michel and Chartres* as well as *The
Virgin and the Dynamo*. He personified the essence of Old and
New Testaments according to their medieval interpretation at
the apogee of the twin faiths' intellectual influence.

Judaism was represented by a muscular, Michelangelesque
woman (to be startlingly reminiscent of Golda Meir) clasping
the tablets of the Law, enveloped by the shattered curtains of
the Ark as the Temple collapsed around her, a prototype of
Hagia Sophia, that Holy Wisdom which would also become the
Fourth Person of the Trinity. Sargent saw Her as the tragic
persona of Israel, doomed to exile, outcast of nations, the voice of
Job and Jeremiah. Christianity was symbolized by a young
woman in mourning robes, enthroned. Between her knees
slumped the corpse of a young man who might have been her
mystic brother (or lover), but who, in essence, was the ageless,
eternal, and incarnate Second Person of the Trinity, above
whom hovered the dove of the Holy Spirit. My father was
much impressed by Sargent's hermeneutics, and later, meditat-

ing on the fact that ideas were formerly of importance behind structures of pure color, design, plasticity within picture frames, I became conscious of a metaphysic in art and "history."

Hence I aspired to write an "historical" novel which would utilize what I knew and felt about my own times in as pictorial a fashion as I might muster. Along with Fitzgerald (who capped his first promise by *Gatsby*), my models (as were also his) were Frank Swinnerton, Compton Mackenzie, Joseph Hergesheimer. Today few read *Sinister Street, Carnival* or *Three Black Pennys*, but when the median literary modes of the time come to be studied by Ph.D.s of the future, it will be seen why their particular brand of vivid characterization and intense atmosphere, quite untouched by cinematic adaptation and dilution, appealed to the young of their time.

To grant that my novel was little more than autobiography would be an understatement. One reason that I never again completed another one was that while I had some sense of background, I was quite unable to realize characters with whom I had no firsthand contact. I could conceive of dramatic, or at least theatrical, situations, but I could not invent three-dimensional characters in any satisfactory depth. I was more interested in the problem of form and structure than in particulars of personality. People seemed to resolve into types and symbols; I had a predisposition to impose a factitious order where there was little apparent evidence. I proposed an episodic narrative in which the protagonist, named Baum (a tree), grew figurative leaves, if not fruit or blossoms. I had taken a famous course in Dante with Professor Grandgent, audited Whitehead's seminar in metaphysics, and was fascinated by J. L. Lowes' exploration of his *Road to Xanadu*. I knew that novels as well as epics should have a structural schedule, and I hoped to build for myself a scaffold, which today must only seem rude, naïve, and pretentious. I conceived of my tale as a parable of *action*, as I then considered physical or nervous energy to be: positive, neutral, negative; comic, tragic, and ironic; thesis, antithesis, synthesis. I'm afraid such elements in their concealed arrangement were so idiosyncratic that they added little to incidents described which hardly rationalize themselves into much of an apparent pattern.

In my search of the past around Cambridge, Concord, Salem, Milton, and Boston itself, I was accompanied by the photographer Walker Evans, who took some hundred pictures of Victorian architecture in the vicinity, many of which are now in museum collections. His lens imitated the eye of architects who designed and built venerable houses. He recaptured history through the quality of his own old-fashioned camera's vision. I wanted my novel to be illustrated by actual photographs, of scenes and persons I'd known, transposed for the sake of decency into a typological gallery. These would not have been literal portraits but symbolic snapshots suggesting an immediacy of time, place, and person with a fresh candor. I thought of my various episodes as post-cards, dashed off to be mailed home or to friends. I strove for a "photographic" atmosphere, which would be at once hard focus but stereo-scopic. I could not then have seen how soft focus the prose proved to be, as it came out in print. The only merit I might claim for whatever got itself written was the urgency which then propelled it, which made its composition seem undoubt-edly necessary and significant. At least I was never hindered by doubts as to its quality as "literature," or whether or not it was sufficiently "artistic" or "well-written." I opted on the side of "life" rather than art; the craft of the novel, in the terms of Morgan Forster or Henry James never daunted me; the book more or less wrote itself. Nothing in it, for better or worse, was invention; it was all far too literally true, however veneered or transposed a detail.

When my father came to read a bound copy, he was

horrified, seriously considering steps toward its suppression. But how to kill it? By buying up every copy and burning each? By paying the publisher, a charming man devoted to the expansion of youthful talent, not to send out the edition? Joseph Brewer, the most unworldly of editors, would have welcomed any chance for scandal. Actually, the book was ignored. I vaguely recall a single notice from a Marxist critic dismissing it as conspicuous waste, its author a trifler typical of his class and college. As for my own reaction: I could not bear to open it from the time it appeared until a few months ago when I was approached by its present publishers. Strangely enough, there had been several offers in the last ten years to reprint, none of which came to much, nor did I take them seriously or push toward any resurrection.

However, now forty years on, simply by letting it gather dust, it seems to have fulfilled some of my original ambitions. One might indeed consider it an "historical" novel, a document of the times in which it was written. The peculiar style of craft featuring the exposition of decorative art in Paris in the mid-twenties has come to popularize itself as Art-Deco. Perhaps my book is an example of Art-Deco, in prose. Certainly I can claim this for the Parisian episode, for Paris was the fount of the special sensibility which forged the style. Objectively regarded, here are the memoirs of a young American born in 1907, a year which was, as far as I am concerned, still in the late nineteenth century. In essence, the twentieth did not start until 1913. Its fanfare was Stravinsky's *Sacre du Printemps*. The Russian ballet was the salient artistic (as well as political) preface to subsequent seminal and tragic decades. Diaghilev brought to Paris and the West ideas demonstrated by dancing, music, spectacle which Russia herself disdained, through the financial agency of a post-Edwardian *entente cordiale*. He threw a bridge from a Byzantine inheritance across to the megalopolitan "modern" world. The succession of the Russian ballet, its diffusion in aesthetics and sensibility, the shock of its physicality, the impact of personalities, its brilliant collaborations and cross-pollination began to make the names of Stravinsky, Picasso, Satie, and Cocteau household words. American exiles in Paris and along the Côte d'Azur spread their particular stylization of postwar behavior through the manners of Fitzgerald and his friends which are clearly delineated in *Tender Is the Night* and Hemingway's *Sun Also Rises*. These were in the heavyweight class. My entry was hardly lightweight, and even to think of it as bantam or flyweight rather strains the metaphor.

I would never pretend to be part of that important environment and its current declarations. The books of this period that I particularly admired and which influenced my thinking and feeling, although hardly my writing, were those of Raymond Radiguet, Edward Sackville-West, René Crevel, and, of course, Fitzgerald. My inadequacies in comparison to their far more professional novels were only too clear to me, and the realization of them precipitated me into other paths. However, now, there seem to me to be two episodes which were eliminated by Joseph Brewer when the book was being readied for the press, which I have wished to include, since I find they reinforce the development of the protagonist's character and fill in chinks or gaps which help its realization as a rounded figure.

Apart from the single name of Sergei Pavlovitch Diaghilev, there are no persons, well known or even moderately renowned, which contribute their figurations, yet the novel might be described as a *roman à clef*, certainly not to the degree of Harold Nicolson's *Some People*, which was also an influence. My cast of characters were simply people I chanced to have met, and claimed for their attraction. Some of the prototypes, recognizing themselves at one remove, from my treatment of them, expressed surprise and dismay by a distorted portraiture. They considered themselves quite irrelevantly considered, by no means subject matter for inclusion in a book by a companion, who, for however else he behaved, certainly represented no one's notion of a writer. Had I been more considerate, focussed, humorous, ironic, my model would not have been Fitzgerald but rather the early Benjamin Disraeli. As a footnote, I can only add that my next three unfinished novels (all destroyed) leaned heavily on *Coningsby, Lothair,* and *Vivian Grey.* After my first effort, I was no longer content to use myself as narrator. The spiritual protagonist of "Choice of Weapons" (my second) was T. E. Lawrence, with whom I had managed to strike up a brief correspondence through David Garnett. In my still-born projection Chapman-Shaw-Ross-Lawrence was an extension of the chief personage in the final episode of *Flesh Is Heir.* In many ways he represented my ideal of Lawrence, for the two resembled each other both physically and in their romantic backgrounds and personal histories. Both were schooled at Oxford, both were archaeologists devoted to Islamic culture, and both dazzled my youth. Whatever merit rests in my work drew from my friend to whom it was dedicated. Mourning his mysterious subsequent career, for he long outlived Lawrence, in a pursuit of the ineffable and ineluctable, I remember a motto he inscribed in a copy of Landor's *Pericles and Aspasia,* which he once gave me, and which was a quotation from it: "There is no word of passionate love repeated of which the echo is not faint at last." Like most literary manifestations of post-adolescence, whatever their flighty presumptions, they usually turn out to be love stories which are really love letters; I hoped mine would qualify also as an historical romance. I was in love with his youth and mine, his world and a world which I hoped we had reason to believe could be equated with a sphere of significant activity.

Now, both seem further removed from any existent present than the Boston of Henry Adams' *Education* or of Henry James' *Bostonians.*

A second narrative of mine, *For My Brother*, through the good offices of Christopher Isherwood and John Lehman was published by the Hogarth Press in London and had the honor of being liked by E. M. Forster. This told of a Mexican working-class boy caught between industrialized Texas and a Mexico still clinging to pre-industrial civilization. It was well received in the English press, but German bombs destroyed the entire edition in a warehouse almost at publication. During the Hitler war, I wrote a narrative in verse concerning much of what I found in the army. Neither of these later books were "novels," but my apprenticeship from *Flesh Is Heir* contributed to the relative security of both. They also were rooted in "history" and both might have been illustrated by photographs.

Textual Note

The text of *Flesh Is Heir* published here is a photo-offset reprint of the first printing (New York: Brewer, Warren & Putnam, 1932). No emendations have been made in the text.

M. J. B.

Lost American Fiction Series

published titles, as of October 1975
please write for current list of titles

Textual Note

The text of *Flesh Is Heir* published here is a photo-offset reprint of the first printing (New York: Brewer, Warren & Putnam, 1932). No emendations have been made in the text.

M. J. B.

Lost American Fiction Series

published titles, as of October 1975
please write for current list of titles

Weeds. By Edith Summers Kelley. Afterword by Matthew J. Bruccoli

The Professors Like Vodka. By Harold Loeb. Afterword by the author

Dry Martini: A Gentleman Turns to Love. By John Thomas. Afterword by Morrill Cody

The Devil's Hand. By Edith Summers Kelley. Afterword by Matthew J. Bruccoli

Predestined. A Novel of New York Life. By Stephen French Whitman. Afterword by Alden Whitman

The Cubical City. By Janet Flanner. Afterword by the author

They Don't Dance Much. By James Ross. Afterword by George V. Higgins

Yesterday's Burdens. By Robert M. Coates. Afterword by Malcolm Cowley

Mr and Mrs Haddock Abroad. By Donald Ogden Stewart. Afterword by the author

Flesh Is Heir. By Lincoln Kirstein. Afterword by the author